SAVAGE TEARS

CASSIE EDWARDS

LEISURE BOOKS NEW YORK CITY

A LEISURE BOOK®

August 1997

Published by

Dorchester Publishing Co., Inc.
276 Fifth Avenue
New York, NY 10001

The name "Leisure Books" and the stylized "L" with design are
trademarks of Dorchester Publishing Co., Inc.

Printed in the United States of America.

THE SAVAGE SERIES

**Winner of the *Romantic Times*
Lifetime Achievement Award for Best Indian
Series!**

**"Cassie Edwards writes action-packed sexy
reads! Romance fans will be more than
satisfied!"**
—*Romantic Times*

PASSION'S PROMISE

How sweet it would be to be taught lovemaking by this
handsome, wonderful man.

But chances were that they might not even see one another
again.

Spotted Horse gently framed her face between his hands.
"*Mitawin*, we shall be together again," he said, as though he
had read her thoughts. "Once this is all behind us, I will
come for you. We shall be together *ah-pah-nay*, forever."

"I want that so much," Marjorie said, then melted into his
arms when he suddenly yanked her against his hard body.
He gave her a deep, long kiss, before letting her go and
riding off.

With much affection I dedicate Savage Tears *to the following fans who have become my special friends:*

KATHY STONE
KAREN COOMER
IDA GRIMALDI
FLORENCE EDMUNDS
ESTHER DITTMER
MAGGIE CAPENER
JO WALKER
LOUISE STRAUSBAUGH
LORI WOODMAN
DIANE DuSCHENE
ELIZABETH WHALEY
GERRI RAWLINS
PAM SIMPSON
MO ROSE

THE SPIRIT OF TEARS
Jennie Rogers

Moisture of the eyes,
Simultaneous South and North lies.
Placed to the West.
Lastly in the East...tears rest.

Why my creator; the turmoil
Souls buried in the soil.
Cries heard all along
Only forgotten, not gone.

Voices in the wind come
Beating like a drum.
Memory of heartache
Visions there to take.

Understand, think back
Such reasoning I lack.
A warrior's pain and pride.
To myself I have lied.

All the while like game
Waiting and trapped by shame.
I am one like the red man
The Spirit has said "I am."

SAVAGE TEARS

Chapter One

The Minnesota Territory—1834

The autumn leaves were brilliant in color. The sky was just turning a soft crimson from the setting sun. The air was damp and cold.

Dressed in a warm wool coat, Marjorie Zimmerman was riding her gentle dark bay mare. She was glad the weather still allowed her to get outdoors. The snows would arrive soon, imprisoning her in her cabin until next spring.

With her long black hair fluttering down her back, she rode through browning, curly buffalo grass and past clusters of pine trees. The meadow angled into woods of oaks, dogwoods, and beeches. She rode beneath trees alive with bird song and tiny animal noises.

Wanting to get to a higher point to see far into

the distance, Marjorie gripped the reins with sure hands, gave her steed a nudge with her heels, and guided her up an eroded hill.

Having topped the rise, Marjorie rode toward a bluff. She loved this land of lakes, trees, and wide, high blue sky. She wished she could make this her home forever. She had lived many places during her childhood with her mother and two stepfathers, but none she loved so well as the Minnesota Territory.

Marjorie gasped when a brightly colored pheasant swept out of a cluster of bushes in bullet-like flight. Laughing at her foolishness, she rode onward. For a moment she had thought it was an Indian jumping out at her. She knew she had traveled far enough from her cabin to be near Chief Spotted Horse's Indian village, which was located on Lake Calhoun.

Marjorie's pulse quickened at the thought of the young Dakota chief. She had become infatuated with him the very first time she had seen him at the trading post. He was a handsome man with burning dark eyes and—

Marjorie's thoughts were interrupted when she reached the edge of the bluff and could see down below her. She felt a churning at the pit of her stomach as she gazed in horror at the small bundles that lay so quiet and stiff on scaffolds in the trees close beside the Mississippi River. She could tell by the size of the bundles that these were children who had been brought to the Dakota burial ground.

She had heard about the whooping cough epidemic at the Dakota village, but she'd had no idea that it was killing so many children. A keen sadness swept over her. Probably she had known some of the children by name.

Not long ago, while she had been at the trading post selling her handmade paper dolls, Marjorie had become acquainted with Sun Bear, a ten-year-old Dakota brave. Intrigued by her paper dolls, Sun Bear had invited her to his village so that she could show them to the Dakota children.

Thrilled at the chance to be near Spotted Horse, who was Sun Bear's adopted father, she had taken as many of her paper dolls as she could spare. She had given them to several little girls, asking no payment from a people who had seemed to have lost so much at the hands of white people.

And now here was another tragedy. Marjorie continued to stare at the bundled bodies. In her mind's eye she recalled that day when she had been at their village.

She would never forget the smiles of the children as they gazed trustingly up at her while she sat amidst them.

She would never forget how precious they had been when they had held the paper dolls to their hearts, thanking her for them in the Dakota tongue.

She would never forget the tiny hands as they touched her face, or their warm lips as they kissed her cheek.

A sob lodged in her throat as she wheeled her horse around. Somehow it seemed wrong to be this close to the burial site of so many

Dakota children, as though she might be intruding on something mystical and private. With tears in her eyes, she headed for home.

Marjorie had taken her horse out today because riding usually helped her temporarily forget a death in her *own* family. Her beloved mother had died two months ago from a tired heart that had just suddenly given out.

Horseback riding usually gave Marjorie a lift. But not today. She couldn't get the sight of the bundled bodies of the dead children off her mind. She couldn't understand why so many had to die.

Deep in thought, Marjorie arrived home. As she dismounted, she gazed uneasily at her cabin. It stood in a clearing of moss and pine, where chickens roamed in a small fenced-off area; a milk cow stood in a nearby makeshift lean-to.

More and more Marjorie dreaded being alone with her stepfather. She had known him for just a short time before their move from Kansas to the Minnesota Territory. Her mother had been married to him for only a year before she died.

Having no living relatives, Marjorie had stayed with her stepfather after her mother's death. In his cabin at least she had a roof over her head and food on the table.

Dispirited, Marjorie walked her horse into the tiny barn and removed the saddle and bridle. As she brushed her mare's sleek mane, she became lost in memories of her troubled past.

Marjorie had never known her true father. When he had discovered that his wife was pregnant, he was already weary of providing for her. He had disappeared without a trace.

Before her mother's pregnancy began to show, she had managed to find another man who would marry her. Then *he* left her high and dry when he discovered that she was with child.

Marjorie had only known the third husband. Although he, also, disappeared from her and her mother's life one day in Kansas, he had left something precious behind for Marjorie—her knowledge of how to make paper dolls, which had given her a way to earn money.

Her third "father" had been an Englishman. "An entrepreneur of goods and services," he had called himself.

In truth, he had been a vagabond peddler who sold his merchandise from a wagon as he traveled from town to town. He sold spices, lace, butter churns, pins and needles, calico well-sweeps, farm tools, and so much more that Marjorie could not remember.

People had always flocked to his wagon and bought what was available for both men and women, in exchange for cash, a meal, or a night's lodging.

Also among his treasures were paper dolls from England. Marjorie had fallen instantly in love with them. But her "father" never gave her any. He told her that if she wanted some for herself, she would have to learn how to make them.

She smiled smugly. She had learned not only how to make them, but had also learned how to profit from them! Paper dolls were something unique and new to most people. Children clamored to have them.

Hugging her horse, Marjorie tried to block out of her mind the most embarrassing, disturbing memories—how her mother had managed to put food on her table and provide lodging for her daughter while between husbands. She had been a paid lady in bawdy houses!

And that was where Marjorie's mother had met her last "conquest." For the fourth time she had managed to get a man to speak wedding vows with her.

Marjorie had seen right away the sort of man Albert Stout was.

He was crude.

He was heartless.

A cynical, suspicious man, he never had anything good to say about anyone.

A trapper, he killed anything and everything without blinking an eye.

Ironic as it seemed to Marjorie, after all the men who ran away, this time it was she who wanted to flee from a father. But she hadn't yet saved enough money from the sales of her paper dolls to go out on her own, to seek a life away from the likes of Albert Stout.

But she would! Lord have mercy, she would!

She gave her horse one last pat and left the barn.

She was sad to know that even if she *did* have enough money saved, there were no river boats at this time on which to make her escape. Winter had almost arrived, and the boats no longer traveled down the Mississippi. None would arrive again until spring.

Marjorie stepped up on the small porch and took a long drink of water from the dipper that hung near a water barrel just outside the door. She removed her gloves and thrust them inside her front coat pocket, then hurriedly splashed water on her face, washing the dust from it. She patted her face dry with a towel that hung from a peg on the wall.

Her spine stiffened when she raised the latch and walked on inside the rustic, stark cabin. It was sparsely furnished, and dimly lighted by a lone kerosene lamp. Her stepfather, a lean, weather-beaten man, sat in a rocker, slowly rocking back and forth close to the fire, smoking a pipe. Under his annoyingly close scrutiny, Marjorie slid out of her coat, put on an apron, and began to prepare supper.

Skilled in the kitchen, and proud of the one possession her stepfather had bought for her mother—a cook stove—Marjorie soon had fried chicken sitting on the kitchen table. She had also prepared moon-white hominy, mashed potatoes, green beans, and her specialty—golden cornbread.

After the platters of food had been passed back and forth across the table between Marjorie and Albert, she sat stiffly and began to eat.

To help hide her uneasiness of being alone with Albert, and at being constantly watched by him, Marjorie forced conversation.

"I saw something terrible today," she said, picking at her green beans with her fork instead

Cassie Edwards

of eating them. The memory of the dead children had suddenly taken her appetite away.

"And what was that?" Albert asked, then gnawed on a fat drumstick with his yellow teeth.

"It was so horrible," Marjorie said, a shiver racing down her spine. She looked over at Albert. "I shall never forget it. Never."

Sighing, Albert glared at her. "What in damnation are you talkin' about?" he asked. He scooped a huge forkful of mashed potatoes up from the plate and shoved it into his mouth.

"The Dakota children," Marjorie blurted out, her voice catching. She gazed at her stepfather. "I saw them. They were dead and placed in bundles on scaffolds in trees close to the Mississippi River." She swallowed hard. "There were so many. I can hardly believe they are dead. Not long ago they were happy, laughing children. I sat among them."

"Yeah, even though I told you not to," Albert said, reaching over for the pot of coffee and pouring himself a fresh cup. "You had no business goin' to that savage Injun village. You're lucky you weren't skinned alive." He looked over at her and smirked. "Your hair would've looked pretty on one of their scalp poles."

"They have no scalp poles," Marjorie defended, her jaw stiffening. "They aren't *savages*. They are more decent and kind than some . . . some . . . white people I know."

Albert laughed harshly. "You'll learn," he said, taking another bite of potatoes. He swallowed them in one fast gulp, then leaned over

18

the table closer to Marjorie. "I'm glad the damn savage kids are dyin'. That means there will be fewer adults to deal with later on. There's already too many Dakota Injuns in these parts. They take too many pelts . . . pelts that could be *mine*."

"How can you be so cold and heartless?" Marjorie said, a sob lodging in her throat. "The Dakota children are so sweet . . . so innocent. And . . . and . . . if anyone should wish anyone dead, I would think it would be the Dakota wishing it on *you*. This has been their land from the beginning of time. We are the true intruders. Not they! If anyone deserves the most pelts, it is they! Not you!"

"Boy, somethin' has really got you goin' tonight," Albert said, closely studying Marjorie. "It surely ain't just the savage kids. It's somethin' else, ain't it? Are you afeared the handsome Dakota chief might get sick, also, and die? I've seen you makin' eyes at him at the tradin' post."

"I have never made eyes at him," Marjorie quickly replied.

Albert leaned back in his chair again and speared green beans with his fork. "You make a fool of yourself starin' at him," he grumbled.

"I never stare at anyone," Marjorie said, her face growing hot with a blush.

"Back to the kids dyin'," Albert said, ignoring Marjorie's last statement. "I heard about it already. Today. While I was at the tradin' post. It's rumored that whoopin' cough is wipin' out the kids like it was the plague."

19

"It's that bad?" Marjorie gasped.

Her thoughts went quickly to Sun Bear, the Dakota chief's adopted son. She prayed that he was all right. She now recalled having not seen him at the trading post for several days.

Her thoughts again strayed to Chief Spotted Horse. Until she had met Sun Bear, she had wondered about the relationship between the young brave and the Dakota chief when she had seen them together at the trading post. At first she had thought that the young brave might be the chief's true son.

When she had questioned the agent at the trading post about them, she had been told that the young brave was the son of friends of Spotted Horse's parents who had died at the hands of renegade Indians when the child was four.

Spotted Horse's parents had taken Sun Bear in to raise, and when *they* died in the Mississippi River when their canoe capsized during a storm, Spotted Horse took over the care of the young brave as though he were his very own son.

Marjorie had learned, also, that the chief had no true sons, or daughters. He had been married once to a small, frail woman who had died one long, cold winter, from consumption.

Her thoughts returned again to Sun Bear. Oh, Lord, what if he *was* one of those who were ill with whooping cough? He was such a special, sweet boy.

"Albert, is there anything that can be done for the Dakota children?" she suddenly blurted out, ignoring the startled look her question brought to his face. "Surely Doc Rose can go and look in on them."

"You mind your own business," Albert spat out. He wiped grease from his mouth with his shirt sleeve. "The Injuns have their own customs and they don't include a white man doctor."

He shoved back his chair and rose from the table. He leaned down and spoke in Marjorie's face, so close that she could feel the heat of his breath. "There's danger in snoopin' in Indian affairs," he coldly warned. "Stay away. Keep your nose clean!"

She glared up at him, then pushed back her own chair and rose quickly from it.

After clearing the table and washing the dishes, Marjorie grew quiet. Nights were always the worst now that her mother was gone and she was forced to be alone with this man who was still no more than a stranger to her.

Trying to ignore Albert, who was sitting in his rocker, slowly rocking and puffing on his pipe, Marjorie settled down at the kitchen table again. But this time with her paper dolls. As she began working on her newest collection, she was keenly aware of being watched. She was so tired of this never-ending staring from her stepfather!

And oh, how she dreaded going to bed. She always delayed it until Albert was overhead in his loft bedroom and she knew that he was asleep by the rumbling snores that wafted down to her.

"Why are you so suddenly quiet? You were

chattering on like a magpie during supper," Albert suddenly said, breaking the silence.

"I'm still thinking of the Indian children," she said softly, which was true.

But she could hear the ticking of the clock and knew that it was time for bed!

She never wanted Albert to know that she didn't trust him.

She had learned to be careful with what she said to him. She never wanted to put ideas into his twisted mind that he might not yet have thought of, ideas of forcing her to be his bed partner since he was now without a wife.

"Hogwash," Albert mumbled.

Marjorie again busied herself making her paper dolls.

But she couldn't get Sun Bear off her mind. She was anxious to go to the trading post tomorrow to see if he was there.

She also hoped to see Chief Spotted Horse. Recently, each time she saw him, she caught him watching her. He seemed more interested in her as each day passed.

Surely he had noticed how her interest in him had grown.

Even now her heart skipped a beat when she thought of his midnight dark eyes, his sculpted facial features, his muscles. . . .

Chapter Two

Early morning frost lay over the land like a fine dusting of snow. At the Dakota Indian village, the power of the *Big Holy* was being prayed for. Tomtoms and large rattles ornamented with beaver claws and bright feathers played in solemn cadence.

Chief Spotted Horse, a tall, sinewy man of thirty winters dressed in buckskins highly ornamented with quills of porcupine and trimmed with fur and feathers, watched sorrowfully as several mothers of his village went to the banks of Lake Calhoun. There, Brown Hair, the village medicine man, awaited them.

Filled with keen sadness and bitter hopelessness over the deaths of so many of his people's beloved children, Spotted Horse watched the mothers carry their children into the swirling smoke of Brown Hair's pipe. The children would inhale a whiff from the mysterious pipe and be blessed before being carried into Lake Calhoun for a ceremonial bath. The bath was supposed to cleanse them of the evil that was causing the coughing disease.

The children wore nothing except sprigs of wild sage wrapped around their ankles and wrists, the symbol of purity and cleanliness.

Even those who sang and prayed today for their children wore sprigs of sage tied to large bone whistles which hung on buckskin thongs around their necks.

Their faces covered with sorrow, the women now stood in the water with their children. Tears flowing down their cheeks like falling rain, they held their small ones tenderly while splashing the blessed water over them.

Hardly able to stand watching any longer, Spotted Horse lifted his eyes to the heavens. Silently he prayed to *Wakantanka*, or *Big Holy*, who was the maker of all things, and asked for the Great Mystery's mercy. He begged the *Big Holy* to spare the children who had not yet become afflicted with the coughing disease.

The children were the future of the Dakota!

Without them there was no hope!

There was no vision!

The children were the saving grace of those Dakota who had lived through the coming of the whites!

The children, their innocence, their utter sweetness, gave comfort to Spotted Horse's people on days they felt despair over the changes

24

brought into their lives since the arrival of the white man.

Spotted Horse prayed to his *Big Holy* that he could retain the courage that was needed keep peace with the whites. He knew that to go against them in war could mean the total annihilation of his people. The white pony soldiers stationed at Fort Snelling and the neighboring forts along the banks of both the Minnesota and Missouri rivers now outnumbered the Dakota people ten to one.

His prayer complete, Spotted Horse opened his eyes.

Despair reattacked his very soul when he turned and looked toward the village, where more dead children were being readied for burial. Gently mothers wrapped them in blankets made fast by buckskin bandages wound around them.

A little hand sliding into one of Spotted Horse's drew his attention from the burial preparations. He knew whose hand it was and relished the warmth of the flesh against his.

He turned smiling eyes down at Sun Bear, his adopted son. He was as proud of Sun Bear as if he were of his own flesh. Ten winters of age, the child was a brave with a good heart and clean thoughts. He was being taught the ways of a chief. Spotted Horse's people looked to Sun Bear as their future leader after Spotted Horse grew too weary and too old for the challenging task.

"*Ahte*, Father, do you blame the whites for the coughing disease?" Sun Bear asked, his dark eyes gazing intensely up at Spotted Horse.

Sun Bear hoped that his father's feelings for the whites had not worsened. If they had, perhaps the white "paper doll" lady would not be welcome at their village again. Sun Bear had seen his father watching Marjorie Zimmerman for many months now since he had first spotted her at the trading post shortly after her arrival in the Minnesota Territory.

Sun Bear had seen Spotted Horse's silent admiration of the woman when she had come to the village, especially after she had given her handmade paper dolls to the children without asking payment for them.

Sun Bear had seen how Marjorie had made Spotted Horse's eyes come alive again. He had taken a vow long ago never to love again after losing a wife he had adored.

Sun Bear had prayed often to his *Big Holy* that Spotted Horse would find a special woman to be his wife, thereby giving Sun Bear a mother. He could not deny watching the other children with envy when they were with their mothers. He hungered for a mother, himself!

He could not help seeing Marjorie as that mother, even though she was only eight winters older than himself.

The age difference did not matter, for while observing her as she sat among the Dakota children, he saw that she had as much love and affection in her as a woman who had borne many children.

Spotted Horse hesitated a moment before answering Sun Bear, for he did not wish to speak his true feelings about what was happening at his village. If he started blaming the whites aloud, it would spread among his people like wildfire, and hate for the whites might reach the boiling point.

He couldn't have that. He was a man of peace! He fought hard to make it so.

His gaze swept over Sun Bear. The young brave wore a fringed buckskin outfit and moccasins. His long black hair was worn loose down to his waist, with feathers braided at the ends and thrust in his beaded headband. He was only ten winters in age, but he already had the intelligence of a grown man.

"*Ahte*, do you?" Sun Bear asked again, softly shaking his father's hand to draw him out of what seemed a reverie. "Do you blame the white-eyes for the death of our Dakota children?"

Spotted Horse sighed heavily.

He bent down and rested on his haunches before Sun Bear. He placed gentle hands on the child's shoulders as he peered into his eyes. "*Ho*, yes, how can I not blame the whites, for was not the disease brought to this land by them?" he said solemnly.

"Yes, it does seem so," Sun Bear said, although he wished it were not true. The lady he wished to be his mother was white.

"*Micinksi*, my son, do not voice my feelings aloud to anyone," Spotted Horse said. "I do not want war to come between our people and the whites because of this. More of our people would die in one day of bloody battle between

27

the white pony soldiers and our warriors, than can die during the duration of this sickness. You have seen. You know how many more pony soldiers there are than there are Dakota."

"*Ho*, yes, I have seen," Sun Bear said, slowly nodding his head. "And, *ahte*, I will tell no one your feelings. *No* one."

"*Micinksi*, there is something more I wish to say," Spotted Horse continued, his voice drawn. "Do not go to the trading post again until we know that it is safe from any more white man's diseases. My son, you might come down with one of the diseases, yourself. I could not bear to stand over you preparing you for the scaffolds, which already number too many."

Sun Bear went silent, for he knew that for the first time ever he would go behind his father's back to do that which had been forbidden. He did not wish to see much time pass before he found a way for Spotted Horse and the paper doll lady to become closely acquainted. There were many men in this area, both white and red-skinned, who did not have wives. Should one of them choose Marjorie Zimmerman before Sun Bear could persuade her and his father that they were meant for one another, Sun Bear would feel the loss deep inside his heart.

Yes, he *must* go to the trading post again, to see if the paper doll lady was there. He *would* find a way to get Spotted Horse and the white woman together. It mattered not to Sun Bear that her skin was white. It was what was inside a person's heart that made him either genuine, or false.

Sun Bear knew that this woman was one who was of a kind heart. She was good, through and through.

Sun Bear had seen her as possibly the one person whose gentle sweetness might banish the sadness from Spotted Horse's lonely heart.

Sun Bear had seen her make the many Dakota children laugh and be happy over her generous gift of paper dolls. That had to mean that she was someone who was filled with love and warmth. Surely she would make a wonderful wife . . . a mother.

"Did you hear what I said, *micinksi?*" Spotted Horse asked, searching Sun Bear's eyes, aware that he was deep in thought about something.

Sun Bear found it hard to gaze directly into Spotted Horse's eyes, for he knew that he could not be altogether truthful with him. It tore at his heart to tell even the smallest lie, for any lie was wronging his father, who was the most important person in the world to Sun Bear.

But this lie was necessary.

Sun Bear was certain that Spotted Horse felt something for Marjorie Zimmerman. He knew that she felt something for Spotted Horse.

Sun Bear knew about destiny, and he believed that it was Spotted Horse and Marjorie's destiny to meet and to love.

And it was Sun Bear's destiny to see that it happened!

"*Hoye*, as you wish, I will not go to the trading post," Sun Bear said, fighting to keep his voice steady, although his heart seemed to pound like many drums inside his chest.

He did not want to feel guilty about how he had falsely answered his father. He had not told a true lie, for, as promised, he would *not* go to the trading post itself. He would be only close by it, where he could stay hidden in the shadows of the huge trees and watch for the paper doll lady.

If Sun Bear saw her with a man besides her father, or saw her even talking to a man, as though she might have singled him out as a prospect for a future husband, only then would Sun Bear intervene and go in to the trading post. He would draw her aside and tell her that a true man awaited her at the Dakota village. Chief Spotted Horse was that true man!

Ho, if Sun Bear was forced to, he would speak in his father's behalf with the lady. He would tell her that his father, who had no wife, found her attractive. Would she consider being his *tawicu*, wife? Would she consider being Sun Bear's *ina*, mother?

He would be bold, as bold as a snake when the rocks grow warm in spring. The idea somewhat frightened Sun Bear, for, in truth, he was not sure how his father would react to the woman arriving at the village by Sun Bear's side.

His only hope was that his father would be so pleased to see her he would forget who had brought her, and why.

"It is good that you see reason in my request that you stay away from the trading post," Spotted Horse said, dropping his hands to his sides and rising to his full height over Sun Bear. "If the *Big Holy* is willing, this time of sorrow will pass quickly and things will get back to normal among our people."

Spotted Horse turned and stared into the forest. He kneaded his brow as he turned and looked down at Sun Bear again. "The fur on the forest animals is growing thick and heavy now," he said. "Soon it will be time for the autumn hunt. We must harvest enough pelts to keep our people warm all winter, as well as enough to sell and trade at the trading post. Then you, as well as all of our people, will resume visits at the trading post. It is my sincerest hope that by then all of this dread disease and death will be behind us."

"*Ahte*, things will change for the better," Sun Bear said, smiling up at Spotted Horse. "You will see. Your prayers and mine, as well as all of our people's, will be answered. This will be behind us. We will look to the future again with hope in our hearts. You will even—"

Sun Bear caught himself just short of speaking Marjorie's name aloud to his father.

No.

This was not the time to bring her name into the conversation. Not while Spotted Horse was still filled with so much despair and sadness. Although Marjorie, herself, brought sunshine inside one's heart, it would be best to wait until later to lure his father into thinking of her.

Sun Bear could hardly wait to see his father in a lighthearted mood again.

Chapter Three

The one room of the log cabin trading post was small and stuffy. It reeked of buckskin, tobacco, and sparkling cider that sold for five dollars a bottle. Kerosene lamps hung low from the rafters, their flames giving off only enough light by which to transact business.

A lone wasp buzzed around a nest that was crumbling into dried dirt on the wood planking of the floor beneath it.

At this trading post, furs were counted, sorted, packed, and shipped. It was the point of rendezvous for a widespread area.

As she watched and counted the coins being placed in her hands after the agent accepted her newest collection of paper dolls, Marjorie still could not get the memory of the many scaffolds of Indian children off her mind.

Today, two days later, when she and Albert had arrived at the trading post, she had noticed the lack of Indian activity there and was afraid to know why. Surely it meant that more children had died.

She was worried now more than before about Sun Bear; since she had not found him at the trading post, or anywhere near it. She was afraid of what his absence might mean . . . that he was ill, or perhaps even buried among the other children who had died.

Percy Allen, the agent, brought Marjorie out of her troubled thoughts. "That's it, young lady. That's payment in full for today's paper dolls," he said. "Now what are your plans for all the money you've been gettin' for those paper dolls? You should have quite a good number of coins by now. I ain't never seen anything like it. You've been bringin' in those dolls weekly. Don't you ever sleep?"

Frowning, Marjorie cast a quick glance over at her stepfather. She was glad to see him so caught up in gathering supplies for their cabin that he had not heard what the agent had said. She had tried to keep him ignorant of how much money she had hidden away. Most certainly she didn't want him to know why she was so earnestly saving the money.

"Young lady, did you hear what I said?" Percy asked in his screeching, irritating voice. He idly scratched his bald head as he stared down at her.

Marjorie leaned over the counter closer to Percy. "Yes, I heard you, and please quit announcing to the world that I have money," she said in a near whisper. "It isn't anyone else's business how much money I have made. Do you want someone coming to our cabin and killing me and my stepfather over a few coins?"

"Sorry, ma'am," Percy said stiffly, then walked away from her and tended to an Indian woman who had come in with an armful of blankets.

As Marjorie dropped her coins into a leather drawstring bag, she gazed at the woman. She had beautiful copper skin. Her black hair was combed smoothly back and worn in two braids, one behind each ear, the ends hanging down on her breasts in front. She wore a long, fringed doeskin dress. It was exquisitely white, richer in sheen than fine broadcloth. It looked softer than velvet.

Marjorie wondered if the woman was from Chief Spotted Horse's village. She badly wished to know how things were there. She especially wished to know how Sun Bear was!

Just as Marjorie started to ask her, Percy began talking to the woman about her blankets as she spread them out on the counter.

"These are the finest I've ever seen," Percy said, smoothing his hands over one blanket and then another. "Let's see. There are how many?"

"There are ten," the woman said in perfect English. Surely she was Dakota. Almost everyone at the Dakota village spoke English well. They had learned it through transactions with the whites.

"I want five dollars a blanket," the Indian

woman said. "That is what you paid me for others I have brought to you."

Marjorie continued to watch the transaction. She gazed at the blankets, moved by their loveliness. Some were made of fine blue cloth, heavily and tastefully adorned with silk ribbons of various colors. Some had a band of embroidered work a foot or more wide, running around the bottom, in a blending of different colors depicting forest animals and plants.

"Ma'am, all I can give you today is five dollars for the lot of them," Percy said, his eyes holding the woman's steadily as he waited for her reply.

Knowing that the blankets should be worth fifty dollars apiece, Marjorie was stunned by how Percy was trying to cheat the lady. Marjorie had been at other trading posts. She knew just what blankets of this quality were worth.

She looked quickly over at the agent. She started to call him a lowdown, filthy cheat. But Albert had become aware of what was going on, and had seen the anger flashing in Marjorie's eyes. He grabbed her by an arm and took her to the far side of the dark, gloomy cabin.

"I've told you not to poke your nose into business that ain't yours," he whispered as he leaned down into Marjorie's face.

"But he's taking advantage of that woman," Marjorie whispered back, her voice tight. "How can you just stand here and allow that?"

"Because I have my own tradin' to do here, that's how," Albert snarled. "If you go buttin' into that Indian woman's affairs and spoil things for Percy, just how much money do you think I'm gonna get for my corn that's layin' out there in the wagon, awaitin' Percy's inspection? If you rile him, he most certainly won't give me a dollar a bushel as is the usual payment."

Albert placed his fists on his hips. "And, damn it, soon I'll be bringin' in heavy fur packs," he said, his jaw tight. "I want a fair trade when I bring in my beaver, elk, deer, and antelope skins. I ain't lettin' you be responsible for me not bein' paid top dollar."

He nodded toward the door. "Now git on outside and wait for me to finish my business," he said. "You've got yours done. Now let me do mine."

Marjorie glared at him as he stamped away from her.

She then turned a slow gaze back to the woman, who had taken the five dollars the agent had paid her.

Marjorie looked again at Albert. The agent was handing him a long coil of rope tobacco. They were laughing and joking. She had to believe they were poking fun at the Indian woman who had just left, her head hanging low.

Dispirited herself, Marjorie went on outside and sat down on the ground beneath a tall oak tree. Its leaves were gold, rosy as old coins trembling in the breeze.

Marjorie looked down at the small leather bag in her hand. She was thankful, at least, that she had received a fair payment for her paper dolls. But the agent had dealt with her many times. A price had been set long ago. He wouldn't dare try to change the price in midstream or she would raise a stink over it at Fort Snelling.

She wondered if she should go there and complain about Percy having cheated the Indian woman.

But no, it was best not to. Albert was right to worry about the agent's reaction to Marjorie's interference. If Percy got angry at her, not only might he refuse to pay Albert what was due him for his vegetables and pelts, but he might also refuse to do any more paper doll transactions with *her*.

Marjorie didn't want to travel farther upriver to other trading posts. When snows set in, that could be a death warrant for both her and her stepfather.

"The soldiers at Fort Snelling wouldn't do anything about it anyhow," she whispered to herself.

No. She wouldn't waste her time going and ratting on the agent. The soldiers at the fort were probably as crooked as Percy. They might even have some deal worked out between them, sharing the profit from the crooked deals!

Trying not to get impatient while waiting for Albert, Marjorie focused her thoughts on other things. She looked past the trading post cabin. At the back, scattered in the long, wide, flat river bottom, lay camp after camp of traders and trappers, and string after string of canvas-covered freighting wagons.

She frowned as she gazed at a tent in which a saloon had been established. Even though it was early morning, men were there drinking.

Albert had said that he wouldn't waste his money there. The alcohol was diluted with water, four to one, and sold at a dollar a drink.

Marjorie's attention was drawn to another tent close by the saloon. A lovely woman had just stepped from inside it, stretching her arms over her head and yawning. She wore a short, full skirt that shamelessly exposed her legs above her knees. Her breasts were all but bare.

Marjorie was reminded of another woman who had worn such scandalous clothes and who worked in such bawdy houses. Her beloved mother!

A noise behind her brought her quickly to her feet. Just as she turned and found Sun Bear standing in the sun-dappled shadows of the forest's outer edge, Spotted Horse rode up on his gelding, a scowl on his face as he glared at his adopted son.

Relieved to see Sun Bear and to know that he was all right, Marjorie at first paid no attention to the Dakota words Spotted Horse fired at the boy.

But when Spotted Horse began speaking English, Marjorie was shocked.

"*Micinksi*, did I not warn you to avoid the trading post?" Spotted Horse said, his voice harsh with disappointment that his son had disobeyed him.

"*Ahte*, I did not go to the trading post itself," Sun Bear said softly, his eyes wide and pleading. "I came only close enough to watch."

Spotted Horse slid a slow gaze Marjorie's way. He locked his eyes with hers for a moment, then gazed at his son again. "Sun Bear, being near the trading post is the same as being in it, for I told you not to come here," he said tightly. "*Micinksi*, do you wish to become sick with white people diseases? Can you not see that you are close enough to the trading post to contract diseases? Do you not see how close this white woman is to you?"

Realizing that Spotted Horse might hold her partially responsible for the deaths back at his village, Marjorie took a bold step toward him.

"I assure you that it is safe for Sun Bear to come near me," she said, trying not to be affected by Spotted Horse's nearness. "Spotted Horse, I carry no sickness with me."

In a sweeping motion she gestured with a hand toward herself. "Do I look ill?" she murmured. "Do I? Do I look as though I am a threat to your son . . . to your people?"

She became aware that Spotted Horse was looking more closely at her. He gazed at her in a silent, intense way, as his eyes swept slowly over her, from her head to her toe.

Under such close scrutiny from a man she silently adored, Marjorie found it hard to stand still.

Her knees were weak.

Her pulse was racing.

And she could feel the heat of a blush rising to her cheeks when the chief's eyes lingered too long on her heaving breasts.

Although covered by her freshly ironed cotton dress, with a comfortable knitted shawl draped around her shoulders to ward off the chill, Marjorie knew that her abundant breasts were quite noticeable. The shawl could not hide their round firmness; her breasts were the only part of her anatomy that was not described as "petite" by those who knew her.

Her voluptuousness had worried her, since that had been the one thing that had attracted so many men to her mother. She wanted to be nothing like her mother!

Self-consciously, Marjorie reached a hand back for her hair and slowly brought the long, wavy ends over her shoulders on each side, to drape down over her breasts.

The minute she did that, she regretted it, for her obvious awareness of Spotted Horse's attention embarrassed her. She could see that what she had done had brought a slow grin to the chief's beautifully shaped lips. She could even see a good-natured humor suddenly light up his midnight dark eyes.

Still Spotted Horse said nothing.

Marjorie shuffled her feet nervously as Spotted Horse resumed studying her. She, in turn, took the opportunity to look at him better. Most times she had seen him in the gloomy interior of the trading post cabin where the light was poor.

But now? Oh, Lord, she could see everything about him, every detail of his smooth copper face, the intenseness of his bright-black eyes, and his lean, muscular physique. He had aquiline features. His shiny black hair hung long and loose down his back. Like her own bangs, Spotted Horse's hair was cut off across the forehead a little above his eyes. But his was confined at his brow with a colorfully beaded band tied around his head.

Attired in a neat and clean buckskin outfit, and sitting so tall in his Indian saddle, Spotted Horse was the epitome of male virility. He was someone Marjorie could not help being in love with.

Spotted Horse could not deny how Marjorie affected *him*. Although he had lost one wife who was dear to him, and he had vowed never to love again, the very sight of Marjorie Zimmerman always licked fire through his veins. She was a glimmering woman, more beautiful than any he had ever known.

She was even more beautiful than his dear, departed wife.

Marjorie's pale skin looked so soft. With perfect features, her face was gentle in outline. She had a delicate, long throat. And her breasts were generous. He hungered to taste them . . . to cup them in his hands!

But now was not the time to be lost in thoughts of a woman . . . *any* woman, he reminded himself!

He had come to get a son who had been disobedient. He would not allow an infatuation to distract him.

And he must hurry back to his village. There were still many ill children.

He was grateful, though, that today had not brought any new deaths.

He turned quickly to Sun Bear. "Go to your horse and follow me home," he said. He motioned abruptly toward his son. "Now!"

Sun Bear gave Marjorie a silent look of apology, then ran to his pony and quickly mounted it.

Marjorie's breath was stolen when Spotted Horse gave her another lingering stare and she saw no trace of anger in his eyes. There was something more that made a ripple of sensual pleasure go through her. His eyes seemed to say what he wouldn't allow himself to speak aloud. She knew now that he had feelings for her that matched hers for him!

She started to walk toward him, then stopped suddenly when he wheeled his horse around and rode off with Sun Bear at his side.

Shaken by the experience of being so near Spotted Horse, under the spell of his midnight dark eyes, Marjorie stood there for a while longer and watched the Dakota chief and his son until they rode from sight.

Then she turned and paled when she found Albert standing there glaring at her.

How long had he been there? Had he seen all that had transpired between herself and Chief Spotted Horse?

"You are just itchin' for trouble," Albert said, his voice low and measured. "I watched you and the Injun chief. Cain't you know what the chief was thinkin' as he stared at you? He mentally undressed you, *that's* what."

"That's a horrible thing to say," Marjorie said. Then, angry at Albert for spying on her, she firmed her jaw. "And what right do you have always watching everything I do?" she spat out. "I don't answer to you."

"As long as you live under my roof, you do," Albert growled out. "You'll do as I say, or *else*."

"Or else?" Marjorie said, her heart thumping as anger swelled within her. "Just what does *that* mean?"

"It means that when I tell you I don't want you flirtin' with that Injun, you won't. It means when I tell you I don't want you goin' horseback ridin' alone again, you won't," he said, his gray eyes flashing angrily. "I don't want you going off anymore on your horse. There's a rumor that the Dakota are going on the war path soon because of so many of their people dying from whooping cough. The Indians blame the white folk for the deaths. There ain't no tellin' what might be on that chief's mind besides wanting you in his blankets with him."

"I don't believe anything you say," Marjorie said, placing her hands on her hips. "Yes, I imagine the whites are being blamed for the whooping cough. But Spotted Horse is a peace-loving chief. He won't start a war over it. But not only because he wants peace. He's an intelligent man. He knows that he wouldn't have a chance in hell of winning against the white soldiers."

"Hah! Since when did *you* become such an expert on Indians?" Albert said, his lips tugging into a mocking smile.

"All I know is that today Spotted Horse's anger was not directed toward me, but toward a disobedient child," Marjorie said softly. In her mind's eye she could see Sun Bear's shame as he was scolded by his father.

"Just shut up and quit arguin' with me," Albert said. "Don't you have any more respect than that for the man who took you and your ma in, and fed and clothed you?"

Marjorie glared up at him. She refused to respond to his remark about what he had done for her and her mother, knowing that her mother had been a slave to this man.

Marjorie slid her bag of coins inside the pocket of her dress, turned, and went to her horse. She swung herself into the saddle and rode away as Albert shouted obscenities at her.

She smiled as she reached down and patted the coins in her pocket. "One of these days I won't have to ever listen to him again," she whispered to herself. "I need only a few more coins. When spring comes, I will book passage on the first steamboat to Saint Louis and. . . ."

Suddenly it came to her that she truly didn't want to leave the Minnesota Territory. If she left, she would be leaving her heart behind!

But how could she make Spotted Horse love *her*? He might never allow himself to care for a woman who was related to those whom he held responsible for so much tragedy.

"Sun Bear," she whispered, smiling.

Yes, Sun Bear was the answer! He had already made her aware of how much he cared for her.

Yes, perhaps there was a chance after all for her to have a future with Spotted Horse!

Chapter Four

Marjorie was jolted awake by her stepfather's loud, abusive voice coming through the thin pane of her bedroom window. He was saying curse words Marjorie had never heard before. Their nastiness . . . their vileness . . . made shivers ride her spine.

She wondered what could make him this angry, especially so early in the morning.

She sighed when he suddenly grew quiet.

Marjorie looked sleepily toward the window. She had slept longer than usual. The morning sun's rays were just filtering through the sheer, white curtain like streamers of velvet. She could hardly believe that Albert had allowed her to stay in bed so long. He usually demanded breakfast at the crack of dawn so that he could leave and be about his business.

Of late, he had been more involved in harvesting what food was left in his garden than setting traps for forest animals.

The fact that the garden was now almost completely harvested was probably the reason he had slept longer this morning, allowing Marjorie some respite from the tedious work of preparing food for canning. She had shelled so many peas, snapped so many beans, and shucked so much corn for canning these past several weeks, her fingertips were almost too raw and sore to make her paper dolls. The cellar in the ground just outside the cabin was already filled to its limit.

Albert's renewed loud curses, and then another sound, the pitiful, pained cry of some animal, made Marjorie's heart skip a startled beat.

"What animal is that?" she whispered, springing to her feet. "What on earth is Albert doing to it?"

She hurried into a cotton dress and a pair of flat leather shoes, ran her fingers through her hair to loosen its tangles, then rushed from the cabin.

She had to go no farther than the porch to see why her stepfather was so angry. When he had gone outside this morning he had found a chicken slaughter.

Marjorie was taken aback by the sight, herself. Hardly a chicken had been spared.

But something else horrified her even more than the sight of the many dead chickens that lay strewn over the ground. Albert had caught the culprit in one of his traps. It was a red fox.

And Albert was so angry over what the fox had done, he was skinning . . . it . . . alive!

The sight of the poor fox being treated in such an inhumane way made bile rise into her throat. She swallowed hard to keep herself from vomiting. It was such a gory sight, she was momentarily rendered speechless.

She couldn't even get her feet to move. It was as though her shoes were frozen to the porch!

But when the fox turned his begging, soft brown eyes her way, sudden anger filled Marjorie.

Yes, what the fox had done would deny her and Albert many eggs for breakfast and fried chicken for supper. But it still did not deserve to die in such a heartless way. The fox had killed by instinct!

Albert was killing from downright meanness and enjoyment. She could see it in his smirk! She could see that each stroke of his knife gave him some strange sort of pleasure.

"Stop!" Marjorie cried, lifting the hem of her skirt as she rushed from the porch and ran toward her stepfather. "Albert! No! What you are doing is wrong! It's cruel! Please stop!"

Albert stopped long enough to send her a dark, scowling glare. "Stay out of this," he said, his voice low and sinister. "This damn fox deserves everything I'm givin' him." He waved with a hand toward the chickens. "Look at what he done!" he shouted. "There are only a few chickens left!"

Tears filled Marjorie's eyes as she stood over the pitiful fox, who now lay only half breathing, his eyes closed. "But no living creature deserves to die in such a hideous way," Marjorie murmured.

When Albert resumed removing the pelt, Marjorie fell to her knees and, without success, tried to grab the knife from him.

Albert quickly placed the bloody tip of the knife to her throat. He leaned into her face. "If you want to take the fox's place, I assure you it can be arranged," he snarled out. "Marjorie, damn it, I've told you over and over again not to interfere in anything I choose to do. Your place is in the house doin' woman's chores. Your place is to keep your damn mouth shut, or . . . be . . . sorry!"

"Take . . . that . . . damn knife . . . away . . . from my throat this minute," Marjorie said, scarcely breathing as she stared into the cold, unfeeling gray pools of his eyes. "I think you've gone mad, or else why would you do such a thing?"

"And so now you revert to swearing and calling me mad?" Albert said, laughing beneath his breath.

"Move . . . that . . . knife away from my throat," Marjorie said, her heart pounding. She *was* afraid that something inside Albert's head might have snapped. He might be capable of slicing her throat.

Since her mother's death, Albert often seemed to be purposely trying Marjorie's temper. And she was not the sort to just stand by and allow it. Whatever the cost, she would defend herself.

She let out a heavy sigh when he finally lowered the knife away from her.

Slowly she lifted a hand and ran a finger over the tiny welt the knife had made on her flesh. When she felt the wetness of blood there and understood that the blade had broken the skin, a fear sliced through her that she had never felt before . . . a deep terror of her stepfather.

"Get back on inside the house and start fixin' breakfast," Albert said, wiping the blood from his knife onto his breeches. "I've got things to finish here."

When Marjorie didn't move, Albert's eyes squinted as he leaned down close to her face again.

"Scat," he growled out. "Or, by God, you'll be the next to be skinned alive!"

Her face snowy white with fear, her eyes wide, Marjorie edged away from Albert. Then she turned and ran into the cabin. Panting, she closed the door behind her. Weak-kneed, she leaned against it.

Her mind went in many directions at once. Her thoughts spun one way and then another. She looked desperately around her. What should she do? What should her next move be?

There was no doubting it now! She was not safe living with that monster. She couldn't stay another moment with him! She couldn't wait any longer to leave! She must leave *now*.

If she waited until spring, for the return of the weekly riverboat excursions between Saint Louis and Fort Snelling, she might not survive the wait.

Her gaze stopped on a rifle that was leaning against the wall. She looked at it for a moment.

She then turned a slow gaze to the window, envisioning Albert still there, taking his time skinning the poor little fox.

She looked at the rifle again. Should she? Should she just pick up that rifle and go outside again and threaten to kill him if he didn't stop?

Or should she just go out there and kill him without first threatening him?

A coldness filled Marjorie's insides when she realized where her thoughts and fears had taken her. She had actually considered killing a man!

Was living with this man contagious? Was he turning her into someone hideous, herself? Marjorie shivered and hugged herself.

"I've got to get out of here," she whispered, falling to the floor on her knees a few feet from the fireplace. She pushed aside the braided rag rug.

Her fingers trembling, she clawed at a loose floor board. She sighed when she finally got it lifted from the others.

Reaching down, she grabbed two drawstring leather bags. They were heavy with coins, but she knew that she didn't have enough to take her far away. Even if the riverboat was there, moored at the embankment close to Fort Snelling, she didn't have enough money to pay passage on it.

But that didn't sway her decision about running away. She would hope that the coins might be enough to pay someone in the area for room and board until spring.

Knowing that she didn't have time even to pack a bag with her belongings, Marjorie slid into her warm wool coat, grabbed her buttery soft leather gloves, and tied a scarf around her head.

She placed a bag of coins in each of her front pockets, then gazed at her paper doll equipment. She was sad to have to leave it behind. But she had no choice. There was too much of it to carry. And she could not get to the barn for her horse and pack mule without Albert seeing her.

No. She had no choice but to leave everything dear to her heart behind.

But somehow, someday, she would build up her supplies again and make and sell her beloved paper dolls.

For now, though, escape must be enough for her.

Her gaze again moved around the room, stopping when she saw a bowl of fruit on the kitchen table. She hurried there and grabbed an apple.

Then her gaze slid to the rifle again and stopped. Yes, she must take the firearm with her for protection. She wasn't sure how long she would be forced to wander in the forest, alone. There were all sorts of threats for a young woman in the wilderness, from both two- and four-legged creatures!

She slid the apple into her front coat pocket.

Then she grabbed the rifle and hurried toward the back door that led into the deep, dark

shadows of the forest. There she would find refuge from a man she wished her mother had
never met. Their life had been pure hell since
those vows had been spoken. Her mother might
even be alive today had she not been worked to
death by her fourth husband!

Putting all thoughts of her mother behind
her, and not even taking the time to go and say
a good-bye over her mother's grave, Marjorie
ran into the forest.

She thought again of where her frantic flight
today might eventually take her. There were
three places where she might go to seek help
until the riverboats returned in the spring.

She could go to the trading post, where Percy
might know of someone who would take her in.

Or she might go to Fort Snelling. She knew
of women who lived and earned their keep there
by working at the Snelling mansion as a maid,
cook, or servant.

Or she could go to the Indian agent who lived
only about a mile through the forest. Louis Eckert, the agent, a widowed man in his late fifties,
seemed the best of her choices.

Yes.

She would go there.

With a destination in mind, she broke into a
mad run.

Then she stopped abruptly when she heard
someone screaming.

She turned and looked in the direction of the
cabin. She paled, for she knew that it was not
the fox making such sounds. It was a human
scream. It sounded like a child's!

Frantic over what might now be happening back at the cabin, Marjorie battled within herself over what she should do.

If she returned to the cabin to see whose scream had filled the morning air with such fear, she would have to drop all hopes of escaping today, herself.

And if Albert saw her with bulging pockets and realized just how much money she had accumulated from the sales of her paper dolls, he would surely take it from her!

But she could not get the frightened screams off her mind.

Nor could she forget the sight of the fox, and what Albert had done to it.

If someone besides herself had happened along and seen what he had done, this person might have intervened and gotten into trouble with her stepfather.

That person's life might be endangered!

"Especially a child's," Marjorie said aloud.

Her jaw set, her eyes filled with angry fire, she broke into a mad run back toward the cabin. Her hand clutched the rifle, and she vowed to use it if Albert posed a threat to some innocent person.

She lifted her eyes heavenward. "Please help me, for I have never been as frightened as I am now," she whispered. "Nor have I ever felt as alone."

Chapter Five

Spotted Horse rode his horse at a hard gallop through the forest toward Marjorie Zimmerman's cabin. When he had awakened early this morning and had discovered that Sun Bear was gone, Spotted Horse couldn't believe that his son had left the village again, especially now, after he had been warned time and again about the dangers of the white man's diseases.

But at least Spotted Horse now understood why Sun Bear kept going against his wishes. Yesterday Sun Bear had confessed that he wanted to draw Spotted Horse and Marjorie Zimmerman together, into a special relationship.

Sun Bear had said that he had observed the white woman many times after she had been at their village giving her paper dolls to the children. They had talked at the trading post. If allowed, he was certain that they could be friends.

Sun Bear had tried to convince Spotted Horse that the woman was special, that she was a woman of gentleness and tenderness . . . a woman of genuine heart.

And even though Spotted Horse had told Sun Bear that it was not the young brave's place to try to match Spotted Horse up with *any* lady, it seemed that Sun Bear's ears were closed to that comment.

Sun Bear's disappearance again today showed that he would not take no for an answer. It was his hunger to have a mother that drove him into such reckless behavior, Spotted Horse realized.

Determined to stop Sun Bear's plans before they advanced any further, Spotted Horse had already gone this morning to the trading post to look for the young brave.

When he had not found him there, Spotted Horse felt that perhaps the boy had gotten bolder in his determination and had gone to Marjorie Zimmerman's cabin. Hoping that he was wrong, yet knowing that he must investigate this possibility, Spotted Horse was now almost at the woman's cabin.

His heart had skipped a beat when he had heard a scream coming from the direction of the cabin. It had been a child's scream! His blood ran cold with fear to think it might be Sun Bear who was in trouble. Spotted Horse found much to like in Marjorie Zimmerman, but he had never found anything good about her father. He seemed evil through and through, a person who might kill his own kin if he would profit from it.

"If the *washechu*, white man, has touched my son—" Spotted Horse whispered through clenched teeth.

He sank his moccasined heels deeply into his horse's flanks and leaned low over the flying mane as he rode at a harder gallop through the forest. He had to see if the one who had screamed was Sun Bear. And if not, who?

His heart did a strange sort of flip-flop at the thought of Marjorie in pain or fear.

"No, it was not a woman's scream," he whispered. "It was a child's."

Spotted Horse rode through a wide break in the trees and wheeled his horse to a shimmying halt when he saw Sun Bear being held by Albert, the white man's knife at his throat.

"Injun, I heard you comin'," Albert grumbled, his hold around the child's waist tightening.

He held the knife closer to Sun Bear's flesh, so close that a trickle of blood flowed from the fresh, open knife wound.

"Drop the knife," Spotted Horse said in a low, threatening growl. He stayed in his saddle, fearing that to leave it might prompt the white man to do something even more foolish. "*Washechu*, if you harm my son—"

"Shut up, Injun," Albert said, interrupting Spotted Horse. "And don't come any closer, neither, or I swear to you I'll slit the boy's throat. He chose the wrong time to come snoopin' here at my cabin. The stupid brat drew his knife on me when he saw me skinnin' a fox." He laughed throatily. "Of course I got the knife away from him."

Spotted Horse's gaze shifted and he saw the dead chickens strewn along the ground. And then he saw the half skinned, half alive fox.

The sight sickened him, for the fox was almost kin to the Dakota! To defile a fox in such a way was almost the same as defiling the Dakota!

Anger welled up inside Spotted Horse over everything, but he still couldn't move. The knife was still at Sun Bear's throat. One slip, and his son would be dead.

"The young brave has done you no harm," Spotted Horse said, his voice wary. "Yes, it is true that he tried to defend the fox. But as you said, Sun Bear is too small. He would never have been able to stop you. So now that you have proven this point, why not let him go? I will take him home. Although I am as disgusted by what you have done to the fox as is my son, it is true that whatever you do on your property is your business."

Spotted Horse gestured with a hand. "Let him go," he said. "*Iciya-wo*, easy. Drop the knife away from his throat. *Slowly*. Let him step away from you. Let him come forward to me. I will take him home. He will not come here again."

"Do you think I'm stupid, or what?" Albert said, laughing nervously.

Albert glanced at the rifle sheathed at the side of Spotted Horse's mount. It was so close to

Spotted Horse's hand he could yank it free in an instant.

Albert looked at Spotted Horse. "If I let the child go now," he said, swallowing hard, "you'll kill me."

"All that matters to me is the safety of my son," Spotted Horse said in a slow and measured voice. "I swear to you that we will leave and that you will be unharmed."

"You'll send your warriors back here to scalp me," Albert said, the knife still at the child's throat.

"I have told you that my only concern is my son," Spotted Horse said. "If you release him now, while he has only a small knife wound on his throat, I give my word to you that no harm will come to you. I am a man of honor who never goes back on his word."

Spotted Horse's jaw tightened and his eyes narrowed. "But if anything more happens to my son, I vow to you that the whole Dakota nation will come for you," he threatened. "You would not want to even think of the kind of pain you will endure before you die. You will be treated with less respect than a *quzeila*, a common ground snake!"

Albert paled and swallowed hard. "You promise I won't die if I release the boy?" he said, his voice drawn.

Spotted Horse saw a movement at the side of the cabin. His eyes widened when Marjorie rushed up behind Albert and placed the barrel of her rifle solidly against the man's back.

"Albert, release the boy or I'll shoot you dead," Marjorie said in a low hiss.

Stunned that Marjorie was there, her voice filled with loathing as she held the gun steady on his back, Albert dropped the knife.

Sun Bear lunged away from him and ran to Spotted Horse.

Spotted Horse swept his son up and placed him on the saddle before him and held him protectively there with an arm around his waist.

His eyes locked momentarily with Marjorie's.

Marjorie stared back at him and saw softness in his gaze. She also saw a silent thank you in his eyes.

Then he rode away with Sun Bear.

Marjorie suddenly felt trapped. If she lowered her rifle and let Albert turn toward her, she expected him to possibly kill her for interfering.

Yet *she* had the weapon, not he. She could get away before he had the chance to run back inside the cabin and get his other rifle. With some luck, she could get on her horse and ride away before he could figure out what to do.

"Albert, walk slowly away from me," Marjorie said. She held her rifle steady on his back as he took slow steps from her. "Albert, as I move away from you and go to the barn for my horse, I will be watching you. If you make one move toward me, I swear I'll kill you."

Stepping over dead chickens, Marjorie edged her way toward the barn. "Hands in the air, Albert," she said, motioning with her rifle as he turned and glared at her.

She smiled smugly as he did as he was told,

his face twisted in an ugly, angry grimace. "Leave your hands there and don't take another step closer," she said. She took much pleasure in being the one handing out the orders, instead of him.

It was good to best him!

She kept her eyes on Albert as she stepped inside the barn only far enough to be able to untie her horse's reins from the hitching post. She knew that she could not take the time to saddle the horse, for that would require taking her eyes off Albert.

She hurriedly mounted the horse. She gave Albert a mocking stare, then, laughing, she rode away.

Albert swung a fist in the air as he watched her ride into the shadows of the forest. "Why did you do this?" he shouted. "Why would you go against a man who has cared for you, who took both you and your mother in and fed you? Why, Marjorie? Why?"

Again Marjorie grimaced over his declaration that he had been so generous to her and her mother. Could he truly believe that? Was he blind to how cruel and heartless he really was?

Marjorie sent her horse into a faster gallop away from this hideous, vicious man. She knew the importance of putting many miles quickly between herself and Albert. If he could be stupid enough to place a knife at a young Dakota brave's throat, knowing what the consequences might be for having done it, who was to say what he might do because she had made him look foolish today in the face of his enemy?

A shiver raced up and down her spine at the thought of how much he must now hate her. Hatred in a man like Albert was like a festering sore inside his dark heart. He would not rest until he found a way to make Marjorie pay for having gotten the best of him!

Chapter Six

The hem of her wool coat flapping around her legs, Marjorie rode at a good clip for a while longer.

Then, believing that she had placed enough space between herself and Albert, she slowed her horse to a softer, easier gallop.

In her mind's eye she kept seeing Sun Bear being held by Albert, the knife at his throat. She kept seeing Spotted Horse as he sat stiffly on his horse, glaring at Albert, trying to talk sense to her stepfather.

Marjorie smiled when she thought of something that pleased her. She would never forget the power she had felt when she had sneaked up behind Albert and placed the rifle barrel against his back.

Her only regret was that she hadn't been able

to see his reaction when he realized that it was Marjorie doing this daring deed. Never had she done anything so bold.

And she hoped that she didn't live to regret it. She realized just how much Albert must hate her.

Now, as never before, she had a desperate need to find a safe refuge away from him.

If he were to. . . .

Her thoughts were stolen away when Spotted Horse and Sun Bear appeared suddenly in front of her on Spotted Horse's mighty steed, blocking her way.

She stopped abruptly and slid a slow gaze from Spotted Horse to Sun Bear, then looked unflinchingly into Spotted Horse's eyes.

Before she got the chance to ask him why he had stopped her, he spoke.

"Why did you go against your own flesh and blood in favor of the Dakota?" he asked, his gaze steady on hers. "No Dakota woman goes against her father, *ever*."

"Albert isn't my true flesh-and-blood father," Marjorie said softly. "My mother was foolish to marry him. Albert is a heartless fiend, someone I have no respect for. I don't approve of hardly anything he does, especially . . . especially the way he chooses to kill innocent animals."

She turned soft eyes to Sun Bear. She returned his sweet smile. "And I especially don't approve of the way Albert threatened this young Dakota brave's life today," she murmured.

She edged her horse up beside Spotted Horse's steed and gently touched Sun Bear's cheek. "Sun Bear, I'm so sorry about what happened to you today," she murmured.

She gazed at the wound on his neck. She gently touched it, then eased her hand away when Sun Bear winced. "I can't believe Albert went as far as—" she began, but was stopped when Spotted Horse interrupted her.

"*Ho*, he wronged my *micinksi*," Spotted Horse said. "*Ho*, the *washechu* also wronged the fox."

Marjorie visibly shuddered. "I still can't believe he actually skinned the fox alive," she said miserably. "The poor animal."

"The worst of it is that it was a *fox*," Spotted Horse said. "Spotted Horse and Sun Bear are of the *Reyata Otonwa* band of Lake Calhoun Dakota, the Fox band. We deeply respect the fox. The Dakota are of fox swiftness and nimbleness. The Dakota formed a lodge in honor of the people's friend, the fox. I am a member of that Fox Lodge. The members are known as peace keepers."

"I, too, will be a member of the Fox Lodge when I grow up and am called warrior by my people," Sun Bear said, proudly lifting his chin. "All of my friends will also be members of the Fox Lodge."

Marjorie felt honored to be with Spotted Horse and Sun Bear in this way, talking with them so openly. Although Spotted Horse was known to be friends with white people, it was common knowledge that there was only one white man he truly trusted and confided in.

Louis Eckert, the Indian agent.

She hoped that Spotted Horse's show of trust in her today meant that he would eventually confide in her about his feelings for her. She had no doubt that he was infatuated with her! It showed in the way he looked at her as he talked. Sometimes his eyes were steady on hers, as though he was looking deep into her very core, touching her insides with a gentle warmth.

Other times, as his eyes roamed slowly over her, she knew that he approved of what he saw by the way the pulse in his neck quickened. Even the black of his eyes seemed to become blacker as he gazed at her.

Under his close scrutiny, Marjorie's own pulse would quicken, and she would feel a strange, delicious stirring in the pit of her stomach.

She could feel something weaving between them . . . something magical and sweet.

"Where are you going on your horse?" Spotted Horse asked. He gazed over his shoulder as if he thought Albert might suddenly appear behind them on his own mount.

He then gazed again into Marjorie's eyes. "You are fleeing this man who wronged my son and the fox this morning?" he asked.

"Yes, I can no longer live with the likes of that man," she said, her voice drawn. "I should've left right after my mother died, but I . . . I . . . didn't have the means by which to support myself. I . . . I . . . hadn't yet made enough coins from the sales of my paper dolls."

Spotted Horse reached a hand out and softly

touched a lock of hair that lay across her shoulder. "It was wrong of Spotted Horse to ride off with Sun Bear and leave you with that man after you showed such bravery and courage saving my son," he said thickly.

"I understand why you felt that you must," Marjorie said, her heart thudding inside her chest at the nearness of his hand. Should he touch her face, she felt that her insides would melt from pleasure.

"Your son," she said quickly. "You had to get your son away from my stepfather. You knew by how I handled my rifle that I could take care of myself."

She looked him in the eye. "You did know, didn't you, that I could take care of myself?" she asked softly.

Why *hadn't* he stayed and waited for her to escape with him? Was she wrong about him? Didn't he care for her welfare, after all?

"*Ho*, I saw that you handled the rifle well enough," Spotted Horse said. He moved his hand away from her. "But I left you with that man because I thought he was your father. I thought you would have to deal with him, father to daughter, in your own way. That is the way of the Dakota. Father-and-daughter business is private business."

"But you saw how I loathed him—"

"Still I saw him as your father—"

At that moment Albert jumped out of the shadows of the forest, his rifle leveled at Marjorie's back. He had been searching the woods for Marjorie when he'd heard the sound of voices. He had dismounted and tethered his horse to a low tree limb and come the rest of the way by foot to catch Marjorie and Spotted Horse off guard.

"Marjorie, take Spotted Horse's rifle out of his gunboot and throw it in the brush," Albert said, his eyes locked with Spotted Horse's. "Then throw your own toward me. I paid a heap of money for that weapon. It certainly wasn't bought to be used against me."

Pale, Marjorie did as she was told. She glanced up at Spotted Horse as she took his rifle from his gunboot. "I'm sorry," she murmured. "I don't have any choice but to do this."

He nodded, all the while keeping his gaze locked with Albert's.

After Marjorie had disarmed both herself and Spotted Horse, she glared at Albert. "Now what?" she said, angrily folding her arms across her chest.

"You are going home with me," Albert said. He nodded toward Spotted Horse. "Dismount. Both you and the boy get off that horse."

With dignity Spotted Horse slid out of his saddle. He lifted his arms to Sun Bear, who slid into them. Spotted Horse helped his son from the horse and stood protectively beside him.

"Now, Injun, walk away from that horse," Albert said, frowning at Spotted Horse. "But first give it a slap. Make it run away from you."

Marjorie's eyes wavered as Spotted Horse gave her a quick glance. She swallowed hard, regret filling her as he looked away from her and slapped his horse on the rump. The animal galloped away, its saddle empty.

"Now take off walking toward your village," Albert said. "And don't even think about comin' back to my home for Marjorie with ideas of attackin' and killin' me."

Albert laughed sarcastically. "You won't be foolish enough to bring warriors to interfere in the lives of a white family," he said, his voice sharp with mockery. "You surely know that you'd be stirring up problems between yourself and the white pony soldiers."

Albert glared up at Marjorie, then looked at Spotted Horse again. "Is Marjorie worth startin' a full-fledged war over?" he asked, his eyes twinkling devilishly. "I think not, savage. The soldiers are just watchin' and waitin' for an excuse to do away with the likes of you."

Finding it hard to stand there and listen to himself and his people being degraded, Spotted Horse clenched his hands into tight fists at his sides. He knew that what the man said was true, that the soldiers would grab the first opportunity they could to start a war with the Dakota.

But that would not stop him. Spotted Horse's lips tugged into a mocking smile. He would pretend to agree with this white man's logic, but he would not let harm come to the woman. Although he had not voiced his feelings aloud to anyone, he was in love with Marjorie Zimmerman. He had fought loving any woman for so long; but now that he had given in to his feelings, allowed himself to love again, he would let no man take her away from him!

"Spotted Horse, what he says is true," Marjorie blurted out. "Please do nothing that might bring war to your people. Let me take care of this in my own way."

"Just shut up, Marjorie," Albert said. He grabbed her horse's reins and led her away from Spotted Horse and Sun Bear, who still stood stoically quiet, watching.

As Albert led Marjorie's horse away, he looked over his shoulder at the Dakota chief. "Get on outta here!" he shouted. "And don't come near my cabin again or I swear I'll have the whole United States cavalry out for your scalp."

Albert howled with laughter when he saw that the word "scalp" caused Spotted Horse's eyes to narrow angrily. "I might ask the soldiers to give me both yours *and* Sun Bear's scalps for my scalp pole!" Albert shouted.

"Albert, you're going to be sorry you insulted Spotted Horse in such a way," Marjorie said, glaring at him. "You just won't let it go, will you? You just keep digging your grave deeper and deeper."

"He ain't got the guts to come and kill me," Albert said, stopping when he came to his tethered horse.

He threw Marjorie her reins. "Now don't try nothin'," he warned. "If you ride away, I'll be forced to shoot."

His face got a pinched look as he glared at her. "Of course, I won't shoot to kill," he taunted. "Perhaps one leg, and then the next—"

"You *are* sick," Marjorie said, gasping. "Oh, how I loathe the very sight of you."

Albert cackled and swung himself into his saddle.

Then he frowned at Marjorie again. "Come on with me," he said darkly. "I've a lesson or two to teach you when I get you home."

Marjorie could not help but be afraid, for who was to say what Albert might be capable of?

As she rode away with him, she looked over her shoulder and searched for Spotted Horse. She saw no signs of him or Sun Bear. They had surely run off into the deeper, darker shadows of the forest.

She was torn with conflicting feelings. A part of her wanted Spotted Horse to risk everything to save her. Another part of her hoped that he wouldn't. She knew that many whites were just waiting for an excuse to kill redskins!

An involuntary shiver raced across her flesh as she envisioned Spotted Horse or Sun Bear taken to Fort Snelling, to be imprisoned, or perhaps tortured.

Marjorie squared her shoulders and tightened her jaw. She vowed to herself that she would not allow anything bad to happen to Spotted Horse or Sun Bear.

Chapter Seven

Spotted Horse placed two fingers between his lips and gave a low, quivering whistle, which he knew his horse would hear and understand. Spotted Horse had long ago trained his steed to come to him when he gave such a whistle.

Spotted Horse had noticed how quiet Sun Bear had been since they had parted with Marjorie and Albert. As he waited for the horse to respond to his command, he turned and placed his hands on his son's shoulders.

"*Micinksi*, what is in your heart that you are not sharing with your father?" he asked, seeing how Sun Bear looked questioningly up at him. "Sun Bear, speak your mind. You know that is the way between you and me. It is not good to have secrets between us. Our hearts and minds have always been as one."

He paused, then placed a gentle hand on his son's head. "This, too, your silence, is also about the white woman, is it not?" he said thickly. "*Micinksi*, what is it that you are keeping inside? Would you not feel better if you spoke it aloud to me?"

"*Ho*, it would be better for me to tell you my feelings instead of letting them burden my heart like a heavy stone," Sun Bear suddenly blurted out. "*Ahte*, I do not understand you today. How could you allow the evil white man to take the nice lady away? Does she not deserve better from the Dakota after having saved Sun Bear's life? Could you not have grabbed your rifle and killed the evil *washechu*?"

"*Micinksi*, you know that violence is not my way when there are other means to achieve one's goal," Spotted Horse said. He sank to his haunches before Sun Bear so that they would be the same height and their eyes would be level.

"But, *ahte*, I would think this time would be different," Sun Bear said, his voice drawn. "How can you stay so calm when you know that Marjorie is now in the hands of a demon man?"

"Because she will not be with him for long," Spotted Horse said, softly smiling at Sun Bear. "I did not want to place you or Marjorie in harm's way today by getting into a shooting battle with the *washechu* in her presence. *Ho*, the man has her *now*. But tonight? I will go and save her."

Spotted Horse's white bay gelding came to

him at a soft trot. He edged up close to Spotted Horse and nuzzled him in the ribs.

Spotted Horse rose to his feet and fondly ran his hand across the animal's withers. "You will be greatly rewarded for your obedience today," he said to his horse. He laughed throatily. "What would happen, though, should I forget how to whistle?"

Sun Bear came and also patted the gelding. "My horse was left tethered close to *washechu's* cabin," he said sadly. "Father, do you think you can get my horse when you go for Marjorie?"

"Both will be saved tonight by your father," Spotted Horse said, patting his son's head.

Sun Bear smiled broadly, for he now saw the good in what *washechu* had done today by taking Marjorie away while Spotted Horse had no choice but to watch. In a sense the white man had done Spotted Horse and Sun Bear a big favor, for he had now forced Spotted Horse's hand. Spotted Horse had no choice but to involve himself in the woman's life, after all. Once Spotted Horse had saved Marjorie from the clutches of the evil *washechu*, they would soon realize their deepest feelings for one another!

As Sun Bear rode behind Spotted Horse, he could not help smiling, for he might soon have a mother after all. What fun it would be to have a mother who knew how to make paper dolls!

Yes, that would benefit Sun Bear! He had seen how the young girls of his village had been enthralled with the paper dolls. The girls would come often to his lodge to see the dolls, where they would admire him as the kin of the woman who made them.

He was just discovering an interest in girls. He could not deny how he had begun to enjoy watching them.

He thrilled at the very touch of a certain girl's hand . . . sweet Sun Shining, a girl of his age, with large, innocent eyes, and beautiful lips!

Ho, Sun Shining, too, would find her way to his lodge after the paper doll lady became his mother! Perhaps Sun Bear could talk Marjorie into making a paper doll just for Sun Shining. Would it not be wonderful if she could make the doll exactly in Sun Shining's image?

His heart warmed at the thought.

Chapter Eight

"You aren't serious," Marjorie gasped when Albert yanked her coat from her, then shoved her down on a kitchen chair. She gasped in dismay when he took all her savings from the coat and shoved the coins into his own pockets. She couldn't believe it when he began winding a rope around her.

She struggled with the rope, yanking and pulling at it, only to have Albert tighten it and make her even more uncomfortable.

"You're insane to think you are going to get away with this," she cried.

Now rendered helpless by the ropes digging into the flesh of her arms, Marjorie stared at Albert as he began pacing the floor. After having seen how he had heartlessly skinned the fox while it was still alive, she knew that he was capable of anything.

But this?

To actually tie her up as if she were nothing better than a criminal . . . or a captive?

Never would she have thought that he would go this far to keep her with him.

"Why do you even care if I am here or not?" she blurted out. "Is it because I cook and clean for you? Is that why I am so important to you?" She swallowed hard. "Or . . . is . . . it something else? Tell me. I deserve to know why I am being held against my will."

"Shut up," Albert said as he continued to pace.

Then he stopped and stood over her, his fists on his hips. "You're just as unpredictable as your ma was," he said. "You've got me in trouble with the Injuns now. But the last laugh is on you. I don't think the Injuns will bother me. I am only one small pea in the pod, worthless to them."

"You are worthless, all right," Marjorie said, laughing sarcastically. "I don't know why my mother didn't see that before she married you. I could see your worthlessness a mile away. But she just wouldn't listen to me."

Albert walked away long enough to pour himself a cup of coffee. Then he stood over Marjorie again, sipping it, his eyes glued to her.

"My mother was so gentle and kind," Marjorie said, her voice breaking. "She didn't know how to fight for her rights. She let you and every man she ever knew walk all over her."

She lifted her chin stubbornly. "If ever I get loose from these ropes, I'm going to show you that I will fight for *my* rights," she hissed. "I swear, Albert, I'll shoot you the first chance I get!"

Albert slammed his empty coffee cup on a table, then leaned his face into Marjorie's. "Your ma only learned to shut her mouth up and be obedient after I beat the spunk outta her," he said darkly. "The same as I'll beat it outta you."

"Obedience, ha!" Marjorie said, her eyes gleaming. "Never!"

Albert stared at her for a moment longer, then dragged a chair over and sat down directly in front of her. "Why do you waste your breath defendin' your ma when you know she was nothin' but a trashy whore?" he grumbled. "For pay, she'd lift her skirts for any man. So don't tell me how wonderful your ma was. You're only tryin' to fool yourself."

"Yes, my mother did things I would never do, but she did them . . . she was *forced* . . . to do them, to live the sordid life of a prostitute, to keep me fed and clothed," Marjorie said, feeling a deep sadness every time she thought of exactly how her mother had lived. But she always thought kindly of her mother, for she had done everything within her power to keep mother and daughter together.

Marjorie was stunned speechless when Albert suddenly slapped her across the face.

"Just shut up," he growled. "Your ma soon learned after marryin' me *never* to give me no back talk. Now you'd best learn to keep your trap shut. From now on, *I* will be runnin' the show."

He laughed into her face. "You will never get the chance to turn on me again," he said, the chair clattering over backward as he rose quickly to his feet. "It's time for supper. I've some fox to cut up and fry." His eyes gleamed as he turned and gazed down at her. "Beautiful Marjorie, won't fox meat be just dee-licious?"

Filled with loathing, and gagging at the thought of him cooking the fox, Marjorie turned her eyes away.

Even when he finished cooking supper—not actually fox, but one of the chickens that had been slain—Marjorie had no stomach to eat. She just sat there and watched him stuff food into his mouth, leaving his lips and chin greasy.

Although her stomach growled from hunger, she still refused to eat when he shoved a forkful of fried potatoes toward her.

She was glad when night fell and Albert retired overhead in his loft and soon fell into a deep sleep.

"I've got to find a way to get out of here," Marjorie whispered.

She strained and squirmed as she again tried to loosen the ropes, but to no avail.

"Oh, God, I can't be here in the morning when he awakens," she whispered, a sob of desperation lodging in her throat. She had no idea what he had planned for her.

But one thing was certain: he couldn't leave her tied up forever. And when he did set her free, he was too adamant about keeping her ever to let her out of his sight again. She would be his virtual prisoner.

The thought sickened her.

Worn out, hungry, and her arms aching from having wrestled so long with the ropes, Marjorie stared bleakly at the window. Moonlight was spilling through the dusty pane. She could hear the lonesome sound of an owl somewhere close by in the trees. A loon gave its eerie cry across the river.

Then Marjorie stiffened when she heard something else. She looked toward the door when she heard soft footsteps outside on the porch.

Breathless, her eyes wide, she watched the door slowly open.

When the moonlight revealed the muscled form of a man, Marjorie could tell who it was. Spotted Horse!

She wanted to believe that he had come to check on her welfare. Yet what if he had come only to kill Albert, to avenge his son's treatment of earlier today?

"Please help me," she whispered, realizing that he saw her there in the milky spill of the moonlight. "Spotted Horse, *please* release me."

Seeing her tied up should not have come as such a surprise to Spotted Horse, for he now knew that Albert was not a man whose mind functioned normally. But still it shocked him deeply to know that Albert could have gone to such lengths with Marjorie. How could anyone be so cruel to her?

And the pleading in her voice and eyes tore

clean into his heart, making him realize more than ever before just how much he cared for her.

He moved stealthily into the room and leaned low over Marjorie. "*Ho-ha-he*, greetings. I am here because I am your friend," he whispered. "I have come to set you free of the bad *washe-chu*!"

Yanking his knife from its sheath at his right side, he soon had the ropes cut and held Marjorie up in his arms. Gently he wrapped her in a blanket to ward off the chill of night, then carried her outside to safety.

"Thank you, thank you," Marjorie whispered, her arms twined around his neck as he ran with her into the darker shadows of night, stopping where he had left his horse tethered beneath an elm tree.

"You will be safe now," Spotted Horse said, placing her on his horse. He secured the blanket around her, then swung himself up behind her.

Marjorie looked over her shoulder at him.

Their eyes locked for a moment.

Then he sank his heels into the flanks of his horse and rode off beneath the jeweled, star-sprinkled sky, saying nothing more. Their togetherness was all that was important for the moment.

He smiled when he thought of Sun Bear's pony. He had promised his son that he would retrieve it when he rescued Marjorie. That had not been necessary, after all. The pony had broken its tether and come home to Sun Bear of its own volition just before Spotted Horse had left on his rescue mission.

Hungry, tired, and sleepy, Marjorie relaxed against Spotted Horse's powerful chest.

And just before falling into a peaceful slumber, she was aware of his muscled arm holding her more securely to him, and of his nose inhaling the scent of her hair.

Feeling protected as never before, Marjorie fell into a sweet sleep with a smile on her face.

When she awakened sometime later, she found herself inside a tepee. She was snuggled between blankets on soft pelts beside the red glow of a cedar lodge fire.

Knowing that she must be in Spotted Horse's lodge, she leaned on an elbow and was disappointed when she looked slowly around her and saw that he wasn't there.

But she did see Sun Bear. He was asleep on a low platform at the far side of the lodge.

She watched him sleep for a moment, glad to know that she had saved him today from a madman. She could hardly wait for him to awaken so they could talk. She already felt his friendship deep inside her heart.

Then she gazed slowly around the inside of the tepee. She was impressed by how neatly it was kept. Clean, green grass had been gathered and spread on the floor. Over this were stiff rugs of rawhide, their hair side up.

She saw how the inside of the tepee was painted with Indian symbols, among them a beautiful horse. Over the inside entrance was a painted rainbow.

On another wall, a tanned hide was tied to two poles, on which she surmised was painted the history of Spotted Horse's family.

Before she had the chance to observe anything else in the lodge, she heard movement behind her.

Expecting to see Spotted Horse, she sat up and looked slowly toward the entrance flap, her pulse racing. Her insides warmed when she saw Spotted Horse standing there, his eyes dark as he stared back at her.

"I have brought you nourishment," he said, coming into the lodge carrying a tray piled high with food.

He sat down beside her and handed her the tray. He smiled as she took it, her eyes wide as she gazed at the meat, vegetables, and fruit.

"How did you know that I was hungry?" she asked, lifting her eyes quickly to him.

Spotted Horse's lips tugged into a slow smile. "Your stomach talked to me on our journey to my village," he said.

"Oh, you mean it growled?" Marjorie said. She laughed softly when it growled again at the sight and smell of the food.

"It just talked again," he said, chuckling. He gestured with a hand toward the food. "Eat. Then we will talk with our mouths, not our stomachs."

Marjorie giggled.

Then, not having to be asked twice, she grabbed up a huge piece of venison and sank her teeth into it. She washed down the food with pine-needle tea that he gave her in a large wooden cup.

Her eyes widened when he offered her something else on a smaller wooden platter. She gazed at the small, round cakes.

"These are *wasna*," Spotted Horse said, having seen the question in her eyes as she had looked at them. "Eat. You will enjoy them."

Marjorie smiled at him, took one of the cakes, and bit into it. She was surprised at how delicious it was. She ate one, and then two.

Feeling stuffed, she gave the platter back to him. "They are so good, but I am too full to eat any more," she murmured. "Would you mind sharing with me how those cakes are made? Do you know the recipe?"

"Recipe?" he said, raising an eyebrow. "*Hoh!* What is this word 'recipe'?"

Marjorie laughed softly. "The word recipe means the listing of ingredients used for making a particular food," she said. "For example, these cakes. Do you know the ingredients used to make them?"

"Chokeberries and dried meat are pounded together, seeds and all, until it becomes fine meal," he said. "This meal is thoroughly mixed with fat skimmed from the boiled bones of a deer. The cakes are not only delicious, but healthy, as well."

"Yes, they are delicious and filling," Marjorie said, placing a hand on her stomach.

He smiled, took the platters, and set them on the ground just outside of the tepee.

Marjorie felt a warm, sensual thrill surge

through her when Spotted Horse came and sat down beside her again. Earlier, when he had come for her, he had been dressed in full buckskin attire. Now he wore only his fringed buckskin breeches. His chest was bare and his hair was shiny and wet. He smelled fresh, like river water and the wind. She could not help but watch the rippling of the muscles in his back and arms as he lifted one hefty log into the flames of the firepit, then put on several thinner, finer strips of cedar wood so that the lodge fire might give off more light.

"Why did you come for me?" Marjorie suddenly blurted out, drawing Spotted Horse's quick attention. "Why did you risk so much for me?"

"I risked nothing," he said, stretching out and resting himself on an elbow. "I do not believe that Albert will involve himself with the soldiers by telling them they should go to war with the Dakota. To do so will place him sorely in danger from the whole Dakota nation."

Spotted Horse paused, his eyes searching deeply into hers.

Then he said, "I was concerned for your welfare ever since Albert took you away today," he said thickly. "I could not leave you with a man of so little heart. I was afraid that no good would come of you being with such a vile man."

"Again, thank you," Marjorie murmured. "I'm not sure how I could have stood another day with that wretched man."

"It is a debt paid to you for having saved Sun Bear," he said. "I, in turn, saved you."

He went to the back of his lodge.

When he returned to Marjorie he held out a pillow from his tripod bed. "It is time for *istima*, sleep," he said softly. "Tomorrow is another day. We will talk more then. *Istima, mitawin. Istima.*"

Marjorie smiled a quiet thank you up at him as she accepted the soft pillow of feathers.

She turned and watched him as he went and stretched out on his bed. She was surprised at how quickly he went to sleep. It was as though he was peacefully content and had no worries in the world.

Marjorie lay down between the blankets, her head resting on the pillow. But too many emotions kept her from sleeping.

Fear, however, was not one of them.

She could hardly believe that she was in a tepee with a man she had fantasized about ever since she had seen him that first time. She could hardly believe that he cared enough for her to save her from a fate that might have been worse than death.

As she lay there watching Spotted Horse sleep, she found her eyelids growing heavier and heavier. Finally she, too, slept, her trust in the Dakota chief complete.

Chapter Nine

A noise downstairs awakened Albert with a start. Remembering that he had left Marjorie tied up in a chair, and wondering if she might have found a way to get free, he yanked on his breeches, then, barefoot, went down the ladder to the room below.

The fire from the fireplace and the moonlight wafting through the windows gave Albert enough light to see that Marjorie was no longer there.

"How?" he cried.

He jumped with alarm when something ran across his bare feet.

Then he kicked at the rat that had taken advantage of the open door and watched it scurry back outside.

"Damn it all to hell," Albert said, falling to one knee beside the chair.

He picked up the ropes and studied them.

"Someone cut 'em," he grumbled. "Someone came and cut the ropes with a knife and took Marjorie away!"

His eyes narrowed, his jaw tight, he rose to his feet and went to the door. Glowering, he peered into the dark shadows of the trees, then looked from side to side at the dawn-flushed land.

"The savage," he said, his teeth clenched. "I *know* it was the damn savage who came and got her."

He scurried back up to the loft and rushed into the rest of his clothes, then grabbed his pistol and holstered it around his waist.

"Yeah, I know of one sure place to look for you, Marjorie," he said, chuckling. "And I'm goin' to get you back. You're mine. *Mine*. You are the same as bought and paid for!"

Even though he knew that he might be walking into danger, especially since he had held the chief's adopted son at knife point only a few short hours ago, nothing would dissuade Albert from going to the Dakota village. He was certain enough of his safety. The chief would not harm even one hair on his head for fear of retaliation from the white pony soldiers. No Injun got away with harming a white man.

Albert laughed boldly as he scrambled down the stairs. He left the cabin, went to the barn, and saddled his horse.

Cassie Edwards

He swung himself into the saddle, almost certain that the Indian chief was only helping Marjorie because she had saved his son. The debt had been paid when he offered her lodging tonight. He shouldn't feel obligated any further where Marjorie was concerned.

In fact, Chief Spotted Horse might be glad to be rid of her, Albert thought, smiling devilishly. Surely the chief held no good feelings these days for any whiteskins . . . not even pretty ones. Too many Dakota children had died recently because of whooping cough that the white people had brought to the land of lakes.

Albert smiled wickedly when he thought of the punishments he was going to bestow on his "daughter" to teach her obedience.

"I'm gonna have some fun with her, that's fer sure," he whispered darkly to himself.

Chapter Ten

The aroma of food and the sound of soft footsteps awakened Marjorie. When she opened her
eyes and recalled where she had spent the night,
in a *tepee*, she smiled, especially since it was
Spotted Horse's.

She held a blanket up beneath her chin and
looked around her, finding neither Spotted
Horse nor Sun Bear there.

Again she was made aware of food as its delicious aroma wafted into her nostrils. She slid
the blanket down away from herself, moved to
her knees, then leaned around the slow-burning
embers of the fire to look for the food.

When she saw the heaping platter of various
meats and the neat pile of sliced apples, she
could not deny how hungry she was.

She smiled when she recalled the prior evening, when she had eaten like a pig in the presence of Spotted Horse. The extra-large helping of food had, no doubt, been put there at his command. He probably thought that she made it a practice to eat as much as a man.

In truth, she had never eaten a lot, but she had eaten regularly. It was a habit learned from her mother, who always had food on the table for Marjorie three times a day.

"Even when we were living alone and so poor," Marjorie whispered, a keen sadness overwhelming her at the renewed memories of her mother. Her mother had made sure Marjorie never went without proper nourishment, no matter how she had to achieve that goal.

"I must quit thinking about my mother's prostitution days," Marjorie whispered, silently cursing Albert for having made sure she never forgot.

"Albert!" she whispered harshly, paling.

She had to wonder what Albert had done when he had found her gone. She was certain he would not give her up without some sort of a fight. She only hoped that he wouldn't come to the Dakota village.

And to make sure of that, she must leave. *Soon.*

No matter how much she hated leaving Spotted Horse, she knew that to keep him and his people out of trouble with Albert and the soldiers at Fort Snelling, it was imperative that she leave today for Louis Eckert's house. Louis was a kind man. She knew that he would give her lodging until spring.

Another urge besides hunger came upon Marjorie. She had to go into the woods and relieve herself. She must do that before Spotted Horse or Sun Bear returned. It would be embarrassing to have to excuse herself for such a private act.

Throwing aside the blanket, she slid into her leather shoes.

She then went to the entrance flap and eased it open. She gazed from side to side, and then farther into the village, where there was much more activity than usual. She saw that some warriors' faces were painted.

Drums were being set up in the center of the village.

Women were leading their children to one side, sitting them down on blankets.

Children, Marjorie thought, quickly remembering the whooping cough problem here at the Dakota village. Today she heard no wailing. She saw no children being bundled for the scaffoldings.

But that did not mean there weren't still many who were ill, perhaps dying, she thought sadly to herself. The faces of the people were solemn. Surely the preparations going on were for some sort of ceremony for the children, perhaps to beg the Dakotas' Great Spirit for mercy.

Needing to get her little chore over with so that she could get back to Spotted Horse's lodge before he returned, Marjorie rushed into the forest and found a thick stand of bushes.

When she hurried back to the tepee, she sighed with relief to find that neither Spotted

Horse nor Sun Bear had yet returned. She had to surmise they might be bathing in the lake, or be in a council with other warriors and young braves, readying themselves for whatever ceremony was to be held at their village today.

Marjorie sat down beside the fire.

She fidgeted with the fringe of a blanket.

She placed small cedar twigs into the embers in the firepit, and soon a nice fire was burning. She held her hands close to it and rubbed them together.

After waiting long moments, Marjorie gazed at the food. She badly wished to eat. But not wanting to be impolite, she continued waiting for Spotted Horse and Sun Bear to return to the lodge.

Rising to her feet, Marjorie began a slow examination of Spotted Horse's belongings. She found a cache of various weapons covered by blankets, at the far back of the tepee. There was a rifle, a bow and quiver of arrows, a lance, and a huge, sheathed Bowie knife.

Also she found a small derringer with an ivory handle. It seemed misplaced among things that were all Indian. She had to wonder where Spotted Horse might have gotten it. It seemed more of a woman's weapon than a man's.

Sliding the blanket back in place over the weapons, Marjorie knelt down beside Spotted Horse's bed and slowly opened a buckskin bag.

When she found a hairbrush, a cracked mirror, and various other women's toilet articles including a round bar of soap that smelled like lilacs and a small bottle of perfume that smelled like lilies of the valley, she had to wonder how Spotted Horse might have come into possession of such things as these unless . . .

"*Hoh*. You are enjoying exploring Spotted Horse's belongings?"

His voice and the fact that he had found her snooping made Marjorie's face turn warm with a blush. She dropped the brush back inside the bag as though it were a hot coal.

Guilt written all over her face, she rose to her feet. She turned slowly and faced Spotted Horse.

"I'm sorry," she murmured. "I shouldn't have gone through your things."

"You found the woman's trinkets," he said thickly. "You wonder about them?"

"Well, yes, kind of," Marjorie stammered out, smiling awkwardly.

"Do not fret over my possession of them, for they belonged to someone my mother knew," Spotted Horse said. He stepped around Marjorie and lifted the bag by its small handle.

She turned to see what he was doing.

Her eyes widened when he thrust the bag into her arms.

"It is now yours if you wish to own it," he said. "My mother is gone, as is her friend. I have only kept it because it meant so much to my mother to have it."

"Then you don't want to give it to me," Marjorie said. "If you give it away, so do you give away your memories."

"Memories hurt," Spotted Horse said.

He went to the fire and sat down beside it. He patted the blanket on which he sat. "*Hiyupo*, come," he said. "It is time to eat. Sun Bear will not eat with us. He is with the other children of our village this morning."

Marjorie felt awkward holding the bag. She truly felt as though she shouldn't have it. He had surely only given it to her because he felt foolish that she had discovered such women's things in his lodge.

Yet if she left it there when she went to the agent's house, Spotted Horse might be insulted that she had refused the generous gift.

Sighing, she sat down beside Spotted Horse, placing the bag at her right side.

"Much food was prepared for your breakfast," Spotted Horse said. He handed a wooden dish of food to Marjorie. His eyes twinkled as he looked at her. "Eat. We do not want to have conversations with your stomach today, do we?"

"But there is so much," Marjorie said softly.

"It is for us both so there is not too much," Spotted Horse said, smiling widely when she took the platter. He touched his stomach when it growled. "You see, my stomach complains the same as yours when I do not eat when I should."

She laughed softly and enjoyed the morning meal with him, at least for the moment forgetting Albert, the whooping cough epidemic, and the realization that, in a sense, she was very alone in the world.

For a while last night she had felt so contented to be there with Spotted Horse. But she now knew that had been a false feeling, for in truth, she did not see how she could ever have a future with him.

There were too many differences in their beliefs. There were too many taboos attached to loving an Indian.

For now, she would take things one step at a time. At this moment she was content just to be with Spotted Horse. Too soon she would be saying good-bye.

After Spotted Horse's plate was empty, he reached around and grabbed the leather bag.

Marjorie scarcely breathed as she watched to see what he was going to do with it. Had he changed his mind? Was he going to keep it after all?

Her own plate empty, she set it aside, her eyes still on Spotted Horse as she waited to see what he was going to do.

When he took the hairbrush and mirror from the bag and gave them to Marjorie, she questioned him with her eyes.

"The Dakota women do not allow their warriors to see them until their hair is groomed in the mornings," he said, his eyes moving to her hair. Then he gazed into her eyes, a slow smile fluttering on his lips. "You now have the tools with which to groom your hair."

Marjorie was almost afraid to look in the mirror to see just what shape her hair was in. Surely it was a fright! She hadn't brushed it since early the prior day.

Smiling shyly and feeling foolish, Marjorie raised the mirror and gazed at herself.

Her smile quickly faded, for never had she

seen her hair in such a mess. Tangles were everywhere. There were even cockleburs stuck in several strands from her early morning trip into the forest.

She realized that he had seen her look of horror. She melted inside when he reached over and gently removed the cockleburs from her hair one at a time and dropped them into the fire.

Then he took the brush from her and began brushing her hair in long, gentle strokes.

"Your hair is the color of a Dakota woman's, but much finer," Spotted Horse said, memories of his wife's hair causing a soft, stinging feeling in his heart. "Your hair is beautiful."

He laid the brush aside, slowly turned her to face him, then lowered his lips toward hers. "As are you beautiful," he said huskily.

When he covered her lips with his mouth in a heated, powerful kiss, a deliciousness Marjorie had never felt before filled her.

As he continued to kiss her, his hands slowly sliding across her back, and then around to the front of her, where her breasts were heaving beneath the cotton fabric of her dress, she became lost in an ecstasy so keen she felt as though she might faint from the wonder of it.

But the sudden sound of tom-toms being played outside and people singing drew them away from one another.

Breathless, her heart pounding, Marjorie stared into Spotted Horse's eyes. She had always envisioned such a kiss, such an embrace. But never had she imagined that it would be this wonderful. She had discovered that reality was far more wonderful than any fantasy could ever be.

Spotted Horse was stunned by the fierceness of his love for this woman, and by her reaction to it. He could tell by the way she returned the kiss that she was his, heart and soul.

Destiny had brought them together.

But was that enough?

There were many obstacles to their love.

Yes, there had been marriages between white and Dakota.

But Spotted Horse had heard of the turmoil those couples had faced because they had crossed the line set down by the white community.

He wondered if Marjorie's love for him was strong enough to fight such odds as that.

"The music, the singing," Marjorie said, breaking the silence. "What is it for? What does it mean? A short while ago I saw your people gathering outside. Are they involved now in a ceremony? If so, are you not required to be there also, since you are your people's chief?"

"The ceremony can last for many days, so it would be impossible for their chief to be there through all of it," Spotted Horse said softly. "*Hiyupo*, come, I shall show you."

He laid the brush aside and took the mirror from Marjorie.

He then placed a hand on her elbow and helped her up from the floor. He walked with her just outside the entrance flap.

Marjorie was taken aback by the frightening

way some of the women dancers' faces were painted with bold, bright colors, while the men's faces were painted black.

And she could not help staring at the way they all danced in a steady rhythm amidst the circle of people.

Then she gazed at the women who were standing back with the drummers, singing. Some of the singing had a weird, unearthly sound. The drum, made of deerskin drawn tightly over the end of a hollow log, was beaten in a very monotonous manner with a single stick. The sound was dull.

The rattles, made of gourd shells into which were put the round teeth of white bass, kept the same beat as the drums.

Flutes made from sumac were piercing and mysterious.

The loud voices of the singers and the dismal sound of the drums, rattles, and flutes caused goose bumps to rise on Marjorie's flesh.

"I see that you have noticed the paint on the faces of some of my people," Spotted Horse said softly, so that his voice would not be heard by others. "The paints are made from baked earth and berries. They wear their paints today for the beginning of the Ghost Dance ceremony, which is being performed in an effort to rid our village of the dreaded coughing disease. The dance is magic to the Dakota."

He slid an arm around her waist and drew her closer when she became frightened. Some of the people were falling to the ground in a trance-like state while others continued to dance, the motion of the dancers unnatural, abrupt, and violent.

"Do not be afraid," Spotted Horse softly explained. "Those who are on the ground are having a vision. This vision can be many things, but none I can explain to you, for each is particular to the individual. This is all being done to make the whooping cough disease go away. My people wish to return to the days when they can live happily on this green, green earth, under a blue, blue sky, and know that their children will grow old enjoying the same."

He paused and smiled down at Marjorie. "Listen to the song that is now being sung by the Fox Dreamers of my village," he said softly. "This song helps lighten the hearts of those bereaved people who have lost a young one to whooping cough."

Marjorie nodded and listened intently to the song. First it was sung in Dakota, and she could not understand the words. Then it was sung in English.

> *"To-ke-ya-inapa-nun-we*
> *To-ke-ya-enapi-nun-we*
> *Sunge la waste take ya inaja nun we,*
> He that goes out first,
> He that goes out first,
> The pretty fox that goes out first."

"And then there is the initial cry of the fox," Spotted Horse said. "*Hui-i-i, hui-i-i.*"

"How lovely," Marjorie murmured. "Thank you for explaining this all to me. It touches my heart that you would care enough to share it."

"It touches my heart that you care enough to want to *know* things Dakota," Spotted Horse said thickly.

"The ceremony, the singing and dancing—does that mean that there are still many who are ill with whooping cough?" Marjorie asked.

She gazed up at him, loving the feel of his arm around her waist, and loving his gentle ways. She had never wanted to be possessed by any man, because her mother had suffered so much at the hands of men. But now, with Spotted Horse's arm possessively holding her next to him, she could not deny enjoying it.

Before her thoughts could go farther, or before Spotted Horse could answer her question, an approaching horse drew both her and Spotted Horse's eyes to the rider.

Marjorie's heart skipped a beat and her knees went weak when she saw that it was Albert. His face was dark with intense hate as he rode right up to her and Spotted Horse, ignoring the ceremony he had so crudely interrupted.

All music, singing, and dancing ceased.

Everyone turned and glared at the man who had dared intrude on a most important, private time in their lives.

"I knew I'd find you here. Marjorie, get on this horse," Albert heatedly demanded. "You are going home with me. Now. Do you understand?"

When she stood her ground, Albert leaned down and glared into her eyes. "Marjorie, did you hear me?" he growled. "Your place is with your father, not total strangers."

He looked slowly around and stopped short of insulting the Indians by calling them heathen savages. Insults would come later when he had Marjorie safely away from the savages!

"I'll go nowhere with you," Marjorie said, placing her hands on her hips. "How could you be so stupid as to think I would? And you have surely gone mad to come here. Don't you even remember having threatened Chief Spotted Horse's son's life?"

His jaw tight, his eyes filled with fire, Albert glared at Marjorie for a moment longer.

He then stiffened when he saw many of Spotted Horse's warriors edging in close around him, grasping long lances, their faces painted hideously.

Realizing that he was close to being taken captive, or killed, and realizing that he *had* been a mite foolish to think he could accomplish anything here among heathens, Albert gave Marjorie another heated stare, then wheeled his horse around and rode away.

But not without a plan. He would now go to Fort Snelling and seek the soldiers' help. He would tell Colonel Samuel Dalton, the man in charge of the fort, that the Dakota had abducted his daughter.

He chuckled when he thought of how he would stir up the wrath of the soldiers against the Dakota in an effort to get Marjorie back. And when she was with him again, she would pay for causing him all of this trouble when he should be readying himself for the busiest hunting season of the year.

If she cost him much more valuable time, she'd be no better off than that skinned fox!

Chapter Eleven

Spotted Horse had seen how Marjorie was shaken by Albert's arrival at the village. He ushered her quickly into his lodge and drew her into his arms and comforted her.

Marjorie reveled in Spotted Horse's embrace, and how wonderful it felt to feel protected.

Yet she felt guilty for having brought danger into Spotted Horse's life by her mere presence.

She eased from his arms. She looked up at him uncertainly. "I truly must leave," she murmured. "My being here is not good for your people. What if Albert manages to get the entire cavalry from Fort Snelling to come with him to your village? For the sake of you and your people I must leave. I will go and request lodging at Louis Eckert's house."

"Stay," Spotted Horse said, reaching a hand

to her face, softly touching her. "The Dakota do not fear the white pony soldiers. My people have never exchanged harsh words with them."

"I still think that I should leave. . . ."

Her words were stolen away when he swept his arms around her, pulled her close to his hard-muscled body, and kissed her.

Marjorie's knees were weakened by the sudden passion that swept through her. She could feel Spotted Horse's own passion in the quivering of his lips and the intenseness with which he held her against himself.

Oh, Lord, she feared this passion even more than she feared staying with the Dakota chief. She now knew that she loved him so much that she might not be able to think clearly about what was right. Not only for herself, but also for Spotted Horse and his people.

She did so badly wish to stay, at least for one more night. She was afraid that once she left, she and Spotted Horse might never get the chance to be together again.

Sun Bear came into the lodge. He went and stood beside Marjorie and Spotted Horse, his eyes absorbing their passionate kiss . . . their show of feeling for one another. His heart leapt with joy at the realization that he had succeeded in getting them together.

But now their love was threatened by the evil white man!

His voice drew then quickly apart. "Marjorie, please stay," he asked softly. "You will be safe here. You will be happy."

Marjorie turned to Sun Bear and took his

hands in hers. "I know that you wish for me to stay, perhaps as much as I would love to," she murmured. "But, Sun Bear, your people have enough problems without me adding to them. I am so afraid that my stepfather is going to make up some big lie to get the soldiers to come here. Their presence, even for just a short while, will put hardships on your people. I don't want to be the cause."

Spotted Horse placed his hands on Marjorie's shoulders and turned her to face him. "Stay this one more night; then if you still insist, I, myself, will take you safely to the agent's house."

The look of soft pleading in Spotted Horse's eyes made Marjorie realize that she just could not say no to this man.

She saw a danger in that. Her mother had forgotten how to use the word *no* while with men. Marjorie had always been afraid of somehow becoming like her mother. She would rather die first!

But she could not deny her heart one more night with the man she loved!

"All right, but just for one night. Then I truly will leave and let you get back to the business of your people," she said, looking from Spotted Horse to Sun Bear.

She smiled when she saw the joy that her agreeing to stay brought into Sun Bear's eyes. She was touched deeply when he suddenly flung himself into her arms and hugged her, then ran from the lodge, a broad smile on his face.

"You have made my son very happy," Spotted

Horse said. He took Marjorie by the hand and drew her into his embrace again. "Also you have made this Dakota chief very happy." He brushed a kiss across her lips that left her weak and dizzy.

But she couldn't get Albert off her mind. She would never forget the hatred in his eyes.

"I wonder how Albert knew that I was here," she suddenly blurted out.

Spotted Horse turned away from her and stood over his lodge fire. He gazed into the flickering flames. "The Dakota have learned from whites that there is a God and a devil," he said solemnly. "*Wakantanka*, the *Big Holy*, is the Good Spirit in the Dakota's lives. The one who is called God is the white people's Good Spirit."

He turned and looked at Marjorie as she stood watching and listening. "*Wakaashica* is the evil spirit in the Dakota's world," he said thickly. "The devil is the white's evil spirit. Albert Stout was led to my village by *Wakaashica*, the evil spirit, the *devil*."

A tremor coursed through Marjorie. "I often think that Albert *is* the devil," she said, her voice drawn.

"*Hiyupo*, come," Spotted Horse said, taking her elbow. "Let us talk no more about the evil man. Let us go and sit among my people as they continue their Ghost Dance. I shall try to explain more about it to you."

He stopped and turned his eyes down to hers. "You do wish to learn, do you not?" he asked softly.

"Yes, I wish to learn," Marjorie said, then

stood on tiptoe and gave him a warm, soft kiss.

He swung his arms around her waist and again drew her against him. Their lips met in a heated, lingering kiss.

Left shaken by the kiss and the passion they felt for one another, they went outside and sat down. They tried to focus only on the ceremony that was meant to bring better health and happiness to the Dakota people.

But it was impossible for Marjorie to think of anything but Spotted Horse. She felt a warm glow to think that he cared so much for her!

But was it enough?

Would he truly fight, if need be, to have her?

Spotted Horse tried to concentrate fully on the ceremony, yet he could not get Marjorie and his feelings for her off his mind. Once the sickness was gone from his village, Marjorie would be there at his side in the capacity of *tawicu*, wife.

He smiled at that thought, taking comfort from it.

Chapter Twelve

At Fort Snelling, Albert stood over the wide oak desk. He stared disbelievingly down at Colonel Samuel Dalton, a gray-haired man with a wrinkle-grooved face.

"What do you mean you ain't goin' to the Dakota village?" Albert asked, his face red with anger. "Didn't you hear what I just said? The Dakota are holdin' my daughter hostage! They abducted her! I need your help to get her outta there before she is raped, or Lord help me, *scalped*."

"Just listen to yourself," Colonel Dalton said, laughing mockingly. "Can you truly stand there and believe what you are saying? Raped? Scalped? Being held hostage? Damn it, man, you know that's virtually impossible. Spotted Horse has never taken captives. He has never raped. And he has never taken scalps. So I don't believe you have to worry about any of that *now*."

"But . . . she's. . . . there," Albert persisted, his voice a low hiss.

"If she's there, I would wager a bet that she went there of her own volition," Colonel Dalton said. He closed a ledger and pushed it aside on his paper-cluttered desk.

"No woman in her right mind would stay among Injuns for any length of time," Albert said tightly. "No *respectable* woman, that is. And you know that my Marjorie is respected by everyone."

"Yes, I have heard about her, and know that she is a sweet, genteel lady," Colonel Dalton said. "I hear she makes paper dolls and sells them. Perhaps that's why she's at the Indian village."

"Never," Albert said, his jaw set. "I would never allow it. I don't trust Injuns any farther'n I can throw 'em."

He leaned down close to the colonel's face. "I plead with you to take a regiment out and check on my daughter's welfare," he said. "I'm afraid that Spotted Horse is up to no good. What if he has taken her captive to force marriage on her? Why, I bet she's prettier than any squaw in that whole damn Dakota tribe."

"I guess I won't be left alone until I do as you ask," Colonel Dalton said, sighing. "All right. I'll get some men together. I'll ride to the village. I'll go and have a peaceful council with the Dakota and see just why Marjorie is there."

Albert went cold. He hadn't wanted the soldiers to actually confront Spotted Horse. He had wanted them to attack him.

Albert knew that the Dakota's defenses were weakened by the whooping cough epidemic. It wouldn't take much to defeat them, to put Spotted Horse in his place.

But if a council was held between the soldiers and the Dakota, Albert would be caught in a bald-faced lie.

"I don't think that approach is right," he blurted out. "What if the Dakota won't allow a council and then, because you interfered, they take my daughter's life?"

"They wouldn't be that stupid," the colonel said, securing his saber at his right side. "Especially not Spotted Horse. He's one damn intelligent Indian."

"If he's so intelligent, why would he abduct a white woman?" Albert said, walking beside the colonel out of the office. He remained beside him as the colonel started shouting orders to his men.

"You've got to attack and get my daughter back," Albert pleaded. He watched nervously as horses were brought from the stable and the soldiers mounted and prepared to leave.

Colonel Dalton swung himself into his saddle. He glared down at Albert. "To please you, to shut you *up*, I will first ride up close to the village and see how things look there." He nodded for a soldier to bring Albert's horse to him. "If an attack is warranted, then most certainly I will attack."

The colonel shrugged. "To tell you the truth, Albert," he said. "I've been worried that peace might be broken because of the whooping cough epidemic at the village. I know that the Dakota must be blaming the whites for the deaths."

"Then see?" Albert said, hurrying into his saddle. "Don't it make sense that they might steal a white woman? To provoke you into a fight?"

"Perhaps, perhaps," the colonel said, kneading his chin thoughtfully. "But still, I don't see any logic in such an act as that. Spotted Horse knows that he is outnumbered and any battle will end in a defeat for him."

"Perhaps he doesn't care about a defeat as much as he wishes to find some way to avenge the deaths of his people's children," Albert said, riding alongside the colonel as they left the fort.

Albert's eyes narrowed and he half smiled as he tried to convince the colonel of the need to attack. "Haven't you heard the gossip about the Dakota quietly planning to go on the warpath over the disease?" he said guardedly.

The colonel looked quickly over at Albert. "No, no such gossip has reached Fort Snelling," he said, his voice drawn.

"Why take chances?" Albert asked, his eyes dancing with mischief. "Attack, damn it. Save yourself the trouble of waitin' for their attack on the fort."

"I just don't know. . . ." Colonel Dalton said, sighing. "I hate like hell to go against Spotted Horse. I truly like the man."

"The hunger for vengeance changes a man,"

111

Albert said, his lips tugging into a slow smile to think that the colonel was finally believing his lies. Yes, by the time they reached the village with their horde of soldiers, he was sure that fear of an Indian raid on the fort would cause the colonel to make a surprise attack on the Dakota.

Thinking that enough had been said, Albert rode onward in utter silence. The sky was blue and clear overhead. An eagle soared on the wing, casting its shadow on the ground. The autumn leaves were falling in the gentle breeze. Squirrels scampered around, burying hickory nuts and walnuts.

When they came within a short distance of the Dakota village, Colonel Dalton exchanged a questioning glance with Albert. "Do you hear the chants?" he said, raising an eyebrow. "Do you hear the loud beat of the drums?"

"Yes, I hear it, and I must tell you that when I was here a while ago, spying on the Injuns, I saw how hideously they were painted," Albert lied, not wanting the colonel to know he had actually been in the village. He had to be careful not to say anything that would lead the colonel to suspect that most everything he'd said today was a lie.

"They were hideously painted?" the colonel gasped out, his voice drawn, his hand suddenly resting on the handle of his saber. "With war paint?"

"Like I said, it is rumored they are going on the warpath," Albert said, feeling smug that the Indians were unknowingly aiding and abetting his plan. "So, yes, I would say the paint they wear today *is* war paint."

Colonel Dalton brought his horse to a quick stop. He raised his fist, the order to halt and dismount.

After securing their steeds, the soldiers went to a butte that overlooked the village and watched the wild dancing. They were stunned when they saw many of the dancers suddenly fall to the ground, as though in a strange sort of stupor.

Colonel Dalton stared through his field glasses, his eyes wide. "By God, it *is* a war dance," he whispered to Albert. "You were right! And, oh Lord, Marjorie *is* among them. She is sitting beside Chief Spotted Horse!"

He slowly lowered the field glasses. He sighed. "Trouble is brewing," he said thickly. "And I do believe now that your daughter was abducted. I must make haste and return to the fort. I will send messengers to the nearby forts to ask for reinforcements before entering the Dakota village."

A quick panic grabbed Albert. "No, you can't wait," he said. "It might take many days for the reinforcements to arrive. What about my daughter? The longer she's in the Indian village, the more danger she's in."

Colonel Dalton stopped and glared at Albert. "Your daughter is only one person," he grumbled. "All the white settlers in the area are at risk. I must consider their welfare first. I must try to stop the war before it starts. Surrounding the village with as many soldiers as I can muster up, to show force to the Dakota, is the best way. And once they see that they can't win against such odds, then I shall get your daughter back for you. Only then, Albert! Let me hear no more about it. I've things to do. I'd suggest you return to your home until I send word to you about when we are going to return to the Dakota village."

He placed a reassuring hand on Albert's shoulder. "Just pray, man, that once the Dakota see the show of force, they will settle this disagreement peacefully," he said. "They won't want their village destroyed, or their people slaughtered."

The colonel dropped his hand to his side, kneaded his chin momentarily, then again looked at Albert. "I have thought of another reason why the Dakota might be angry," he blurted out. "Just yesterday I sent word to Chief Spotted Horse to stop putting the bodies of their dead in trees along the river. I ordered many pine caskets taken to the village. Perhaps the chief resents my interference in his people's burial customs . . . and resents being told what to do. That might have been the straw that broke the camel's back."

Hearing about the caskets gave Albert another idea.

He smiled as he nodded farewell to the colonel.

He rode off, having his own idea of how he would get Marjorie from the Dakota.

"And to hell with the soldiers!" he muttered angrily. "Who needs 'em?"

Laughing wickedly, he sent his horse into a hard gallop. He had a certain destination in mind—the casket maker's cabin!

Chapter Thirteen

Albert slid slowly from his saddle as he gazed
with apprehension at the casket maker's cabin.
He shuddered at how unkempt the cabin was.
The wood shingles of the roof were half gone.
And the cabin leaned precariously sideways, as
though one sudden wind might blow it over.

It sat in a small clearing in the forest, where
trees hovered over it, their bare, twisted limbs
taking on the appearance of old men's bones
that had been bent out of shape by disease.

But what was even more unnerving to Albert
were the stacks of newly made pine caskets at
one side of the cabin. The casket maker also
served as the area's mortician.

The smell of coffee wafting from the open
door of the cabin was the only pleasant thing
about Albert's arrival at the mortician–casket

maker's lodge. It somehow seemed to make the man more human, for in truth, almost everyone avoided him unless they had the need of his services. He was a bent, small man, called Snow because of his snow white hair and pink eyes. He was an albino.

Remembering Marjorie, and how badly he wanted to get her from the Dakota village, Albert drummed up the courage to proceed with his plans. He tethered his reins to a hitching post and walked toward the cabin.

His steps became more hurried as he considered his plan to get into the Dakota Indian village without being detected. This scheme would give him quick, easy access to Marjorie. He would steal her back from Spotted Horse. When Albert married Marjorie's ma, he had got Marjorie in the bargain. No one but him would have her!

Suddenly the casket maker was standing at the door, sipping coffee from a tin cup, watching Albert approach.

Albert smiled awkwardly and stepped up to the man. "Good morning, Snow," he said, extending a stiff hand even though he loathed the thought of touching the man.

Who was to say where his hands had just been? What if there was a dead body inside his cabin being prepared for burial?

That thought sent a shudder across Albert's flesh.

"Mornin', Albert," Snow said, squinting his pale eyes up at Albert, who stood a head taller than he. "What's the cause of your visit? You got a need for my services?"

A nervous twitch began on Snow's right cheek as he leaned closer to Albert. "It ain't that pretty Marjorie, is it?" he asked, his eyes showing anxiousness in their depths. "She ain't died, has she? I'll never forget her ma, so pretty and all. It was a pleasure preparin' her for burial, Albert. A pleasure."

"No, it ain't Marjorie," Albert said, frowning, and trying to ignore the vile man's mention of his wife. "But, yes, I do have a need for your services."

Snow nodded toward the caskets as he poured the last of his coffee on a high pile of coffee grounds beside his front door, which he dumped there each morning as he made a fresh pot.

"I've got the finest caskets in the area," Snow said, nodding. Then he raised a pale white eyebrow as he gazed up at Albert again. "But you don't need a casket if no one has died. What is your reason for bein' here? What sort of services are you after?"

Albert scrunched up his shoulders and looked cautiously from side to side.

Snow could see his uneasiness. He reached out and grabbed Albert's arm. "Come on inside where we can talk in private," he said.

Albert yanked his arm away, shuddering at the thought of entering Snow's cabin, for fear there might be someone in there being prepared for burial. He'd seen many a corpse in his day, but none in the process of being readied for the ground!

"Come on," Snow said, nodding toward the door. "Have a cup of coffee while you tell me why you're here."

Albert's eyes wavered. He swallowed hard.

Then, wanting to get this behind him so that he could get away from this undesirable man, Albert sighed and went inside with Snow. The cabin was so dark and dank and crowded with things he did not recognize that it took a while for Albert's eyes to get used to the darker interior after being in the bright sunshine.

But once he could see things more clearly, he made out a slab table at the back of the cabin, opposite the wall where flames glowed in a large fireplace. He felt the urge to turn around and run from the cabin. He knew that he was looking at the very place so many people had been prepared for burial.

It came to him like a bolt of lightning that his own wife had been on that table as she was readied for the grave. In his mind's eye he could see her lying there, her beautiful eyes closed, her long and flowing black hair encircling her angelic face like a wreath.

He could see the tiny, pink-eyed man undressing her, enjoying the wonders of her body.

Albert turned his eyes quickly away. He anxiously accepted a cup of coffee as Snow placed it in his hands.

"I know how you're feelin'," Snow said, leading Albert by an elbow to a rocker before the fireplace. "That's why most people won't come to my house to make arrangements for their loved ones. My business is usually done at the individual's house, or at Fort Snelling."

Snow sat down on a straight-backed wooden chair and drew it up close to Albert. He looked him square in the eye. "Now tell me why you are here," he said. "What can I do for you?"

Albert took another quick swallow of coffee, then cradled the cup in his hands as he gazed at Snow. "My daughter is no longer with me," he blurted out. "For reasons I won't get into, she's at the Dakota Indian village. I can't persuade her to come home. So I plan to go in and get her. That's why I'm here. I need your help."

"Oh?" Snow said, his eyebrows raising. "How can *I* help? I only make and sell caskets and bury people in 'em."

"All of those caskets I saw outside your cabin? They appear to have just been made," Albert said. "Ain't that so?"

"Yep, that's so," Snow said, nodding.

"You've made them to take to the Injun village?"

"Yep, early in the mornin' I should have enough made to set out for the village. But how'd you know the government paid me to do this?"

"I was at the fort. Colonel Dalton told me about the Injuns bein' forced to bury their dead in caskets instead of on scaffoldings in the trees."

"That's so. But what does that have to do with you?"

"I'll pay you good when I sell my autumn pelts

if you'll let me hide in one of those caskets that you are going to take into the Injun village," Albert said guardedly. "Once I'm in the village, I can sneak out of the casket. No one will ever know that you were in on my scheme to steal Marjorie away."

"And you're not about to tell me why she chose not to live with you?" Snow said.

"That ain't none of your business," Albert growled, his jaw tightening. "Now, will you or will you not let me hide in one of the caskets? Like I said, you'll get paid well for helpin' me get my daughter back."

Snow shrugged. "Yep, I'll help. I don't know why I shouldn't," he said, laughing throatily.

Albert broke into a broad smile. He set the cup aside and clasped a hand on Snow's shoulder. "Thanks, man," he said. "You don't know how much I appreciate it."

"You'll show me how much when you pay me double the pelts that you've got in mind to pay," Snow said, cackling when that statement caused Albert to draw his hand from his shoulder as though he had been shot.

"Double?" Albert gasped. "You will make me pay double?"

"Yep, guess so," Snow said, rising. He lifted a large log and laid it on the grate of his fireplace. He bent and blew into the glowing coals, standing up again when the fire caught hold on the log.

Albert smiled wickedly, knowing that Snow had no idea just how many pelts he had been planning to give him, so how would he know if

121

the payment was double or not? Whatever Albert paid him he would have to accept, for by then he would have no other choice. Albert would have already gotten what he wanted from the pink-eyed man, and there was no way Snow could take it back from him.

"A bargain is a bargain," Snow said, turning to smile at Albert. "Do we have one or not? I've got to get back outside and put the finishin' touches on a casket."

"Yeah, we have one," Albert said, his lips curling into a sly sneer.

"Then be here before dawn tomorrow," Snow said, walking outside the cabin as Albert followed close beside him. "I won't wait on you if you ain't here. I've things to do. I ain't used to no one interferin'."

"I'll be here," Albert said, walking toward his tethered horse. He swung himself into his saddle and gave Snow a mock salute. "Yeah, Snow, I'll be here with bells on."

He wheeled his horse around and rode off. "Like hell I'll pay you *any*thing," he whispered harshly to himself. "You pink-eyed, no-good thief."

Chapter Fourteen

The sound of people singing and wailing awakened Marjorie the next morning. She leaned upon an elbow and looked around her. By the dim light of the slow-burning fire she could see that she was alone.

The wails soared into the morning air, filled with such torment and grief that they caused shivers to ride Marjorie's spine. Fearing that the Ghost Dance had not worked its magic after all, and that there were more deaths in the village, Marjorie rushed to her feet. Except for her shoes, she still wore her clothes.

Not worrying about her hair or her wrinkled clothes, she ran outside, barefoot. It was a crisp dawn. The morning star was just fading in the violet sky. The corn crop in the distance was fringed with a heavy frost that had overnight changed the vivid colors of the trees into something faded and ugly as the withered leaves rustled mournfully in the bleak autumn forest.

Marjorie gasped and stared at what was going on in the village. Horrified, she watched two children being placed in pine caskets just outside the Medicine Man's lodge. This large tepee stood out from the rest by being painted with the symbols of the Medicine Man's particular dream-given power: two huge grizzly bears in black, below which were circles of moons in red.

Spotted Horse saw Marjorie standing there. He hurried to her side and slid an arm around her waist. "More children have died," he said, his voice drawn. "Two pregnant women have also died. They were weakened from caring for the children and came down with the disease, themselves."

He placed his hands on Marjorie's shoulders and turned her to face him. "You must go, or *you* might become ill with the whooping cough disease," he said somberly. "Until today I thought the disease claimed only children. I was wrong."

His eyes burned into hers with soft pleading. "I want nothing to happen to you. *Please* go."

"Yes, I will go," Marjorie said. "But I will return. I will bring Doc Rose back to your village. He can bring his medicine to the Dakota. He will help stop the deaths."

Spotted Horse's eyes narrowed. His jaw tightened. He lowered his hands quickly from her shoulders. "No," he said tightly. "No white doctors are needed. The powers of our Medicine Man come from the west and from the Thunder Beings. It will insult our Medicine Man and our Thunder Beings if a white doctor is brought amidst the Dakota people."

"Please, Spotted Horse, *please* give Doc Rose a chance," Marjorie pleaded. She grabbed his arm. Unknowingly, her fingers dug into his flesh. "The children! So many are dying!"

He placed his hand over hers and slowly lifted it from his arm. "Brown Hair, the Dakota Medicine Man, is close to the source of all things," he said thickly. "Mother Nature is the source of all things. She is the mother of all things. Brown Hair is wise. His is the power of medicine and the protection of faith."

Suddenly the wailing stopped. A lone man began singing, his voice seeming to reach beyond the clouds.

Marjorie turned and watched Brown Hair walk to the center of the village. His brown hair hung long and straight down his back. He wore a tight-fitting fur headpiece, from which hung a single eagle feather. He also wore a simple buckskin tunic decorated with a porcupine-quill breastplate, trousers, and beaded moccasins. In one hand he carried a coup stick bound with leather and fur. In his other hand he carried a deer-hoof rattle.

Spotted Horse leaned closer to Marjorie. "He sings the song of the sun," he whispered. "The words are those of the sun delivering his power to the Medicine Man to be used for the sick. The sickness is carried out of those who are ill, into the sun. Listen. You will be moved deep inside your soul by the song."

He paused, then added, "Of all the deities, Sun Father wields the greatest power, for just think of what life would be like if he withheld the sun from us, or how damaging the rays of the sun would be if Sun Father let them shine day and night without cessation."

He leaned even closer to Marjorie. "Listen," he whispered. "Listen."

Although Marjorie could not understand the words being sung in the Dakota tongue, she could feel the force of the song in the way it was sung. She listened, for the moment lost to the song. . . .

> "Wanka tan han he ya u we lo,
> Wanka tan han he ya u we lo,
> Meta wi cohan topa wan la.
> Ka nu we he ya u we lo,
> Anpe wi kin he ya ue we lo,
> A ye ye ye yo."

Then Brown Hair sang another song, parts of which Marjorie did understand, for he spoke some in his tongue, and some in hers.

> "Chiksuya-waoewe,
> Change shica waowe,
> He-o-he! He-o-he!
> I remember you, wa-o-we!
> Heart bad, heart sad,
> Wa-o-we,
> He-ohe!
> He-ohe!"

Brown Hair then walked away and entered his lodge.

The wailing resumed.

Spotted Horse took Marjorie by the hand and led her back inside his lodge. "You are trembling," he said. He led her over to the fire. He eased a warm bear robe around her shoulders, then bent low and placed small strips of cedar wood into the flames.

"Sit," he said, gesturing toward the blankets she had used for a bed the previous night. "Let us talk some more. I have already given instructions to bring us food."

"I don't think I can eat," Marjorie said solemnly, unable to get the thought of the dead people off her mind. "I am saddened by so much."

Spotted Horse sat down beside her as they both watched the tangled flames wrap themselves around the wood. "You must eat for strength for your journey to the agent's home," he said. "I will escort you safely there as soon as your stomach is comfortably filled with food."

"I refuse to leave your village unless I can go to the fort and get Doc Rose," Marjorie said, giving him a stubborn stare. "The Medicine Man can do only so much for your people. Can't you admit that having someone else looking in on your people might help them?"

"No white doctor has ever been needed by the Dakota," Spotted Horse said, looking back at her just as stubbornly. "Our Medicine Man feels a kinship with the Thunder Beings. A deep joy comes from feeling a oneness with our Medicine Man. It gives our people a sense of belonging. Because of the Medicine Man, my people are attuned to the powers of nature that envelop them. The joy they feel makes any fear of the afterlife needless. My people have a firm belief in the immortality of the soul. When they die, they go to the country of spirits. To them it is an unknown country, but a real one."

"Yet the wails fill the air even now," Marjorie said. "Where is your people's joy now?"

"They do not cry over lack of joy, or over fear," Spotted Horse said. "They cry over their loss."

"Such losses might be prevented if you would only allow Doc Rose to come with his medicine," Marjorie said, then grew silent when his cold stare seemed to cut her heart in two.

She knew that her arguments were in vain. She knew that nothing she said would change his mind.

And it hurt to know that he did not trust her enough to give what she suggested a try.

A young maiden brought a tray of food into the lodge and set it on the floor between Marjorie and Spotted Horse. She then went to the back of the lodge, got two wooden platters, and gave one to Spotted Horse, the other to Marjorie.

She left as quickly as she had come.

"Eat, for you will leave soon after," Spotted Horse said, sighing deeply when Marjorie did not make a move toward the food. "It is important that you take nourishment into your body.

All things that help sustain the body—food, pure air, water, and sun—are medicine. It will help protect you against the whooping cough disease."

Marjorie's eyes wavered as she looked down at the food. There was no question how hungry she was. And she knew that it might be many hours before she got the chance to eat again. She would be leaving. He was adamant about that.

She had never met anyone as stubborn as Spotted Horse. He seemed even more stubborn than she.

She watched Spotted Horse fill her plate with blue and white corn scrambled with duck eggs and wild onions. He lifted slices of meat onto the plate, as well. Also slices of apples and an assortment of berries.

She accepted the plate, and with her fingers began eating. She got so involved in the wonderful taste of the food, she paid no attention when he left for a moment.

When he returned, he had a wooden jar of juniper tea and two cups. He offered this to her.

They both ate and drank in silence.

Then he left again.

When he returned, he carried a lovely buckskin dress across one arm, a towel across the other. "The women are bathing in private in the river," he said, handing her the dress and towel. "You can join them. You will be refreshed for your journey to the agent's house."

She gazed in wonder at the lovely dress, then looked into his eyes. "Thank you," she murmured. "I . . . I do feel as though I haven't bathed in weeks."

He reached a gentle hand to her cheek, then turned to leave. "I will go now and find Sun Bear," he said over his shoulder. "He has been with a friend, consoling him over the loss of a sister. He will travel with us to Louis's house."

Now alone, Marjorie was overwhelmed by her emotions. She felt deep sadness over what was happening at the Dakota village. She felt a gnawing emptiness at the thought of leaving Spotted Horse. But she had no choice *except* to leave, and she must not allow herself to continue thinking about the need for Doc Rose at the village. Spotted Horse would never allow it.

Just as she stepped outside the tepee she saw a wagon filled with freshly made pine caskets enter the village. She shuddered as she recognized the pink-eyed man who was removing the coffins from the wagon and placing them in stacks near Spotted Horse's tepee, where the trees made a shady, secluded spot.

She lifted an eyebrow when she saw how Snow struggled with one casket in particular. It seemed to weigh more than the others, as though a body might already be inside it.

Shrugging, and watching Snow leave with his empty wagon, Marjorie stepped outside and walked toward the river. She shivered as she was forced to walk past the caskets, the trees on one side, the caskets on the other.

She stopped and paled and took an unsteady step backwards when she saw the lid of one of the caskets slowly opening.

Marjorie felt faint with fright when she saw a hand circle around the edge of the lid of the casket.

A scream froze in her throat.

She dropped the dress and towel to the ground when Albert slid free of the casket.

Quick as lightning he grabbed her and dragged her into the shadows of the trees. Before Marjorie could scream, Albert had a gag tied around her mouth and her hands tied behind her back.

Helpless, Marjorie looked frantically around her as Albert dragged her farther into the forest, and then into a clearing where Snow waited in his wagon.

"You thought you'd gotten away from me, didn't you?" Albert said, lifting Marjorie into his arms and placing her in the buckboard wagon. He climbed up beside her and held her in place as Snow started the wagon. "Well, little miss smartie pants, you'll never get away from your pa. Never."

Marjorie tried to wrestle her hands free, but the more she worked at the ropes, the more she caused them to bite into the flesh of her wrists.

She settled down, knowing that for now she was again at this evil man's mercy. But at her first opportunity she would escape again. He would be sorry he ever knew her. He would pay for all he had done to her mother, and now, herself.

She watched with bated breath to see where Snow was taking her. When she saw Snow's cabin a short distance away, she cringed, for she knew what he did there. He prepared the dead for burial! Was there someone even now in his cabin, awaiting his special touches?

She was glad when he turned the wagon to the right and instead took her and Albert to a small shack so well hidden from view that she had not noticed it on the day she had come with Albert to bring her mother to the mortician.

She tried to wriggle free when Albert yanked her up into his arms and took her from the wagon. She tried to speak, but the gag stifled the words. Also, the more she tried to talk, the drier her mouth became.

She became stone silent as Albert carried her inside the shack. She was relieved that it was only a storage shack for tools and supplies.

"This'll do for a hiding place until Spotted Horse gives up searching for you," Albert said, placing her on her feet.

Carrying a straight-backed wood chair, Snow scurried into the shack.

Marjorie grimaced under Snow's leering stare as Albert slammed her down on the chair and tied her to it.

"Now that oughta take care of you for a while," Albert said, stepping back. "You'll be untied long enough to eat and to pee. But otherwise, you'll have to stay tied. You've proved you can't be trusted."

He studied her, then untied the gag from her mouth. "I might as well let you get some air, for no one's anywhere near to hear, not even if you scream your lungs out," he said.

She scarcely heard what he was saying. Her

eyes were on Snow. She hated the way he continued to leer at her hungrily. But she could see that he was infatuated with her, which gave her a ray of hope that she might be able to use that infatuation to her advantage. She would use it against Albert!

"I need a drink," Albert said, wiping his mouth with the palm of a hand. He gazed over at Snow. "Snow, have you got anything that'll sting the gut?"

"There's a bottle of whiskey in my cabin," Snow said, his eyes never leaving Marjorie. "Just inside the door to your right."

Albert left the cabin with eager steps.

Snow went closer to Marjorie and knelt down before her.

When he reached a hand to her face and traced her features, she tried not to show her loathing for him. He was a strange man with strange habits.

"You're as pretty as your ma was," Snow said huskily. "So pretty and soft."

Knowing that he was playing right into her hands, Marjorie fought against showing her revulsion to him. She tried not to think about how he had been alone with her mother as he had prepared her for her burial. Yes, if she thought about that, she might retch.

As it was, she had to concentrate on getting free while Albert was gone, or she might never again get the chance.

"Snow, do you truly think I'm pretty and soft?" Marjorie said, forcing herself to speak in a seductive tone.

"Very," Snow said, eagerly nodding, his pink eyes wide as he peered at her.

"Snow, would you like to see just how soft I am?" Marjorie said, her pulse racing.

"I'm touching you now," Snow said, smiling. "I can feel just how soft you are."

"But you can touch more than my face, if you wish," Marjorie said, playing on his loneliness. "I'll go to your cabin with you. You . . . can . . . touch me all over, if you wish."

"Really?" Snow said, his face taking on a pinched sort of eagerness.

"Really," Marjorie said. "But first you've got to get rid of my stepfather. He's an abusive man. Please help me. If I'm forced to live with him again, he'll beat me like he beat my mother. Snow, you don't want me to have bruises all over my soft body, do you?"

"No, no bruises," Snow said, visibly shivering. "Never bruises."

"Then, Snow, do what you must to stop my stepfather," Marjorie said. "Then you and I can be alone. You do want me, don't you, Snow?"

Snow nodded, then stood up and walked over to his supplies. He picked up a hammer from a table and went and stood behind the door and waited for Albert to return.

When Albert stepped inside the shack, lifting the whiskey bottle to his lips, Snow rushed from behind the door and knocked him on the head with the hammer.

Albert's body lurched with the blow. He dropped the bottle, then tumbled onto the floor, blood seeping from a wound at the back of his head.

Marjorie winced as she stared down at Albert. The sound of the hammer hitting his skull had been similar to the sound made when she cracked walnuts.

And by the way he was lying there she was not sure if Snow had rendered him unconscious or killed him.

"I'll get you untied and outta here," Snow said, bringing a knife from his cache of supplies. "I'll take you to my cabin."

He cut through one rope and then another until Marjorie was freed of her bonds.

She noticed that Snow kept the knife as he led her out of the shack and toward his cabin. Perhaps he wasn't as dumb as she had thought. It was obvious that he didn't trust her by the way he kept lifting the knife out for her to see.

"Come on inside," Snow said, stepping aside to let Marjorie enter his dark, dank cabin. "But pardon the mess." He cackled. "In my line of business, I don't have much time for worryin' about messes."

He led Marjorie to a bed at the far side of the room, away from the part of the cabin that was used for preparing bodies. She cringed at the sight of the yellow blankets and soiled pillows.

But she had no choice but to get on the bed. Snow still held the knife.

"I haven't had women in my cabin,'cept for those"—he stopped to chuckle—"who are dead."

Marjorie was struck so numb by what she had

gotten herself into, she was speechless. She smiled awkwardly at Snow, silently praying that he wouldn't rape her at knife point. Oh, Lord, things weren't going at all as planned!

Snow started pacing, looking only occasionally at Marjorie. "No, I ain't had no women in my cabin," he said, his voice drawn. "And to be truthful, it's been a while since I had a woman at *all*."

He turned quickly toward her. "Do you want somethin' to eat or drink?" he said nervously.

Marjorie couldn't believe her luck. She was with a man who was awkward with women! There was a chance that he wouldn't even want her!

Yes, she would play along with him for as long as she could, until she could find a way to outsmart him and get that blasted knife away from him. Yet she kept thinking about Albert.

Was he or was he not . . . dead?

"Yes, I'd like something to eat, *and* drink," Marjorie said in a soft, sweet murmur. "That is, if you are going to eat and drink with me."

"Yes, yes," Snow said, nodding.

He scurried around the cabin gathering up food, dishes, cups, and a bottle of vodka, always keeping an eye on Marjorie so that she did not have the opportunity to get away.

"You are the first," Snow kept mumbling, his cheeks red with excitement. "You . . . are . . . the first. . . ."

Marjorie swallowed hard, thinking that if she was the first, just how long would she be able to hold him off? Surely he would not be able to stand the waiting much longer. Not with someone there, offering him all that he had been denied for so long.

Chapter Fifteen

When Spotted Horse returned to his tepee and discovered that Marjorie was gone, he thought that she was still at the river, bathing.

Sun Bear had lingered outside to look at the pine caskets that had just been delivered. When he went inside the lodge, he said, "*Ahte*, I found this dress and towel outside by the pine caskets." He held the buckskin dress and towel out for Spotted Horse to see.

When Sun Bear saw alarm leap into his father's dark eyes and heard him gasp, he took an unsteady step from him. "*Ahte*, what is it?" he asked, flinching when Spotted Horse grabbed the dress and towel from him.

He silently watched in wonder as Spotted Horse stared down at the dress and then looked quickly at the entranceway.

Then, his eyes flashing, Spotted Horse turned his gaze back to his son. "You found these beside the pine boxes?" he asked, his voice drawn.

"*Ho*," Sun Bear said, his voice barely a whisper.

Then he spoke more loudly, sudden fear grabbing him. "Whose dress and towel are they?" he asked guardedly.

"I gave them to Marjorie to use for a bath in the river with the other women," Spotted Horse said, puzzled that she had not used them.

And where was she?

Had she gotten so upset at him for refusing to allow her to bring a white doctor to his village that she had just left on her own to go to the agent's house?

Or had she decided to go against his wishes? Had she gone for the white doctor after all?

Or had Albert managed to get into the village somehow and abducted her?

That thought, that possibility, gave Spotted Horse a sudden foreboding feeling. If the white man had managed to get Marjorie back in his clutches, she was in mortal danger, for her stepfather would surely find ways to punish her for having gone against him.

"Where *is* Marjorie?" Sun Bear asked softly. "Did she leave without a good-bye? Did she not want our escort to the agent's house?" He sighed heavily. "*Ahte*, did you and Marjorie argue over something? Did she leave in anger?" he asked wearily.

"I know not the answers to any of your questions," Spotted Horse said, evading especially the question about having argued with Marjorie.

Spotted Horse wished now that he had used more tact with Marjorie about the white doctor. If she had left because of him, and any harm came to her, he would never forgive himself.

"Sun Bear, show me the exact spot where you found the dress and towel," Spotted Horse said, dropping them to the floor. "Now, Sun Bear. Take me there *now*."

Sun Bear stared at his father for a short moment. When he saw quiet desperation in his father's eyes, he grabbed Spotted Horse's hand and left the lodge with him.

"There," Sun Bear said when he reached the spot of Marjorie's abduction. He pointed to one casket in particular. "They were there beside that pine box, the only one whose lid is open."

Sun Bear stood back and watched Spotted Horse search the ground around the casket, fearing as each moment passed that harm had come to the white woman.

Spotted Horse bent to his knees and studied the ground more carefully when he saw that there were more than Marjorie's footprints there. There were also larger footprints! A man's!

And the man did not wear Dakota moccasins. He wore flat-soled boots with a large heel.

The abductor was a white man.

He reached a slow hand toward the prints, realizing that the footprints were not those made by two people who were standing and speaking on friendly terms.

There had been a struggle.

The footprints were scattered here and there, one over the other.

He looked slowly at the open casket, then looked at the others with their lids securely in place.

"Coward that he is, the *washechu* came in a pine box," Spotted Horse said. "He knew that he could not just ride into our village and be greeted as a friend. He knew that the only way he could get to Marjorie was to sneak in, in a box made for the dead. Then he stole her away!"

"Who, *ahte?*" Sun Bear asked, raising an eyebrow. "Who are you saying came in the pine box?"

"Marjorie's stepfather," Spotted Horse growled.

"Her stepfather came and took her?" Sun Bear gasped out.

"*Ho*, he came in the pine box, but—"

Spotted Horse didn't finish what he was saying. He began following the footprints into the darker depths of the forest.

Sun Bear walked beside him, his eyes also studying the prints.

"She did not go willingly, that is for certain," Sun Bear then said, anger filling his heart. "You can see by the prints, and how the leaves are scattered here and there on the ground, that she was being dragged."

"*Ho*, I am also aware of that, which means that she feared her abductor," Spotted Horse said.

"But where did he take her?" Sun Bear asked,

141

ducking to walk beneath a low-hanging branch. "If he came in the pine box, he could not have brought a horse."

"That is so, which means there was an accomplice, for it is too far to his cabin to walk, especially with a prisoner in his possession," Spotted Horse said dryly.

"But most people they might run into would not see Marjorie as a prisoner," Sun Bear said, giving Spotted Horse a half glance. "Only we know that she is his captive. Most who know them from the trading post and forts see them as father and daughter. It would look natural for them to be together, except that . . ."

Spotted Horse gave Sun Bear a slight, sly smile. "Except that no father would be manhandling a daughter in such a way," he said, completing Sun Bear's words.

"We must get her back, *ahte*," Sun Bear said, swallowing hard. "She is such a good woman. She would make a good mother. A wonderful wife."

"*Ho*, she is everything we both have envisioned in a woman, and more," Spotted Horse said, wishing she were with him now, safe, loved, and smiling at him.

He suddenly stopped, and his heart skipped a beat when they stepped out into a clearing and found more tracks. They were the tracks of a wagon being pulled by a mule.

"Snow!" Spotted Horse said.

His eyes narrowed angrily as he sank to his haunches and ran his fingers along the tracks made from the wooden wagon wheels. "Snow brought Marjorie's stepfather to our village in the pine box! After he abducted Marjorie, Snow took them both away in his wagon!"

"How could Snow involve himself in such a plan as this?" Sun Bear said, looking at the wagon wheel tracks himself. "Did he not know that we would find his tracks and that they would lead us to him?"

Spotted Horse rose quickly to his feet. "The man called Snow is not intelligent, and I am sure he was promised a large payment for his part in what happened today," he said.

He turned and broke into a hard run in the direction of his village. "*Hiyupo*, Sun Bear," he cried. "We must gather together many warriors! We must get Marjorie away from those madmen!"

As he continued to run through the forest, Spotted Horse lifted his eyes heavenward. "*Hunhunhe*! Will things ever again be right?" he cried to his *Big Holy*. "And my woman! Why does she have to pay for the sins of others? Why?"

Hearing the despair in his father's words, Sun Bear felt as though his heart was being ripped in shreds, and tears came to his eyes. He, too, lifted his eyes heavenward and said his own prayer, but in silence.

Sun Bear prayed for Marjorie, and also for his people's children, for the mothers and fathers, and for the grandparents and aunts and uncles.

But most of all he prayed for Spotted Horse, the man who was everything to him.

When they finally reached the village, word

spread quickly. Many warriors armed themselves and mounted, and Spotted Horse led them away on his strong steed. The horses' hoofbeats sounded like distant thunder.

Sun Bear rode tall, straight, and proud beside his father.

And today he rode no mere pony. He rode a great black stallion.

Today Sun Bear carried a man's weapon in the gunboot at the side of his horse—a rifle that Spotted Horse had trustingly thrust into his hand, telling him that it was his now, to do what must be done to save the woman.

And Sun Bear knew that he would not flinch while firing the powerful weapon, not if it meant getting Marjorie back safe with Spotted Horse!

They rode hard until they came close to Snow's cabin.

Then they dismounted, secured their horses, and went the rest of the way by foot.

When they got just beyond Snow's cabin, and stood at the edge of the forest, Spotted Horse sent his men in two directions until the cabin was totally surrounded.

Spotted Horse watched the cabin for a moment longer, his eyes roaming slowly over it. He then gazed at the stacks of pine caskets, some finished, others in parts, ready to be nailed together.

Sun Bear sidled closer to Spotted Horse. "I see Snow's buckboard wagon, but no mule or horses," he whispered, his hands clutching his rifle. His gaze swept over to the chimney. Slow spirals of smoke reached heavenward from it.

"Pass the word around from man to man that I will go to the cabin first, alone," Spotted Horse whispered to Sun Bear. "My men know what to do if I need assistance."

Sun Bear nodded.

Spotted Horse waited a moment longer, watching Sun Bear scamper from warrior to warrior with the message.

Then when he felt that enough knew his plan, he moved stealthily out into the clearing that led to the cabin.

When he reached the lopsided dwelling, he stopped and braced his back against the log siding and took a deep, heaving breath.

Then again he moved stealthily, so quietly he made no more sound than a panther moving toward its kill. He stopped, turned, knelt, and then inched himself upward until his eyes were just above the sill of a window and he could peer inside.

What he saw made his heart leap with hope.

His woman! The woman he loved with all of his heart was there.

And he could tell that nothing about her had been harmed, except perhaps her pride.

She was tied to a chair facing the open door.

But no one else was there! She was in the dank, dark room alone!

Spotted Horse frowned. "It must be a trap," he whispered. "Perhaps we were spotted!"

He watched for a while longer, his eyes slowly searching the shadows inside the cabin. Still he saw nothing, no movement of any kind, no telltale signs of someone lurking in the shadows.

But, still afraid it might be a trap, Spotted Horse did not rush right into the cabin. He rose to his full height and placed his back to the cabin.

He moved quietly along the side of the dwelling, then made a slow turn that took him to the front, where he knew he could be a target for anyone who might be watching for him.

Desperate to free Marjorie, Spotted Horse went to the door and stood beside it for a moment. Taking a deep breath, he jumped out and rushed into the cabin.

The sudden movement frightened Marjorie, but the gag tied around her mouth stifled her scream.

When she realized who was there, so close, so dear to her heart, tears of joyous relief fell from her eyes.

Spotted Horse slid his rifle to his left hand, grabbed his knife from his sheath with his right hand, then quickly cut the gag and the ropes from his beloved.

"Spotted Horse, oh, Lord, thank you," Marjorie cried, rubbing her raw wrists.

"Where is Snow?" Spotted Horse asked, looking cautiously around him. "Where is Albert?"

"I thought Albert was dead," Marjorie said in a rush of words. "But he isn't. Only a moment ago . . . he . . . came. He took Snow away at gunpoint. I . . . think . . . he plans to kill him, do away with his body, then return later for me. Spotted Horse, how did you know where I was?

If you had not come, I don't know what Albert would have done with me."

"I have so much to tell you," Marjorie went on breathlessly as he swept her up into his arms and carried her from the cabin. "It's been horrible! Oh, so horrible!"

"You do not need to tell me, for to speak of it would be reliving it," Spotted Horse said as he ran with her to the cover of the forest. "I will take you to Louis Eckert's house. My men will search for Albert and Snow. You are to forget about them. When we are done with them, they will never bother you again."

"But if you kill them, the . . . the soldiers will hold you accountable," Marjorie said, her eyes pleading with him. "Please do nothing that will bring danger to you or your people. I will be safe enough at Louis's house. And I truly doubt that Albert will stay in these parts once he realizes you have rescued me. He knows I will tell about his part in the scheme. He will know that every breath he takes is one that you allow. He will run scared, Spotted Horse. None of us will ever see him again."

"Especially you," Spotted Horse said.

When they reached his horse, he gently placed her in the saddle, took her hand and lifted it to his pounding heart, then reluctantly released it and went to speak with his warriors.

Marjorie sat on the saddle as Spotted Horse's warriors moved around him in a tight circle. He spoke purposely low so that she could not hear him give the orders to kill both Albert and Snow at first sight.

Cassie Edwards

He told his warriors to hide the dead men's bodies so that no one would ever find them.

Without proof, without bodies, no white pony soldiers would have the right to arrest the Dakota warriors, or their chief for having ordered the killing.

Sun Bear had stayed back from the others, on his horse beside Marjorie. "It is good that you are safe," he said, drawing Marjorie's eyes to him. "I found the dress and towel that Spotted Horse gave to you. I took them to Spotted Horse. He knew then that someone had wronged you."

"Because of you I am safe?" Marjorie asked, reaching over to take his hand. "Sun Bear, thank you for caring so much."

"I do, so much that I hope once things are better for my people, you can return and live with us," Sun Bear said, circling his fingers around hers. "You are a special woman. You touched my heart the very first time I saw you. I knew then that you would be the one who would draw my father into loving a woman again."

He smiled broadly. "I am proud that I have had a part in making it happen," he said.

"Because of you I am still alive," Marjorie said. She reached over, twined an arm around his neck, and gave him a soft kiss on his cheek. "Again, Sun Bear, thank you."

Spotted Horse came to them. He stood for a moment as he watched the affection between his son and his woman. He smiled at the beautiful sight, for one day soon they would be a family with all of this unhappiness and danger behind them.

"We must go now," he said, hating to interrupt them.

"Yes, we must go," Marjorie said, easing away from Sun Bear.

They rode off together, the three of them on their two horses, while the warriors all went in many directions in their search for the two white men.

On the saddle in front of Spotted Horse, with his arm protectively around her waist, Marjorie saw how the warriors separated. She knew why. They were going in all directions to search for Albert and Snow.

She gave Spotted Horse an uneasy glance over her shoulder, yet said no more of how she felt about his warriors searching for the culprits.

No. She would not think any more about it. It was out of her hands. She would just hope and pray that no danger would be brought to his people because of her. She worried that many of Spotted Horse's men might be imprisoned at Fort Snelling if they were known to have killed two white men.

But Marjorie feared something else more than anything—that the love she and Spotted Horse had found was never meant to be.

In a sense, *they* were the true prisoners of all that was happening, for unless things changed, they would never have the freedom to be together, to love as they wished to love.

Dispirited and weary, Marjorie tried not to

think any more about it. For the moment, she was with Spotted Horse. His arm felt so wonderful as he drew her back closer to him, their bodies touching.

She closed her eyes and let her thoughts wander to how it might be if they were alone . . . making hot, passionate love!

Chapter Sixteen

Marjorie gazed in wonder at Louis Eckert's house as Spotted Horse guided his mount down a long lane covered with fine, white gravel. Sun Bear followed closely behind them.

Marjorie had been at the agent's house once before with her mother and stepfather soon after their arrival in the Minnesota Territory.

She would never forget his kindness. He had told her family that should they ever need anything, he would do what he could to help them, for he was not there only to assist in Indian affairs, but also to help the settlers.

She had since learned that all travelers were received at his house with a cordial reception. He often invited weary travelers to spend the night in his fine, two-story stone house, to rest their bones and to get a decent breakfast before venturing onward.

Marjorie smiled to think that she might be sleeping in a nice, clean bed, with soft, thick pillows for a change. Not since her mother had lived in Saint Louis with her third husband, who for a while had lodged Marjorie and her mother in a grand hotel with all sorts of fancy trimmings, had Marjorie known anything but drudgery and grime. Especially after her mother had married Albert Zimmerman.

As Spotted Horse drew his horse to a halt before the lovely house, Louis opened the large oak door and stepped out onto his wide, pillared porch. When he saw them he gave them a hearty smile of welcome.

Marjorie returned his smile, knowing that he would offer her lodging. Widowed, and fifty years of age, he was a lonely man, since only occasional visitors came his way.

Marjorie would enjoy being in his company. He was from Germany, yet now spoke English, as well as many Indian tongues, fluently. He loved to talk of Germany, and of his wife, who had died on their voyage to America.

"Hello, there!" Louis said, his smile fading as he gazed from Marjorie to Spotted Horse. "Has something happened to your father, Marjorie? Is that why you are with Spotted Horse? Has he come to your assistance in your time of need?"

"Yes, he came to my assistance," Marjorie said, giving Spotted Horse a smile across her shoulder.

Then her smile faded as she once again

peered up at the agent. "I have left my stepfather," she said. "He . . . he has proven to be an untrustworthy, undesirable man. I must make my own way in life now, without him."

"He abused you?" Louis said, paling. "The man harmed you?"

"Not physically," Marjorie reassured him as Louis came down the steps stiffly.

"Here, let me help you down from the horse," he said, reaching up for her. "Then we can go inside. You can tell me all about it."

Spotted Horse slid his arm from around Marjorie's waist and watched Louis help her to the ground. He then swung himself out of the saddle and circled his reins around the hitching rail. He waited for Sun Bear to also dismount, his eyes still watching Louis and Marjorie as they went up the steps, chatting.

Sun Bear slid out of his saddle, smiled over at his father, then both of them went inside and sat down in the parlor with Marjorie and Louis.

Marjorie scarcely heard the conversation between Spotted Horse and Louis. She knew that Spotted Horse was explaining the situation to the agent, but she was lost in a world of grandeur. She was awe-struck, gazing at gilt-framed paintings, plush, thickly cushioned chairs, oak tables upon which sat beautifully painted kerosene lamps, and a handsome upright piano beneath a gold-fringed tapestry hanging on the wall.

A fire burned low, yet warm, in the huge grate of a large stone fireplace. The oak flooring shone as though it had just been waxed.

Cassie Edwards

Cassie Edwards

Her gaze was distracted when a maid came into the room, carrying a tray of refreshments.

After everyone was served tea and iced cakes, and the maid left the room, Marjorie stared down at the lovely porcelain cup and the sparkling silverware. She was dazzled by the pretty iced cake on the tiny plate. She had never been served anything as delicious-looking as this.

She looked quickly over at Sun Bear and smiled when she saw that he was just as impressed as she. She noted his awkwardness as he looked from the table at his right, back to the cup and saucer and cake, then at the table again.

Marjorie leaned closer to him. "You don't want them?" she whispered.

He gave a slight, nervous smile as he glanced her way and shook his head.

"Then just place them on the table," Marjorie whispered. "No one will be insulted by you not wanting the tea and cake."

Sun Bear nodded and did as she suggested.

She glanced over at Spotted Horse as he also set his aside, followed then by Louis Eckert, who obviously was trying to lessen the awkwardness between himself and Spotted Horse by following suit.

Marjorie was not shy, or worried about what anyone else thought. She picked up the fork and dove into the cake, the sweetness swirling around inside her mouth like nothing she had ever eaten before.

She gobbled up the cake, swallowed down the tea, then blushed when she realized that every-

154

one was quietly watching her, amusement in their eyes.

As she set the empty cup and dish aside, her lips curved into a slow smile. "I was hungry," Marjorie said, then sat up, straight and square-shouldered, her hands clasped politely together on her lap.

There was another moment of silence, then Spotted Horse rose quickly from the chair. "I really must go now," he said. "There is so much sadness at my village. I am needed."

Louis took an Indian pipe from the table beside him. "Would you wish to share a smoke with me before you go?" he asked, offering the pipe out to Spotted Horse. "Will it not ease your feelings of sadness somewhat to share a smoke with your friend? As you know, I always have on hand the tobacco of your choice—smoked, dried bark of the dogwood mixed with a small portion of tobacco."

Marjorie had never seen such a pipe before. Its long stem was made of the shank-bone of a deer, cut off at each end. The marrow had been punched out and the mouth-end had been pared down and made smooth. The stem was wrapped with ligament from the back of a buffalo bull's neck. Its bowl was made of red calumet, and red feathers from a woodpecker hung from it.

"It does give me peace to smoke, but now is not the time," Spotted Horse said. With the wave of a hand he gestured for Sun Bear to come with him.

Marjorie rushed from her chair and walked with them outside.

Louis stayed on the porch as Marjorie walked Spotted Horse to his steed.

"Thank you for everything," she murmured, wanting so badly to be drawn into his arms.

Under different circumstances, surely he wouldn't have insisted she leave his village! Then they could have explored their deep feelings for one another with much more leisure. Oh, how sweet it would be to be taught lovemaking by this handsome, wonderful man.

But chances were that they might not even see one another again.

If things worsened back at his village, or if Albert found Marjorie and forced her to leave the agent's house, who was to say what either of their futures was going to be?

Spotted Horse gently framed her face between his hands. "*Mitawin*, we shall be together again," he said, as though he had read her thoughts. "Once this is all behind us, I will come for you. We shall be together *ah-pah-nay*, forever."

"I want that so much," Marjorie said, then melted into his arms when he suddenly yanked her against his hard body. He gave her a deep, long kiss, before letting her go and riding off.

Marjorie touched her lips with her fingers as she watched Spotted Horse and Sun Bear ride away.

"Come on inside before you catch a chill," Louis called, breaking through her reverie.

Startled she looked up at him, then blushed

when she realized that he had witnessed the passionate kiss. She wondered if he had heard the spoken promises between herself and the Dakota Indian chief.

She was glad when he didn't question her, only held his hand out for her as she walked up the steps.

"Now, I want you to feel at home in my house for as long as you wish to stay," Louis said, escorting her inside and closing the door behind them.

Once again they went into the parlor. Marjorie stood before the fireplace. She placed her hands close to the flames, absorbing the heat.

Louis sat down close by the fire. "Spotted Horse told me about your stepfather and Snow," he said solemnly. "I assured him that you will be safe here with me."

Marjorie turned slowly around and faced him. "I knew that I would be," she murmured. "But . . . but . . . you must know, I have come without any personal belongings of my own. I was forced to leave everything behind."

She gazed down at her dress and shuddered when she saw that it was ripped, wrinkled, and soiled. She was even barefoot. "I look such a fright," she said softly.

Her fingers went to her hair. She smiled awkwardly at Louis as she ran her fingers through it in an attempt to remove the tangles.

"I have just what you need," Louis said, rising from his chair. He reached over and took Marjorie's hand. He then swept a long, gangly arm around her waist and led her from the parlor.

He walked her toward the grand oak staircase at the far end of the foyer.

"Come with me upstairs," Louis said, smiling down at her. "I shall show you your room. And something more than that. I have the trunks of my wife's clothes. Although she died on the passage from Germany to America, I kept her things." His gaze swept over her. "Yes, her dresses will fit you. She was your size, oh, so petite and lovely, my Eugenia."

"Eugenia was her name?" Marjorie asked as she went up the stairs beside him, strangely at peace with herself. But, of course, being with this gentle man, who would not feel peaceful and safe?

"Yes, Eugenia Marie," Louis said, stepping up onto the top landing. He led her down a narrow corridor, lighted by afternoon sun pouring through a tall window at the far end. "She was my first and only love. I shall never love another."

"I have heard that a person only has one true love in a lifetime," Marjorie murmured.

"Yes, that is true," Louis said, smiling at her as he recalled witnessing the kiss between Marjorie and Spotted Horse.

"I have found my one true love," Marjorie said. "But I fear I may not have the opportunity to share my life with him."

"I'm sure you are speaking of Spotted Horse," Louis said, stopping to slowly open a door. "If so, I assure you that you will be with him. He is a man of goodness . . . a man with much strength. Once things improve at his village, you will be sent for."

Marjorie's breath was taken away when she was ushered into a wide, spacious room where the scent of perfume lay sweetly in the air.

She found herself in a room where the bed and curtains were dressed in lacy fabrics. The floor was not bare. There was a white carpet from wall to wall, so sparkling clean she was almost afraid to walk on it with her soiled feet.

A dressing table with a three-sided mirror reflecting many bottles of perfume, a silver hairbrush, and a hand mirror sat at the far side of the room, between two tall windows.

Marjorie went with Louis to a trunk at the foot of a massive oak bed. She watched wide-eyed as he unlocked the trunk with a small golden key, then raised the lid, revealing piles of folded, beautiful dresses.

"These belonged to my wife," he said, gesturing toward them with a hand. "It is foolish to leave them locked away like this. Please choose what you wish to wear while you are my guest."

Speechless, Marjorie only stared at the clothes, then knelt down beside him on the floor to take a better look.

She dared move a hand toward them, then quickly ran her fingers over one of the velvet dresses. "I have never seen anything as beautiful, or felt anything as soft," she murmured.

"I'll leave the room so that you can go through the trunk and choose what you wish to wear to dinner tonight," Louis said, rising to his feet. He looked slowly around the room. "This is your room for as long as you wish to be my guest. The perfumes are there for your use. The clothes . . . the bed. And I shall have Edith, my maid, prepare a hot tub of water for you in the next room." He laughed softly. "I call it my bathroom."

Touched by his kindness in sharing his beloved wife's clothes with her, Marjorie bolted to her feet and flung herself into his arms.

"Thank you," she sobbed. "You are so kind . . . so generous."

He said nothing, only stroked his long, lean fingers through her hair, his eyes brimming with tears. He had been so lonely for so long. And while Marjorie was there, he would relish the company of such a fine young lady. He had missed having children.

Marjorie hugged him. She closed her eyes and knew that if she could have chosen a man for a father, it would be Louis Eckert. And while she was with him, she would pretend that he was.

But what she wanted more than life itself was to be with Spotted Horse. She would pray each night that things would soon right themselves at his village. She would pray that Albert never entered her life again!

If Albert found out she was here . . . ?

No.

She would not think any more about Albert. He was finally out of her life!

She would keep that thought. To keep sane, she *must*.

Chapter Seventeen

Screams of panic and the sound of horses approaching drew Spotted Horse from his council house with several of his warriors. His heartbeat quickened as he watched soldiers from Fort Snelling surround his village, their rifles drawn.

Sun Bear ran up to Spotted Horse and clutched his arm when Colonel Dalton broke away from the other soldiers and entered the village, his hand resting on his saber.

Everyone in the village was now quiet. Children were clinging to their mothers, their eyes warily watching Colonel Dalton rein in in front of Spotted Horse.

"*Hoh*! Why are you here?" Spotted Horse asked, his eyes locking with the colonel's. "Why have your soldiers surrounded my village?"

"We have come today to prevent bloody warfare in the Minnesota Territory," Colonel Dalton said stiffly. "Yesterday I observed your village. I saw your people performing a war dance. I have come today with my men to stop the bloodshed before it starts.

"*Hunhunhe*? You witnessed a war dance?" Spotted Horse said, lifting an eyebrow. "How can that be? There has been no war dance at my village since I have been chief. There are no plans for warring with your people."

"I would like to believe that is true, Spotted Horse, for peace is best for everyone," Colonel Dalton said, uneasily shifting in his saddle as Spotted Horse stared at him.

"Nothing has changed to lessen that friendship," Spotted Horse said, forcing himself to be cordial when, inside, he was seething with anger.

He knew who was behind the interference in his life today! Marjorie's stepfather! The evil *washechu* had taken his lies to the colonel!

With all his heart, Spotted Horse regretted the fact that his warriors had not found Marjorie's stepfather. The search had been long and hard, but they had found no trace of the man.

And now, because of Albert and his lies, peace was threatened!

Colonel Dalton looked around, at the children, at the mothers, then farther still where small pine caskets were lined up at the edge of the village.

Frowning, he again looked at Spotted Horse. "Can you honestly stand there and tell me that you hold no resentment inside your heart against white people after so many of your children have died?" he said, heaving a sigh. "Can you honestly say that you don't resent my forcing you to use caskets instead of being able to bury your dead in the traditional way?"

"I cannot honestly say that I do not hold resentment, but it remains inside me," Spotted Horse said, slowly folding his arms across his chest. "My people have gone through enough hardship and heartache over the deaths. I would not start a war with whites that would bring *more* hardship and heartache to my people. *Oyate nimkte wacin yelo*, I want my people to live, not die."

"But, Spotted Horse, I witnessed the dance," Colonel Dalton said dryly. "Those who were dancing were painted hideously. The dance was frenzied."

"What you witnessed was a Ghost Dance," Spotted Horse said somberly. "For the past several days my people have been performing this dance to bring healing to our people."

Colonel Dalton straightened in his saddle. He thoughtfully kneaded his chin. Then he looked over his shoulder and shouted at two of his soldiers. "Come and seize the chief!" he cried.

He looked at another soldier. "Get the chief's horse!" he shouted. "Bring it to him! He'll pay dearly for lying! A few months in prison should sober him enough to forget warring!"

Everything happened so quickly, the people were stunned by how their chief was being mistreated. They gasped almost in unison as Spotted Horse was grabbed and forced onto his horse, then tied as though he was nothing more than a renegade.

Sun Bear wanted to speak up in behalf of his father, but he knew that Spotted Horse would be better served if Sun Bear kept quiet and found ways to help him once he was taken away. The soldiers knew that Sun Bear was Spotted Horse's son. It would be easy for them to grab him and place him in the dungeon with his father!

Sun Bear looked warily from warrior to warrior, hoping they, too, would keep their silence. There was a better way to help his father than fighting the whites! Louis Eckert, the Indian agent, would see to his release, for Louis knew that Spotted Horse was innocent of any wrongdoing.

Also, Marjorie had been at the village while the Dakota had danced. *She* had known the true purpose of the ceremony. She could also go and speak in Spotted Horse's behalf. Before the sun set tonight, Sun Bear's father would be free again!

Spotted Horse sat stiffly, but with much dignity, on the horse, his hands tied behind his back. He stared straight ahead. He only hoped that his warriors would do nothing foolish after he was taken away. Any attack on the fort in an attempt to free Spotted Horse could mean the total annihilation of his people. The white pony soldiers had more powerful weapons, and their soldiers far outnumbered the Dakota warriors.

"I have something else to tend to before we

head back for Fort Snelling," Colonel Dalton said, edging his horse closer to Spotted Horse's. "Chief, where is the white woman? Where is Marjorie? When I was watching the frenzied war dance, I also saw Marjorie Zimmerman sitting among your people. I received word that she was being held captive in your village. Seeing her here proved it was true. Now. Tell me where she is being held captive."

Hearing the colonel speak of Marjorie as a captive infuriated Spotted Horse. Again he knew who was responsible for the lie.

Marjorie's stepfather! He had done everything he could to bring trouble between the whites and the Dakota!

He had succeeded.

But still Spotted Horse said nothing. He stared straight ahead, yet a faint smile fluttered across his lips to know that his woman, his *Zit-kay-lah-skah*, White Bird, was safe. Now that he knew the colonel was no friend, after all, but instead conniving and untrustworthy, Spotted Horse would not want his woman to be anywhere near him.

Ho, he thought, still trying to ignore the colonel as he asked him again about Marjorie. The name White Bird fit his woman well. The name's meaning was "pure." From now on he would call his woman White Bird!

"All right, ignore me!" Colonel Dalton shouted, his face beet red from embarrassment over the chief acting as though he was not even there. He waved a fist in the air as he turned and looked at his men. "Several of you go through the village and search each dwelling for Marjorie Zimmerman. She has to be here somewhere! Find her!"

Women cried and wailed as the soldiers entered their private domains and ransacked as they searched intensely for Marjorie.

The hunt continued until every lodge had been searched. One tepee was now burning after a soldier had accidentally set a blanket on fire as it fell into a firepit, its tail end hanging out enough to spread the fire along the mats on the flooring.

Sun Bear watched the flames reaching into the sky. He watched the man and woman whose lodge was burning stand there and look on in despair; the flames were now too high to stop them.

Sun Bear then turned glaring eyes up at the colonel. But still he said nothing. Inside his heart he was feeling many things. He circled his hands into tight fists at his sides, wishing that he could yank the colonel from his horse and toss him into the burning tepee!

But he fought such feelings . . . such intense anger. He had his father's welfare to think about. He would make things right in a peaceful way, which was his father's way.

"She isn't here," a soldier said, stepping up to the colonel. "We looked everywhere. There are no signs of her."

"But she *was* here," Colonel Dalton said, idly scratching his brow. "Damn it, I saw her."

He turned slow, glaring eyes to Spotted Horse. "What'd you do with her?" he spat out.

"If I discover that harm has come to that woman, more than *you* will be taken to the fort and imprisoned. All of your people will pay for the wrong you have done a white woman!"

Spotted Horse still didn't speak. He knew that silence was better than words while he was filled with such loathing for the colonel. If he spoke his mind now, the colonel's saber might be used to silence him!

"Take him away!" Colonel Dalton shouted.

One of the soldiers grabbed Spotted Horse's reins and led him slowly through the village while Spotted Horse sat proud and tall in his saddle, his eyes unwavering, his chin lifted.

It was hard for Sun Bear to watch. His love for Spotted Horse was so strong, it was as though a piece of Sun Bear's heart was being separated from his body.

When Spotted Horse was swallowed up by the dark depths of the forest, Sun Bear looked slowly around him. Hopelessness and fear were etched on all of the Dakota people's faces. Even the warriors seemed suddenly rendered weak and helpless in the absence of their chief.

Then everything seemed to happen at once. The warriors seemed to come to life again. They began running around, grabbing their weapons, going for their horses.

Sun Bear quickly intervened.

"*Ah-ah*, listen! Stop!" he cried, bringing a quick silence to the village again.

The warriors all turned and stared at him.

The women and children clung to each others, their eyes wide.

"We must not do anything in haste that could cost not only the life of our chief, but your own as well," Sun Bear shouted. "Remember what my father has taught you all! That peace is the best way! That means *now*. I know of a way to help my father. Give me a chance. If it doesn't work, then perhaps we will have to resort to fighting. But first let me see if my father's way will work just this one more time."

"And what will you do?" one of the warriors said as he stepped away from the others. "You are but a mere brave!"

"I am my father's son!" Sun Bear said, proudly thrusting out his chest. "I *will* get him released! You stay behind, all of you, and protect our women and children. Without a chief, our village and our people become vulnerable!"

No one questioned him any further, for although Sun Bear was only a brave of ten winters, he was speaking the words of an adult.

His heart pounding, praying that what he was doing was right, Sun Bear quickly mounted his horse and rode from the village. He prayed that Louis Eckert's reputation of being a powerful man was true!

For today the agent's true power of persuasion was going to be tested!

And Marjorie? Ah, yes! *She* would be the best proof of all that the colonel had been wrong to take Spotted Horse into custody!

That thought alone made Sun Bear smile.

Chapter Eighteen

Marjorie was fresh out of the bathtub. Her skin was soft and smelled of lilac from the wonderful bubblebath. She had gone through the dresses in the trunk, and, not used to wearing silks, satins, or lace, she had chosen simpler attire.

Dressed in a fully gathered pale green skirt, with a matching cotton blouse, she sat down at the dressing table and slowly pulled the silver hairbrush through her hair.

Ah, but it did feel so good to have her hair washed and smelling good. She had already brushed it until it shone, yet she still wanted to brush it some more.

She felt special sitting at such a grand dressing table surrounded by fancy perfume bottles filled with perfumes that had probably been purchased in such faraway places as France.

After she lay the brush down, her gaze swept over the bottles of perfume, trying to choose which one to try. Just as her hand went to the fanciest of all the bottles, a horse approaching outside caused her to jerk her hand back. When she heard the horse stopping at the house, she looked toward the bedroom window.

She felt a chill when she recognized Sun Bear's voice as he shouted something she could not understand.

But the note of frightened panic in his voice was enough to tell her that something bad must have happened.

"Spotted Horse," Marjorie whispered. Oh, Lord, why else would Sun Bear be there alone, so afraid?

Marjorie rushed to the window and shoved it up. Just as she leaned her head out, Louis came from the house and went to Sun Bear. He began questioning him as the young brave dismounted and tied his horse's reins to the hitching rail.

Marjorie tried to hear what Sun Bear said in response, but he was talking too quickly.

"What's wrong?" Marjorie shouted from the window. She didn't make it a practice of interrupting people, yet she could hardly bear not knowing what had happened. "What's happened? Sun Bear, where is Spotted Horse?"

Her voice brought a quick silence between Sun Bear and Louis. They both looked up at her.

Marjorie leaned her head further from the window. "Good Lord, Sun Bear . . . *Louis, tell* me," she cried. She clutched the windowsill so tightly her knuckles were white. "Where is Spotted Horse?"

"Marjorie, come down here and then we can talk," Louis said, reaching a hand toward her.

"I want to know now!" Marjorie said in a half scream. "Tell me!"

"Spotted Horse was arrested and taken to Fort Snelling," Louis said. "Marjorie, please come on down. Let us speak without shouting back and forth. We have decisions to make."

Marjorie was so shaken by the news, her knees scarcely held her up. Her throat was dry. Her stomach was churning, as though at any moment she might throw up.

Spotted Horse's face swam before her eyes as she felt a fainting spell coming on. She fought with all of her might to steady herself and to keep from fainting, or retching. Spotted Horse! Her beloved Spotted Horse had been taken away like a criminal and placed in the dungeon at the fort.

But why? she thought as she lifted the hem of her skirt in her hands and ran from the room. Why would Spotted Horse be arrested? He had done nothing wrong! Nothing! He was a good man. Against all odds he had kept the peace between himself and the white people.

"And now?" she whispered harshly. "They arrested him? They . . . unjustly . . . arrested him?"

Determined to get him set free, no matter what she must do to achieve it, Marjorie scurried down the stairs.

Outside, she placed her hands on Sun Bear's shoulders. "Tell me everything," she said breathlessly. Her heart skipped a beat when she saw the utter fear in the boy's eyes. She paled. "Oh, no, Sun Bear, don't tell me he was harmed during his arrest. Please don't tell me that."

"No, he was not harmed," Sun Bear said. His body stiffened when he recalled how brusquely his father had been forced onto his horse, his hands tied behind him. "His dignity has been harmed, but not his body."

"Why did they come and arrest him?" Marjorie asked in a rush of words.

Louis placed a gentle hand on Marjorie's shoulder. "Marjorie, calm down," he said softly. "Take a deep breath. Then I shall explain everything to you."

Marjorie sucked in a nervous breath. She dropped her hands away from Sun Bear's shoulders and faced Louis.

"Here's what happened," Louis said, gently taking her hand and holding it affectionately.

He explained to her how the soldiers had come to the Dakota village and accused the Indians of having been involved in a war dance.

He explained how the colonel wouldn't listen to reason when he was told that it was not a war dance at all but instead a Ghost Dance, which was used for healing.

"The colonel still arrested him after being told the truth?" Marjorie gasped out, again feeling frantic.

"Yes, and all because of your stepfather," Louis explained. "You see, Marjorie, the main reason the soldiers went to the village in the first place was not because of any dancing. Albert told them that the Dakota had kidnapped you. When they came to see if that was true, that was when they saw the people participating in the Ghost Dance. They also saw you sitting among the Dakota. They actually believed you *were* there as a captive. They left and made their plan of attack. When they returned, they arrested Spotted Horse, not only for thinking he had planned to attack the fort, but also for having abducted you, for you were not there to tell them any different. You were here with me, Marjorie."

"I never should have left the village!" Marjorie said, stifling a sob of regret behind a hand. "I could've been there for him."

"You are only part of the reason why my father was arrested," Sun Bear said. "It was the Ghost Dance that drew their attention and gave them true cause to arrest my father. It gave them an excuse to arrest him, for nothing would please the white pony soldiers more than to see the Dakota leave this land, so that it can be taken over completely by settlers. Yes, Marjorie, it was just an excuse. Do not blame yourself."

"We must go to the fort and get him freed," Louis said, walking in his long-legged, stiff gait toward the stable at the back of his house. "I shall have the stable boy ready my horse, and one for you, Marjorie. We must all go and speak on behalf of Spotted Horse."

Marjorie paced until the young stable hand brought a horse to her. She mounted as she watched Louis ride out of the stable on his lovely strawberry roan.

Then she, along with Louis and Sun Bear, rode in a hard gallop toward Fort Snelling.

When they arrived, they were not denied entrance through the wide gate. Louis was perfect for the job of Indian agent, for he was held in high regard by everyone.

Marjorie's heart pounded hard inside her chest as she dismounted before the colonel's quarters. She was not afraid of the man . . . just of his power. By wrongly arresting Spotted Horse, he had already abused this power. She prayed to herself he would not abuse it a second time today!

Marjorie walked between Sun Bear and Louis as they were taken to the colonel's private office. He was at his desk working on a journal.

He slid his hands slowly from the journal and gazed up at his uninvited guests. "What can I do for you?" he asked, mainly centering his attention on Louis Eckert. He avoided Marjorie's cold stare, now certain that he had been wrong about her having been held captive at the Indian village. He hated being wrong about anything.

"Chief Spotted Horse's son brought me news today that greatly disturbs me," Louis said stiffly.

"And?" the colonel asked blandly, still avoiding Marjorie's steady stare.

"We have come to ask for Spotted Horse's release," Louis said. "The Dakota were *not* performing a war dance." He gestured toward

Marjorie with a sweep of his right hand. "And as you can see, Marjorie is not being held captive by the Dakota. Nor has she *ever* been their captive. So wouldn't you say that you are unjustly holding Spotted Horse prisoner in your dungeon? Wouldn't you say he deserves an immediate release, and just as swiftly an apology?"

Marjorie edged closer to the desk. "Let me speak for myself," she said, her voice filled with pride and conviction. "Colonel, I am shocked by your treatment of Spotted Horse. He has fought hard to keep peace between his people and the whites, and you reward him with treatment such as this?"

Her eyes narrowed as the colonel stared up at her. She placed her hands on her hips. "I was never a captive of Spotted Horse," she said tightly. "I was there because I wished to be. I only left because Chief Spotted Horse asked me to, and that was only because he was concerned about my safety. He did not want me to come down with whooping cough. Had he asked, I would have stayed among his people forever."

She glared down at the colonel. "Had he asked, I would have stayed in the capacity of *wife*," she said proudly.

She wanted to laugh out loud when that confession caused the colonel's face to lose its color.

Louis smiled at Marjorie.

Sun Bear slid a hand into hers.

Colonel Dalton jumped from his chair. He went to the door and leaned out. "Go and get

175

Spotted Horse," he shouted to one of his men. "Bring him here. Immediately!"

He then went back to his desk and sat down. He nervously shuffled through his papers in an effort to look busy as he waited for Spotted Horse.

Marjorie's pulse raced as she waited for her beloved to enter the room. Surely once he was released he would ask her to go back with him to the village! It had been wrong to ask her to leave. She would let no fear of disease keep them apart, ever again!

She turned quickly when she heard footsteps enter the room. She had to hold herself back when she saw Spotted Horse standing there flanked by two soldiers. Where they had tied his wrists together, there were rope burns. His beautiful hair was tangled. His buckskin clothes were soiled. His moccasins had been removed. He was barefoot.

Spotted Horse's gaze went first to Marjorie. Their eyes locked.

Her insides grew cold when he didn't offer her a smile. He seemed to be looking at a stranger!

Did he, deep inside his heart, blame her for his arrest? she silently despaired. Had it changed his feelings about her?

They had been so close to declaring their feelings for one another when he had told her it was best that she leave the village during the epidemic. Or had that just been a way of telling her that he didn't want her after all?

She swallowed hard and fought back the

tears that were burning in her eyes when Spot-ted Horse looked over at Sun Bear, offered a gentle smile, and then smiled and nodded toward Louis Eckert.

Marjorie felt as though she were dying a slow death. He had not even given her a friendly smile or nod. She was certain that things had changed between them.

Hardly able to bear the hurt, she turned her eyes away.

"Chief, it seems you were wrongly arrested," Colonel Dalton said. He rose from his chair and went and placed a hand on Spotted Horse's shoulder. "I apologize. Go home. Please try to forget this ever happened. Let us resume the relationship we had before Albert's interference. Can we be friends again?"

Feeling a deep loathing for the colonel, Spotted Horse glared at him.

Tight-lipped, and rubbing his sore wrists, he continued to give the colonel a silent glare.

Then Spotted Horse turned and went to Sun Bear and took one of his hands. "My son, let us go home," he said thickly.

He then turned to Louis Eckert. He reached out a hand of friendship. "Again you have proved your friendship," he said. *"Pila maye*, thank you. I shall always be in your debt."

"You owe me nothing," Louis said. He gave Marjorie a quick, nervous glance. He then again looked into Spotted Horse's eyes. "Just return to your people. They need you."

Marjorie wanted to scream out that she also needed him. She loved him! How could he be so cold to her? Was he not even going to say good-bye? Was he not going to offer her at least a thank you for having come to the fort to speak in his behalf?

She was so hurt she could not stand another moment of the humiliation of being ignored by the man she would always love. Tears streaming from her eyes, she turned and fled the room.

Louis walked with Spotted Horse and Sun Bear from the room and stood outside in the corridor and talked for a moment longer.

"That woman loves you with all her heart," Louis said, watching Spotted Horse's expression. "Why are you treating Marjorie this way? Do you blame her for what has happened to you? If so, don't you think that's a mite unjust? It's not like you."

"It is not that I blame her," Spotted Horse said. "It is because I have had a lot of time to think while imprisoned. Did you not see how quickly the soldiers came to my village and endangered my people? The soldiers could have opened fire with their weapons. If Marjorie is living among my people when the soldiers decide to come again, she will be looked at as one of the Dakota. She will not be spared hurt, humiliation, perhaps even death, by the whites, for they will look down on her for being as one with the Dakota."

Spotted Horse inhaled a nervous, quavering breath. "I only wish to spare her those things," he said, then turned and walked away, with Sun Bear close beside him.

Marjorie waited on her horse for Louis to

come from the colonel's office. When Spotted Horse came out with Sun Bear and turned her way to gaze at her for a lingering moment, she stubbornly said nothing. Although her heart was breaking, she just returned his stare.

Then trembling overtook her when he turned away from her without as much as a word or smile, mounted the same horse as Sun Bear, and rode away. She watched them until they rode through the wide, open gate.

Then she turned her eyes down and wiped the tears from her cheeks.

"He didn't do that to hurt you."

Louis's voice breaking through her heartache caused Marjorie to look quickly at him as he swung himself into his saddle and edged his horse closer to hers.

"What?" she asked, swallowing a sob away into the depths of her throat. "What . . . did . . . you say?"

"I said that Spotted Horse didn't ignore you to hurt you," he said solemnly. "He did it because he felt that it was in your best interest."

"My . . . best . . . interest?" she gasped out.

Louis tried to explain to her, but nothing he said took away the hurt, or made her accept Spotted Horse's reason for being outright rude and cold to her.

"Can I stay with you until spring?" she blurted out, now having no hope of her and Spotted Horse ever being together. "Until the riverboats resume their travels on the Mississippi between Saint Louis and the Minnesota Territory?"

"Why, yes," Louis said, searching her face,

taken aback by how she refused to accept the explanation about Spotted Horse's attitude toward her. "You can stay at my house for as long as you wish. You know that I enjoy having you."

"Thank you," Marjorie said, flicking her reins as she and Louis left the fort behind them.

She glanced over at Louis. "I might have to stay with you just a slight bit longer than I thought," she said guardedly. "But only long enough for me to make enough money to pay my passage on the riverboat."

"Make enough money?" Louis asked, raising an eyebrow. "Oh, yes. You are talking about making money from the sales of your paper dolls."

"Yes, and perhaps I can borrow enough money from you to buy supplies at the trading post so that I can start making my paper dolls again," Marjorie said softly. "You see, when I fled my stepfather's house, I was not only forced to leave my clothes behind, but also my supplies to make my paper dolls."

"I will gladly make you a loan," Louis said, smiling over at her. "I will do anything you wish to make you happy. In you, I see the daughter that my wife and I never had. You see, I didn't tell you . . . but . . . she was pregnant when she died."

Marjorie looked quickly over at him. Suddenly her own troubles and heartaches didn't seem so bad, for this man had suffered so much.

It was strange. She, too, found it easy to look at him as a father figure. Had she ever known her father, she would have wished him to be exactly like Louis Eckert!

But she knew not to allow herself to get too attached. She seemed to lose loved ones so easily. First the father she had never known . . . then her mother. . . . then Spotted Horse!

Yes. She would guard her feelings well from now on. She would not give of herself so easily to anyone ever again!

Chapter Nineteen

A hard coughing spell had awakened Marjorie. She leaned up on an elbow in the bed and grabbed at her throat as the coughing persisted. Even her chest ached. And her head seemed so hot.

When she had gone to bed the previous evening, she had noticed that her nose was running and she had a slight cough. She had even felt slightly feverish.

Thinking it was only exhaustion from her trying day, she had thought nothing more about it.

Until now. She knew the symptoms of whooping cough. Although she had heard that usually it came on more slowly than this, she knew now that she had the dreaded disease.

Suddenly chilled, Marjorie grabbed a blanket

up around her. The cough was now deep and hard, coming from the depths of her lungs. She was coughing so hard she couldn't even respond verbally to the knock on the door.

Trembling from the mounting fever, Marjorie crept from the bed. With the blanket wrapped around her shoulders, she went to the door and opened it.

Louis paled when he gazed at her. In the sunlight pouring through the windows behind her, he could see that Marjorie was feverish.

Her face turned crimson as she continued to cough. Then her face turned a strange sort of blue, which meant that her hard, persistent coughing wasn't allowing her to get enough oxygen into her lungs.

"Whooping cough," Louis whispered beneath his breath. "Lord, she's come down with whooping cough."

Marjorie dropped the blanket from around her and clawed at her throat as the coughing persisted. She tried to get her breath, feeling desperate when she couldn't. Then, just as she felt as though she might black out, the coughing ceased.

Gasping for breath, she fell into Louis's arms. As she kept on making a strange low whooping noise, Louis swept her into his arms and carried her to her bed.

"I'm so sick," Marjorie whispered, her chest heaving as she fought off another coughing spell. She closed her eyes and welcomed the warmth of a blanket as Louis drew it up beneath her chin.

"I'm going to send for Doc Rose," Louis said. "And my maid, Edith, will be here soon to bathe your brow. We've got to get that temperature down."

Marjorie smiled weakly up at him, then closed her eyes as her body was wracked by another bout of coughing.

Louis quickly left. Edith came into the room. She placed a basin of water on the table beside Marjorie's bed and began bathing her brow with a cold, wet compress.

Again the coughing spell overtook Marjorie and she was lost to everything but the pain and memories of the small bundled bodies placed on scaffolds in the trees along the Mississippi River.

As her body was wracked by the coughing, she recalled the wails of the mothers at the Dakota village as they prepared more children for burial. She recalled the pine boxes that had been brought to the Indian village for the dead.

"Marjorie?"

A voice, sounding as though it came from a dark, deep tunnel, broke through Marjorie's dark thoughts. She was filled with dread at the realization that she had the same disease that had killed so many innocent Dakota children. She had just begun to imagine her*self* being prepared for burial, and the thought of Snow tending to her body excited a horror in her even worse than dying.

"Marjorie, can you hear me?" someone said, and Marjorie felt a heavy, thick hand on her brow.

Gasping, she slowly opened her eyes.

When she saw Doc Rose standing beside the bed, with his tousled head of gray hair, his red, pudgy cheeks, bulbous nose, and friendly brown eyes, she smiled weakly up at him.

"You're quite a sick young lady," Doc Rose said, his hand slowly sliding along her brow as he felt to see just how hot she was. "But I'll get you fixed up real soon. You'll be back on your feet before you know it."

"I'm . . . not . . . going to die?" Marjorie stammered out, her voice hoarse from coughing.

"I won't allow that," Doc Rose said goodnaturedly. "Nope, I wouldn't allow a pretty, sweet thing like you to die."

"How bad do I have it?" Marjorie asked, fighting off another urge to cough.

"I've seen much, much worse," Doc Rose said. He took a small bottle of cough syrup from his black bag. "In fact, I don't think you'll be sick more'n a day or two. You see, you aren't vomiting, which is usual in the worst of cases. If we can get the fever checked and the coughing controlled at least somewhat, then you'll be back to makin' those paper dolls of yours in no time flat."

"Yes, I need to make my paper dolls so that I can earn enough money to book passage to Saint Louis in the spring," Marjorie said, finding it hard to say so much at once. She closed her eyes and heaved in a deep breath.

Then she began coughing again.

When that coughing bout was over, Doc Rose placed a spoon filled with red liquid to her mouth. "Here's my remedy for whooping cough," he said. He poured the syrup slowly through her parted lips. He gave her two more spoonfuls. "It knocks it out every time."

He sighed as he set the empty spoon in a saucer on the table beside the bed. "If I could only get the cough syrup to the Indian children," he said, screwing the lid back on the medicine bottle. "I know I could've saved more than half of those children. The main thing in this battle of whooping cough is to get the coughing itself checked. That way the body isn't as weakened. Small children, in particular, have a hard time combatting this weakness. That makes them more vulnerable to other diseases. Often it is that something else that kills them, not the whooping cough itself."

"I tried to talk Spotted Horse into allowing you to take your medicine to the children," Marjorie said in between wheezing. "He . . . just . . . wouldn't listen to reason. They believe too much in their Medicine Man to allow a white doctor to administer cures to their children."

"In time that'll change," Doc Rose said, lifting the bottle for Marjorie to see. "Now, I'm leavin' this bottle beside your bed. After each coughing spell, take a spoonful."

He smiled at Edith as she entered the room with a tray of things that were not familiar to Marjorie.

Marjorie raised an eyebrow when an aroma similar to bacon wafted from the many things on the tray.

She looked in wonder at Doc Rose when he

reached over and took the tray, then set it down on the edge of the bed. "I've told Edith some things to get from the kitchen that I'm going to use as a poultice to place on your chest," he said. His pudgy fingers slid the blanket down, leaving it resting around her waist.

He then slid the straps of her nightgown down so that her chest was exposed. She watched as he reached his hand into a small dish and dipped something from the dish onto his fingers.

As he rubbed the salve on her chest, she questioned him with her eyes.

"All right, I can see that you want to know what I'm usin'," Doc Rose said, chuckling. "Let's see now . . . there's bacon grease, some flour, baking soda, and mustard. It'll seep into your chest and help pull the germs from your lungs."

"I'm beginning to smell like a kitchen," Marjorie said, laughing softly, trying to find some humor in her illness. "And your cough medicine seems to have worked. I no longer have the urge to cough each time I open my mouth."

"Yep, works every time," Doc Rose said, his eyes dancing. "My own concoction." He laughed softly. "I oughta go on the road from town to town, sellin' my cough medicine, don't you think?"

"I just wish you could take it to Spotted Horse and prove to him how effective it is," Marjorie said. She was disappointed when the coughing returned and she could hardly get her breath until it was over.

She closed her eyes and felt as though she

were drifting over soft clouds. Then she was aware that there was more in the cough medicine than medicine. There was a good portion of alcohol. It was numbing not only her lungs, but everything in her. She felt suddenly giddy and wonderful, and ah, so sleepy.

"Get some rest now," Doc Rose said. He covered her chest with a warm cloth, then pulled her gown back up in place. He covered her with the blanket again, then picked up his bag, and started to leave.

He turned to Edith. "Keep bathing her brow," he whispered. "Keep the water cold. That will combat the fever."

Edith nodded, then sat down on a chair beside the bed and continued bathing Marjorie's brow. She watched as Marjorie's eyes twitched in her sleep and wondered what she might be dreaming about.

In her dream, Marjorie was walking, hand in hand, in the forest with Spotted Horse. It was spring. Everything around them was beautiful and new. The scent of wild roses filled the air. Marjorie wore a low-swept silk dress, the skirt rustling around her legs in the soft breeze of evening.

Suddenly Spotted Horse stopped and drew Marjorie around and into his arms. His mouth covered hers in a sensual, long, and deep kiss.

As his hands cupped her breasts through her dress, the warmth of his flesh bleeding through the thin material, her breasts tingled. The sexual excitement within her was building.

She was floating and clinging as he rained

kisses across her brow, her closed eyelids, and then her cheeks, his hands gently stripping off her clothes.

In her dream, Spotted Horse tossed her clothes away, then knelt down before her on one knee and worshiped her flesh with his hands and mouth, awakening feelings inside her that she had never known existed.

Soaring with joy, Marjorie let her head fall back and sighed as his hands caressed her.

Then he eased her down to the ground.

She watched him undress; then she held her arms out for him.

She welcomed him above her as he imprisoned her against him. She took a deep breath of pleasure as he thrust himself inside her and began his rhythmic strokes.

His mouth found hers. He forced her lips open as his kiss grew more and more passionate.

Just as her senses began to swim with rapture, another coughing bout thrust her back to reality. Edith held Marjorie's hand as she coughed until she began to choke.

Louis rushed into the room. He sat down on the bed beside Marjorie and drew her into his arms and held her until the coughing subsided.

Aware of strong arms around her, Marjorie sobbed with joy. "You've come to me," she whispered, clinging to Louis. "Oh, Spotted Horse, you do love me after all. Thank you for coming to me. Oh, how I love you."

Louis stared at Marjorie, not sure what to do when she suddenly opened her eyes and discovered who was truly there, holding her. He could see the disappointment and embarrassment in her expression as she gazed with parted lips at him.

Marjorie died a slow death inside when she saw that it was not Spotted Horse who sat there with her, holding her.

She turned her eyes away and eased herself from Louis's arms. "I feel so foolish," she murmured. "I truly thought—"

"Don't feel bad about mistaking me for the man you love," Louis said, helping her down beneath the blankets. "If he knew you were ill, he would be here for you."

Marjorie looked quickly up at him. "Please don't tell him," she said in a rush of words. "I don't want him here. I don't want him to place himself in danger. It is apparent now that adults *can* get whooping cough."

She didn't want to tell Louis the truth . . . that she feared Spotted Horse wouldn't come even if he knew, for the Dakota chief had shown her by his coldness that he truly didn't care for her, after all.

Yes, she felt foolish, all right, but not so much over having mistaken Louis for Spotted Horse. She felt foolish for having ever allowed herself to think that such a man as Spotted Horse could truly care for her.

The dream.

Oh, damn the dream!

It made it even harder to have lost him.

Chapter Twenty

Spotted Horse rose from his bed and went and knelt down before the fire pit. Slowly he began adding strips of cedar to the simmering coals.

He felt stiff from having not slept all night. He hadn't been able to get Marjorie off his mind and how he had treated her so coldly, as though she meant nothing to him, when, in truth, she was everything!

But for many reasons he felt that it was best to deny their feelings for one another.

Yet he couldn't deny the terrible emptiness he felt at her absence. Now that he had allowed himself to fall in love again, he missed Marjorie with every fiber of his being. It was impossible to think of life without her!

He turned with a quick jerk when Sun Bear awakened on his bed behind Spotted Horse, his body wracked by a fitful bout of coughing. Thinking that his son might have whooping cough caused a quick fear to leap into Spotted Horse's heart.

Feeling strangely numb, he hurried to Sun Bear's bedside.

Spotted Horse realized by the soft pleading in Sun Bear's dark eyes that he knew, also, that it was more than likely that he was coming down with the dreaded disease that had taken so many of the Dakota children's lives.

"*Ahte*, I feel so ill," Sun Bear said, his chest heaving as he fought off the urge to cough again. His eyes slowly closed. "I . . . feel . . . so hot."

Spotted Horse placed a gentle hand on Sun Bear's brow, flinching when he felt his son's heat. Sun Bear had a ragingly high temperature!

And when Sun Bear started coughing again, his face growing blue when he was unable to stop, panic seized Spotted Horse. He lifted Sun Bear into his arms and held him close until once again the coughing momentarily subsided.

Spotted Horse now recalled that Sun Bear had coughed several times during the night. But it had been so slight. Spotted Horse had thought that it was just from Sun Bear having taken a late bath in the river the evening before.

When Sun Bear had coughed, Spotted Horse had gone to check on him in his sleep. He had seen his nose slightly running, but he had thought that his son was just getting a cold.

Spotted Horse had taken a soft piece of buckskin and had gently wiped Sun Bear's nose clean, and when his son hadn't started coughing again, Spotted Horse had returned to his bed and to his troubled thoughts about Marjorie.

Now he felt guilty for having ignored his son's cough during the night. If he had gone for Brown Hair at the first hint of illness, perhaps the Medicine Man's prayers to the *Big Holy* might have been enough to stop the terrible disease.

Now if anything happened to Sun Bear, Spotted Horse would blame himself. He felt guilty that he had been thinking of Marjorie, his White Bird, when he should have been thinking of Sun Bear. He had been ready to go to her and apologize and tell her he wished to have her love forever. He was going to tell her that his love for her was as strong as the marriage of the stars to the heavens!

Sun Bear began coughing again, this time more deeply.

"*Ahte . . .*" Sun Bear whispered as the coughing stopped again. He laid his head against Spotted Horse's chest. "Help . . . me . . . Father."

Without further hesitation, Spotted Horse carried Sun Bear from the lodge.

Through a slowly falling rain he took him to the communal *initi*, sweat lodge.

When they entered the small, cone-shaped structure of tightly bound willow poles, bark, and earth, he laid Sun Bear on the floor, which was covered with branches of sweet-smelling and healing sagebrush. In the center of the lodge was a small space, slightly hollowed out in the ground, where hot stones would be placed.

While Sun Bear coughed, Spotted Horse disrobed him of his loincloth, then left long enough to go and get Brown Hair.

When they returned together, Brown Hair carrying his medicine with him as well as a whistle made from the wing-bone of an eagle, Brown Hair disrobed, then went inside the sweat lodge.

Breathless, and with an anxious heartbeat, Spotted Horse stayed outside. Not far from the door of the sweat lodge he prepared a fire of cottonwood bark in which he placed smooth stones to heat. While the rocks were heating, Spotted Horse went to the river with a buckskin bag and filled it with water.

Then, with hurried steps, he went back to the stones. They were hot enough now to continue the ceremony.

With large wooden tongs, Spotted Horse placed these rocks in a basket.

Before entering the lodge, he disrobed. Then he carried the basket of hot stones and the bag of water into the lodge and closed the entrance flap behind him.

Sun Bear continued to cough. Brown Hair knelt over him, chanting and sprinkling his body with herbal medications.

Spotted Horse placed the hot stones in the pit in the ground. Then he slowly poured the water over the stones, softly praying to his *Big Holy* that none of the stones would explode. That would be a precursor of misfortune.

He held his breath until all of the water had been poured on the stones and none had broken. He closed his eyes and made a wish on the unbroken stones that his son would soon be well, for a wish made on such a stone would come true.

A heavy steam soon filled the lodge.

Enduring the intense heat and steam, hardly aware of it in his concern for Sun Bear, Spotted Horse knelt opposite Brown Hair, who was performing his magic over the ailing young Dakota brave.

And as Sun Bear benefited from the purifying steam, Brown Hair sang sacred songs over him and played soft tunes on his whistle to invoke the aid of the deity.

And then Brown Hair chanted again, requesting aid from the *Big Holy*, seeking the solace of a spiritual force greater than himself.

Brown Hair stopped his ceremonial performance and looked over at Spotted Horse. "Now lift the entrance flap so that the stones can be allowed to cool," he said softly. "I will then dry your son's body with sage leaves."

Spotted Horse nodded and did as he was asked.

Sitting just inside the entrance, where the open flap provided enough light to see Sun Bear, Spotted Horse was not at all encouraged. Although the steam was expected to cause a sick person weakness, it was Sun Bear's listlessness and the way his eyes slowly rolled to the back of his head while he coughed that made Spotted Horse think the ceremony had not helped him. Just like the other children in the village who had not benefited from the same ceremony. Was his son going to die?

Had Spotted Horse waited too long?

The fear of his son dying caused panic to grab at Spotted Horse's insides. Had the Medicine Man lost his power? Had he, for some reason, lost favor in the eyes of the Sun?

Too many children had died! Brown Hair had not been able to help *them*. Oh, why had Spotted Horse had such faith that he would be able to help his own son?

Spotted Horse left the lodge and yanked on his clothes. He paced frantically back and forth in the cold, misty rain. He ran his fingers through his long hair. He grimaced and closed his eyes when the image of pine caskets flashed before his mind's eye.

Spotted Horse lifted his remorseful eyes to the gray heavens. "There has to be something more that can be done!" he cried to his *Big Holy*. "Too many have died. Must my own son be a part of the sacrifice? Why? Why is this happening to the Dakota? My people are good! Why must so much sadness come to our lives?"

Then it came to him as if someone had laid a heavy hand on his shoulder and spoken to him with words that only he could hear and understand. He had felt this strange occurrence before, as though his father had stepped down from the hereafter long enough to speak to him . . . to guide him.

A sob lodged in his throat when he looked slowly around him, wishing that it *were* his father! Spotted Horse needed not only his father's wisdom and guidance, but also his comforting embrace.

"*Ahte* . . ."

The voice, not that of his father, caused Spotted Horse to turn with a start. He stiffened when Sun Bear spoke his name again.

"*Ahte*," Sun Bear cried, lifting a hand toward Spotted Horse.

Spotted Horse went back inside the small lodge and saw that Brown Hair had left, and that Sun Bear was now dressed again in his loincloth.

"What is it?" Spotted Horse said, lifting Sun Bear into his arms. "What is it you wish to tell me? Do you feel better? Has the ceremony eased your coughing?"

Sun Bear was seized with a terrible bout of coughing. His son was no better.

There had to be another way to help him!

To lose Sun Bear would be the same as losing Spotted Horse's own soul!

His chest heaving, his face crimson, Sun Bear reached a hand to his father's cheek.

The heat was so intense from his son's hand that Spotted Horse flinched.

"*Ahte*, Marjorie spoke of her doctor to you," Sun Bear said in a faint whisper. "Would . . . he . . . make me better?"

Spotted Horse's eyes wavered as he saw the soft pleading in his son's. He recalled how Marjorie had begged him to allow the white doctor to come to his village. Perhaps it *was* time to allow it! Things in life were ever changing. Was this just another change that had to be tried? Perhaps accepted?

He was torn. He had always believed in the power of his Medicine Man. Just like his ancestors before him, he had always depended on his Medicine Man.

But now?

With the diseases of the white people invading the Dakota's lives, perhaps it might take the white man's medicine to rid them of such ailments.

And had not his father come to him moments ago, advising him, encouraging him to go beyond their usual beliefs? To find other ways to help cure the ailing children?

Did not his father, during his brief time with his chieftain son, give him his blessing to go beyond their village to seek help?

"*Micinksi*, I am not certain of the white medicine man's powers, but I must see if he can help us," Spotted Horse said. He carried Sun Bear from the sweat lodge and hurried toward their tepee. "I shall go and speak with the white doctor named Doc Rose. If he has some hidden powers that can stop the coughing disease, then we must allow him to use these powers here at our village."

Sun Bear snuggled against Spotted Horse's chest. "Bring Marjorie, too?" he said, then drifted off into a momentary sleep, until he was awakened again by a bout of coughing as Spotted Horse took him into their tepee and placed him on his bed.

"*Ho*, I shall bring Marjorie back with me," Spotted Horse said. He drew a blanket up to Sun Bear's chin. "Try to sleep while I am gone. *Istima*, sleep. Rest."

Spotted Horse brushed Sun Bear's fevered brow with a kiss, then dressed warmly for the ride through the rain. He would first go for Marjorie. They would go together to see if Doc Rose would still offer his help to the Dakota.

Outside, the wind whined and the air was cold. Wearing a coat made of a blanket that was fastened in front by a coil of steel wire, Spotted Horse rode hard from his village on his mighty, snorting steed.

Yes, he would go for Marjorie.

He would seek her help in going to the doctor to plead his case, for Spotted Horse had been rude to the white doctor more than once and was afraid that he would now ignore Spotted Horse.

Yes, it might take Marjorie's sweetness to convince him!

If Marjorie could forgive Spotted Horse for having treated her so coldly when they had last been with one another! What if his White Bird's love for him had turned to hate?

That thought, that fear, tore at the very core of his being.

Chapter Twenty-one

Spotted Horse wheeled his horse to a sudden stop when he saw Doc Rose's horse and buggy outside Louis Eckert's house. The presence of the white doctor at the agent's house surely meant that someone in the house was ill.

A sense of foreboding swept over Spotted Horse. Was it possible that Marjorie was sick? Had she stayed among his people too long? Was she now ill, herself, with the whooping cough disease? Was he going to lose her as he had lost so many loved ones?

Hoping that he was jumping to conclusions, Spotted Horse rode onward. He guided his horse up the narrow gravel path and drew a tight rein before the house.

As he dismounted, Louis came from the

house and stood on the porch, gazing down at him.

Spotted Horse wound the reins around the hitching post, then returned Louis's steady gaze. It was hard for Spotted Horse to read the other man's expression. It seemed to be a mixture of many emotions, but what seemed lacking was the good-natured easiness with which Louis usually welcomed Spotted Horse.

"Good morning, Spotted Horse," Louis said, walking to the steps, offering Spotted Horse a handshake as he came up them. "It's nice to see you again. Have you come to have council?"

"I have no time for council," Spotted Horse said, taking Louis's hand and gripping it tightly as he shook it. "I have come to talk with White Bird."

"White Bird?" Louis asked, arching an eyebrow.

"Marjorie," Spotted Horse said, softly smiling. "White Bird is the Dakota name I have chosen for her, yet even she is not yet aware of it. Do you think she will wear the name, or reject it?"

"I think it's best if you ask her, yourself," Louis said, easing his hand from Spotted Horse's. "But first there is something you need to know about Marjorie."

Spotted Horse's heart leapt with sudden apprehension. He looked over his shoulder at the white medicine man's horse and buggy, then looked at Louis again. "And what is it you need to say about White Bird?" he asked guardedly.

"Come with me," Louis said, gesturing with a hand toward the door. "Come inside. We will talk for a moment, and then you can see Marjorie."

His heart pounding, fearing the worst now, Spotted Horse practiced restraint by not forcing answers out of Louis. He could not bear to think that not only was his son ill, but also the woman he loved with all his heart.

No. He was not sure if he could stand losing the two most important people in the world to him! His son? The woman he wished to marry?

"She is going to be all right," Louis said, stopping inside the foyer to face Spotted Horse. He slowly closed the door behind them. "I'm sorry I caused you such alarm. Lord, I see it in your eyes! I should've come right out and told you that, yes, Marjorie is ill. But today she is so well she will be up from her sick bed and able to do as she wishes. It was a brief illness, thanks to Doc Rose's quick attention to Marjorie. She coughed hardly at all through the night. And like magic, her fever is gone today."

"She . . . had . . . the coughing sickness?" Spotted Horse asked hesitantly. "But she is well this quickly? I have seen the children in my village suffer for days upon days before they either got well, or died. How could White Bird have the disease and then get well so quickly?"

"It's not altogether a miracle," Louis said, taking Spotted Horse by an elbow, slowly ushering him toward the stairs. "Like I said, Doc Rose took care of her with his medicines. Thank God, they worked for Marjorie."

As he and Spotted Horse took the steps, he continued. "It doesn't always work that way for everyone, Spotted Horse," he said. "Sometimes the white man's medicines don't work. Marjorie was strong to begin with. I'm sure that is why the doctor's medicine worked so quickly on her."

"And you say that she is well today?" Spotted Horse said, taking the last step that took him to the upstairs landing. "Well enough to ride with me?"

He stopped. He turned and faced Louis. He placed his hands on the agent's shoulders. "You see, Louis, my son is very ill," he said, his voice drawn and solemn. "He asked not only that I come for Doc Rose, but also Marjorie. Is she well enough to ride with me back to my village? Seeing her seems so important to my son."

"Your son has whooping cough?" Louis said softly. "I'm sorry, Spotted Horse. So sorry. Just how bad is he?"

"He is so ill that our Medicine Man's prayers rose above him instead of wrapping themselves protectively around him," Spotted Horse said thickly. "Nor did the sweat lodge ceremony heal him."

"And you say he has asked you to bring the white man's medicine to him?" Louis asked, surprise in his voice and his eyes. "You will allow it?"

"I will do anything possible to help save my son from the pine boxes," Spotted Horse said. He lowered his eyes to the floor. He slowly dropped his hands to his side. "My pride may have cost my people many children. The white doctor might have saved them."

"But you are not to blame even if that is true," Louis said, placing a hand of encouragement on Spotted Horse's shoulder. "Your people do not believe in the white doctor. Even if you had brought him to your village earlier, you know that most mothers and fathers would have shunned him and preferred the Medicine Man over him. You know that most see the white doctors as witch doctors."

Hearing Louis saying what Spotted Horse himself knew to be true, Spotted Horse felt some of the guilt leave his shoulders.

He raised his eyes again and gazed into Louis's. "*Ha-ye-e-e, ha-ye-e-e,* thank you," he said, gripping Louis's hand. "In my grief, guilt, and heartache, I am not thinking as clearly as I am normally able to."

He gazed down the long corridor of closed doors, then turned to Louis again. "My woman is in one of those rooms?" he asked softly.

Louis smiled. "Yes, your woman is in one of those rooms," he said thickly. He started to walk with Spotted Horse toward the door, then stopped and faced him again. "You call her your woman now and have given her an Indian name, yet it was not so long ago that you turned your back on her. I take it you have had second thoughts on why you did this?"

"That is so," Spotted Horse said, slowly nodding. "Times are hard for this chief. But soon all of these problems will pass and the lives of the Dakota will be lives of sunshine and gladness again."

"Yes, sunshine and gladness," Louis said, again walking toward Marjorie's bedroom door.

When he reached it, he stopped and placed his hand on the doorknob, then turned toward Spotted Horse before opening the door. "And the woman in this room will bring much sunshine and gladness into your life," he said softly.

"Yes, that is true," Spotted Horse said, his lips quivering into a slow smile. "She *is* sunshine and gladness. She is everything good."

Louis's eyes twinkled. He nodded, then turned and opened the door.

He stepped aside as Spotted Horse entered the room, his eyes wide as he gazed at Marjorie, who was sitting up, a food tray on the bed before her.

Busy sipping soup from a spoon, Marjorie did not at first notice the door open.

Doc Rose sat beside the bed chatting with Marjorie while putting his medicine back in his black bag.

"Young lady, I think you're almost fit as a fiddle," Doc Rose said, snapping his bag closed.

He became quiet and looked quickly over his shoulder when he realized that Marjorie was no longer listening to him but was absorbed in something else. He soon saw what. Spotted Horse stepped out of the shadows, his eyes locked with Marjorie's.

Doc Rose looked slowly from Marjorie to Spotted Horse and saw something between them that was even more potent than the medicine that Doc Rose had used on Marjorie. He smiled to see that Marjorie was still suffering from a disease, all right, but this time it was love sickness.

Without saying anything else to Marjorie, Doc Rose stood up and, carrying his bag at his right side, slipped past Spotted Horse after offering him a nod of hello, which was not seen. He went on outside into the corridor with Louis.

"Well now, Louis, did my eyes see correctly, or are that young lady and that powerful Dakota chief enamored with one another?" Doc Rose said, chuckling.

"Quite," Louis said, smiling.

"Well, I'd best be on my way, then," Doc Rose said, walking toward the staircase. "Seems that young lady has someone else who's going to make her feel better now."

"No, don't go yet," Louis said, grabbing the doctor by the arm.

"Why not?" Doc Rose said. Then he laughed. "Oh, yes, a cup of coffee. You want me to take time for a cup of coffee. Well, I think I can oblige, Louis." His eyes gleamed as he leaned closer to Louis. "That is, if Edith has baked some of those sweet things to dunk in my coffee."

"Yes, Edith always has something sweet to offer everyone," Louis said. "But that's not why I've asked you to stay awhile longer." He heaved a heavy sigh. "It's the chief's son. Sun Bear has come down with whooping cough. He needs your help."

"You don't say . . ." Doc Rose said, his eyes

widening. "I find that hard to believe. I've offered Spotted Horse my help many times. I even went to the village. I was always turned away."

"Sun Bear, personally, has asked for you to come," Louis explained, walking beside Doc Rose down the stairs. "Come on downstairs. We'll have that cup of coffee and something sweet while Marjorie and Spotted Horse patch things up between them. While we're having refreshments, I'll explain more about Sun Bear."

"Is he very ill?" Doc Rose asked solemnly as he descended from the last step, then made a turn toward the parlor.

"Bad enough for the young brave to ask for help from a white doctor," Louis said, his voice drawn.

"Then I'd say he's damn bad," Doc Rose said, kneading his chin as he sat down in a plush chair before the roaring fire.

Chapter Twenty-two

Marjorie's pulse raced as Spotted Horse moved slowly toward her. Now that they were alone, she could hardly wait to hear why he was there.

Yet even when he knelt at her bedside, his eyes still looking intensely into hers, he said nothing.

"You heard that I was ill?" she blurted out. "Louis sent word? You . . . cared . . . enough to come see how I was faring? The other day, you . . . you . . . acted as though you cared nothing at all for me."

"I was wrong," Spotted Horse said, taking one of her hands. "But believe me when I tell you that I did it for *you*, not because I wanted to."

"What do you mean?" she asked softly, loving the feel of his hand in hers. "Spotted Horse, it broke my heart to see you ride away without a word. I truly thought you somehow blamed me for what had happened to you."

"You are not to blame for anything but making this Dakota chief want and need you like nothing else before in his life," Spotted Horse said thickly. "*Tecihila*, I love you. I need you. I will never hurt you again." He swallowed hard. "That is, if you forgive me."

"How could I not forgive you when I love you so much?" Marjorie said, a wonderful, joyful bliss flooding through her. "Yet I still wish to have an explanation. Please tell me why you treated me in such a way. I need to hear it from *you*."

"I thought it was best that you not associate yourself with me and my people when it is so obvious the white pony soldiers will try to find fault with anything my people do in order to destroy us," Spotted Horse said. "I would not want *you* to suffer because *we* must suffer. Your life would be safer and more peaceful if you did not live among the Dakota. That is why I turned my back to you. I wish for you to be safe. I wish for you to have a peaceful heart."

"My heart would never be peaceful were I not able to share it with you," Marjorie said, happy tears filling her eyes. "Have you come today to ask me to return with you to your village, to live among your people, as your woman? Or did you just come and apologize because you heard that I was sick and did not want the guilt of what you did lying heavy on your heart should I die?"

"I came for many reasons, but mainly because my love for you burns inside my heart so fiercely it is hard for me to eat, sleep, or think clearly," Spotted Horse said softly.

"I do so love you," Marjorie said, sliding her hand free of his. She lifted the tray from her lap and set it on the table at her side.

Then she held out her arms for Spotted Horse. "Hold me?" she murmured. "Please . . . hold . . . me?"

Filled with joy that she still cared so much for him, and that her illness was all but gone, Spotted Horse sat on the edge of the bed.

He pulled her into his embrace. As she twined her arms around his neck, Spotted Horse's lips moved over hers. She melted into Spotted Horse's embrace and sank into a chasm of desire as his kiss deepened. His hands slid between them and cupped her breasts through the thin fabric of her gown. She abandoned herself to the torrent of feelings that washed over her.

And when he slid the straps of her gown down and his flesh met hers as he molded her breasts in his hands, her breath quickened with yearning.

Suddenly she recalled the sensual dream that she had experienced two nights in a row, in which they had made love.

She hungered for him to cover her body now, having never been joined with him in such a way, except in dreams.

"Spotted Horse," she whispered against his lips. "I need you. Please . . . ?"

When he suddenly drew away from her, her breath quickened and her eyes widened.

Sudden shame washed through her to think

that she had practically given herself to him, and he . . .

"This is not the time," Spotted Horse said huskily, his pulse racing, his loins so hot they pained him. "You see, my woman, I have not yet told you all the reasons why I came to you today."

"Why else?" Marjorie asked, almost afraid to hear the answer.

"Sun Bear is very ill," Spotted Horse blurted out. "He has the whooping cough disease. He has asked for you, *and* for the white doctor."

"Sun Bear is sick?" Marjorie gasped, paling. "Oh, no, Spotted Horse. Please don't tell me that he's dying."

"I have prayed that he will not die, but I prayed, also, that none of the other children in my village would die, and you saw the many bodies on the scaffolds," he said, his voice breaking. "You also saw the many pine boxes that were delivered to my village for the others who will die."

He raked his fingers through his hair. "I do not want to place my son in a pine box!" he cried, his voice filled with torment.

Marjorie's thoughts were scrambled. She was thinking about him having come to her, but not only because he wished to have her as his woman. He had come for his son! Was that the real reason?

"You would do anything for your son, wouldn't you?" Marjorie found herself saying. "Even come and tell me you love me when . . . when . . . perhaps you truly don't."

Marjorie's words were so hurtful to Spotted Horse he felt as though she had slapped him. "You do not believe that, do you?" he said, his voice drawn. "You do not think I am guilty of lying to gain something for my son? I am a *wi-casa-iyotanyapi*, a man of honor. Especially with the woman I love."

Filled with shame and regret for having wrongly accused him, Marjorie looked quickly away from him. She lowered her eyes. "Yes, I know that you wouldn't do that," she murmured. "I don't know why I said such a thing."

He placed a finger beneath her chin and brought her eyes around to hold with his. "*Mitawin*, my woman, I have not slept since I last left you," he said thickly. "I have not been able to swallow food. I have not been able to think clearly. White Bird, you are my life. Come back with me to my village. Never leave again. Tonight let us sleep between my blankets together. Let my hands touch you all over and teach you the things that should be between a man and a woman in love."

"Yes, I want this," Marjorie said, flinging herself into his arms. "I love you so. Please forgive me for doubting you for even one moment."

"There is nothing to forgive," Spotted Horse said, and gave her an all-consuming kiss.

Then they drew apart.

Marjorie gazed in wonder at him as she rose from the bed and began to dress. "Moments ago you called me White Bird," she said softly. "You have never called me that before. Why did you today?"

"It is a name I wish to give you if you do not mind," Spotted Horse said softly.

"You don't like the name Marjorie?" she asked, buttoning the last button of her fully gathered cotton dress. She then sat on the edge of the bed as she slid her feet into flat, leather shoes.

"It is not that I do not like it," Spotted Horse said. "It is just that since you are going to be my *tawicu*, wife, it would be best that you are called something that is more Indian in nature. Your soft, white skin reminds me of white birds I have seen flying in the sky as summer turns to autumn. Do you like the name? Do you like birds?"

"Yes, I like the name," she said, smiling up at him as she grabbed a wool coat from the trunk and hurried into it. "And yes, I love birds."

"And you love my son?" Spotted Horse said, as he grabbed her into his arms. "You love him enough to talk the white doctor into going and giving him his medicine?"

"I love you enough to do anything you wish of me," Marjorie said, placing a gentle hand to his soft, copper cheek.

"I shall remember that when we are between my blankets together," Spotted Horse said, chuckling.

Blushing at what he might be implying, Marjorie laughed softly as she left the room with him.

When they got downstairs, Doc Rose was waiting for them with his bag beside the door.

Marjorie knew that Louis had already talked

with the doctor about Sun Bear having asked for him. Doc Rose was ready to make the journey to the Dakota village. Finally he was going to be able to help their children!

Louis swept his arm around Marjorie and hugged her, then held her away from him and gazed at her in question. "Are you certain you are strong enough to travel on horseback?" he asked softly. "If not, I can go with you. You can ride in a buggy."

"Or she can ride in mine," Doc Rose said, opening the door. "Come on, Marjorie. I think it is best if you ride in my buggy. Must I remind you that you had quite a high temperature yesterday? Surely you are weaker than you will admit to, for a temperature takes a lot out of a person."

"Yes, I do think it best if I ride with you," Marjorie said, going outside with them.

She climbed into the buggy as Spotted Horse took his reins from the hitching rail.

"I shall come soon to the village with all of the paper doll materials that you will ever need," Louis shouted, waving as they all rode off.

"Thank you," Marjorie shouted back, waving at him. "How can I ever thank you?"

"By pretending to be that daughter I never had," Louis shouted back, smiling at her.

"I shall!" she said, returning his smile. "Oh, yes, I shall!"

With Spotted Horse riding on his mighty steed at their right side, the horse and buggy made a wide turn out of the lane, then headed on down the narrow road that edged alongside the forest.

Soon numb from the cold and the bone-chilling wind, Marjorie accepted a blanket that Doc Rose handed to her.

"A cold blast of arctic air has arrived," Doc Rose said. "Perhaps that will help clean the air of germs!"

"I hope it all ends soon," Marjorie said, then looked up into the sky when she heard a whining sound. The wind howled like a thousand wolves as snow began to fall in white sheets from the heavens.

"Snow," Marjorie murmured. "I love snow. There is something spiritual about it . . . as though things are given a new, fresh beginning."

She gazed over at Spotted Horse and found him looking at her.

They exchanged warm, knowing smiles.

Yes, fresh beginnings, she thought to herself. Now if only Sun Bear could be well again!

Chapter Twenty-three

Finally at Spotted Horse's tepee, Marjorie sat on warm, thick pelts spread on the floor near the fire. She gazed at Sun Bear as he lay huddled beneath blankets on his bed at the far side of the lodge. Her heart bled for him when he coughed until his face reddened, then rested beneath his blankets when the coughing subsided.

Spotted Horse knelt down beside Sun Bear, his face etched with concern as he watched Doc Rose sit down on the opposite side of the bed. Doc Rose had been at the village all day, doctoring Sun Bear first, then offering his medicine to those Dakota who would take it for their children.

Sun Bear had already shown signs of improvement. His coughing bouts were less frequent now. His breathing seemed easier. He no longer had a frightened look in his eyes. When he gazed at Marjorie, there was a quietness, a warm sense of gratitude.

Now, as he looked at her and smiled, her heart melted, for she knew that his love for her was genuine.

"Just one more dose of cough medicine should do it for now and then the young brave can get a peaceful night of sleep," Doc Rose said, pouring the liquid into a spoon.

When the wind whistled ominously down through the smoke hole, Doc Rose gazed up at it and frowned, yet he knew that for the most part the snow and wind were being kept out of the tepee by two flaps that served as wind breaks. If the wind blew too hard from the north, the flaps on the north side rose. If it blew from the south, the southern flaps would rise.

"Yep, one more dose of medicine for Sun Bear and then I'd best head back for home or I might get stranded by the weather," Doc Rose said.

"You will be escorted home by my warriors," Spotted Horse said, glad to see that his reassurance calmed the anxious look in the doctor's eyes. "My warriors could travel blind on this land and find their way back home. Their memories become their eyes when tracks are hidden beneath a heavy layer of snow. Should the snowstorm worsen, do not fret. You will make it safely home tonight."

"I appreciate the offer," Doc Rose said. He slid the spoon gently between Sun Bear's lips, making sure the boy swallowed the medicine before taking the spoon away.

He smiled when Sun Bear took the spoon from him and eagerly licked it. Doc Rose had made this cough syrup especially for children, making sure to give it a taste that would be pleasing.

Doc Rose smiled at Sun Bear as he gave the spoon back to him. He cleaned the spoon with a rag soaked in alcohol to remove any contagious germs that might be clinging to it, and then gazed at the closed entrance flap, which was whipping in the wind. "The weather is worsening," he noted. "Not long ago I heard wolves howling. Now all I hear is the wind, for the wolves understand when it becomes too dangerous to stir from their warm shelters."

He looked over at Spotted Horse. "I believe you Indians call this worsening weather *Poudries*, don't you?" he said, setting the cough medicine and spoon on a tray.

"*Ho*, and the weather is nearing that danger point," Spotted Horse said, well aware of the dangers of being outside now. The temperatures were not much below the freezing point, but the wind would now pierce the garments of any traveler like a sharp knife.

"The storm will worsen until the snow whirls about in a thousand eddies, obscuring everything."

Spotted Horse did not like the idea of sending his warriors out in such weather. But the white doctor had repeatedly said that he needed to return home. His wife had an ailing heart. Should the white doctor not arrive home as expected, she might worry herself into a heart attack.

Spotted Horse wondered if that was the real reason the doctor wished to leave for home tonight. Or was it because he was afraid of the village Medicine Man who was not pleased by his presence in the village and his interference in the lives of the Dakota people, who until tonight looked only to him to heal their children?

Yes, Spotted Horse knew that Brown Hair was angry, and hurt and humiliated by the white doctor's presence in the village. His Medicine Man had stood back in the shadows and watched those who had invited Doc Rose into their lodges. Brown Hair had smiled when there were those who were not as cordial to the white doctor.

Spotted Horse had watched, himself, wishing that he had brought Doc Rose here earlier. Yet he would not allow guilt to blind him to the truth. Until the situation had deteriorated to the point that so many children were ill or dead from the dreaded disease, the white man would not have been invited into that first lodge in his village.

"Yes, winter has come to stay, that's for certain," Doc Rose said, pushing himself up from the floor. He nodded down at the cough medicine and spoon. "I'll be leaving those with you. Give him the cough medicine whenever his coughing gets out of hand."

He again looked toward the entrance flap. "Soon there'll be more than whooping cough to deal with in the area," he said. "With winter come many sorts of ailments."

He grabbed up his bag and smiled. "But I'm ready for it all," he said. "I'll just take my black bag wherever there is a need for it."

Marjorie went to Sun Bear's bedside and ran her fingers slowly through his hair. She was so glad that he no longer felt feverish. "Doc Rose, thank you so much for everything," she murmured. "Please have a safe trip home."

"Why, Marjorie, aren't you leaving with me?" Doc Rose asked, a look of quiet wonder in his eyes as he gazed down at her. "Don't you want me to take you back to Louis's house?"

Before Marjorie had the chance to answer, Spotted Horse rose to his feet and placed a gentle hand on the doctor's shoulder. "She stays," he said, his eyes locked suddenly with the doctor's.

Doc Rose gazed a moment longer into Spotted Horse's eyes, then he looked quickly down at Marjorie. "Marjorie?" he said, his voice guarded.

"I'm staying," she said softly, yet offered no more explanation than that. She knew that if Doc Rose asked, Louis would feel free to explain everything to him.

Oh, how it thrilled Marjorie to know that she was in Spotted Horse's tepee, and that she *was* staying.

But most of all she was happy to know that Spotted Horse wanted her there. And not for only tonight. He wanted her to stay with him forever!

They would soon be married. She would be his wife. She would be a wife to a great and powerful Dakota chief!

"Well now, if that's your decision, Marjorie, I'll be on my way without you," Doc Rose said, still staring down at her.

"Yes, it's my decision to stay," Marjorie said, smiling up at him.

Spotted Horse was again aware of the howling of the wind and knew that the snow was still falling in thick, white sheets. He thought again about how dangerous it was outside.

He went to the back of his lodge where he kept his warm robes. He sorted through them and removed a hooded robe sewn from a thick bear pelt.

Spotted Horse took the robe to the doctor. "I offer you this as one gift of many you will receive for having come today to help my people," he said, holding the robe out for the doctor. "Wear it on your journey home. While wearing it, I assure you that you will not feel the wind. And when the weather improves, I will bring you many more gifts from my people. I will be certain that among those gifts will be something special for your woman."

Spotted Horse smiled widely when the doctor set his bag down and put on the robe.

"Warm as toast," Doc Rose said, sliding the hood up over his head. He ran his hands up and down the soft pelt. "Mighty nice. Yep, this is a *mighty* fine pelt."

Doc Rose then held out a hand toward Spotted Horse. "Thank you for the gift," he said softly. "I shall wear it with pride."

Beaming, Spotted Horse clasped the doctor's hand, then walked Doc Rose outside. He watched the doctor until he rode from the village in the company of several of his warriors, who were also dressed warmly in blankets and robes.

Then Spotted Horse turned and reentered his lodge. He stopped just inside the entrance flap to gaze down at Marjorie and Sun Bear. While Marjorie was stroking her fingers through his son's hair, she was singing softly to him. Sun Bear was asleep, his coughing silenced by the white man's medicine.

The sight was a wondrous one to Spotted Horse, for he now knew that his son was going to be all right, and he now knew that Marjorie was there to stay!

Now if only his people's children could be well, Spotted Horse would think that things were finally right in his world again!

For now, having Marjorie with him, and seeing his son sleeping peacefully, were enough for him. He was filled with contentment.

And there was something more that was beginning inside him, something he had long denied himself after the death of his wife. He had a deep longing now to fulfill those needs that had eaten at him ever since he had allowed himself to think of Marjorie as someone he could love. Only when he had finally given in to those feelings and shared them with her, had he felt alive again.

He had never felt as alive, or as filled with expectation at having a woman in his bed, as now.

As he gazed at her, his heart pounding with hungry need and a love so intense he felt dizzy from it, he saw her as more beautiful than the stars. The moon. The snow. Or an eagle soaring majestically overhead.

Yes, she was more beautiful than the spring flowers that dotted the land with their exquisite colors, their scent wafting through the air like perfume.

"I want you," he suddenly said aloud, drawing Marjorie's head up. "Tonight, White Bird. Tonight."

As she saw the hungry intent in his eyes, and heard it in his voice, Marjorie's heart began to race, for surely his need could not compare with her own.

As he walked slowly toward her, she could feel the pulsing of the blood through her veins. Even without him actually touching her, pleasure was spreading through her body.

It was the way his gaze was scorching her flesh, igniting all of her senses.

It was the remembrance of his kisses and how they left her so weak and wanting.

And now she would finally be with him, sexually. He would open up the mystery of lovemaking to her, for he was the key to her heart and soul.

She was filled with euphoria at the thought of his body against hers. She could hardly bear to wait while he saw to Sun Bear's comfort.

223

Breathlessly, she leaned back, thinking that Spotted Horse would take more time with Sun Bear.

But instead he leaned down and kissed her, his tongue thrusting between her lips, seeking. Ecstatic waves of passion rippled through her.

She could feel his hunger in the hard pressure of his lips. She answered his hunger with her own as she reached up and twined one arm around his neck to draw him closer.

But the sound of Sun Bear coughing drew them back to reality.

Marjorie gazed down at Sun Bear and discovered that he was still asleep. She made sure that he was covered warmly with several blankets and pelts.

She stroked his cheek, brushed a soft kiss across his brow, then stood up and stepped away from the bed as Spotted Horse took his turn with his son. She was touched deeply to see his deep tenderness for his son. She could not hear what Spotted Horse was saying as he bent low next to Sun Bear's ear, but she knew that he was telling him how much he loved him and how happy he was that he was going to get better.

Spotted Horse gently touched his son's brow, kissed him on the cheek, then rose and slid a blanket across a rope that would give Marjorie and Spotted Horse privacy.

Spotted Horse turned to Marjorie. "I shall draw it back open when you and I are ready to go to sleep, for I do not want Sun Bear to be cut off from the fire for too long," he said.

He slid his arms around Marjorie's waist and pulled her to him. "But will you and I truly want to sleep tonight?" he said huskily, his eyes dark with passion. "Or do you think we will want to make love all night?"

With Spotted Horse's hard, taut body against hers, Marjorie was finding it hard to bring her breathing under control.

Yet there was a part of her that was still rational about things, causing her to remember just how ill she had been, and the weakness from the illness that she was fighting even now. She wanted nothing to stand in the way of their finally being together intimately. She would fight the weakness with all her might!

"I doubt that I shall ever want to sleep again, not if I must choose sleeping over being with you," Marjorie said, laughing softly.

Spotted Horse swept her up into his arms. While kissing her, he carried her around the lodge fire to his own bed.

As she clung to him, he slid another blanket across a rope, to truly assure their privacy should Sun Bear awaken and push his blanket aside.

While the storm raged outside, the firelight gilded all within. Spotted Horse and Marjorie stood behind the drawn blanket and took turns undressing one another.

After Marjorie was fully nude, Spotted Horse stood back and gazed at her. He enjoyed looking at her nakedness. Her shoulders were so white and soft. Her ivory-pale breasts were generously rounded, the nipples taut with anticipation.

Her waist was small. Her belly was flat. The hair between her legs, like a puff of smoke, beckoned to him.

Marjorie, in turn, gazed at him. She had not been able to help seeing many men nude before. Her mother had not thought to keep the men she bedded hidden from the eyes of her daughter.

As Marjorie recalled, some of the men even seemed to purposely flaunt their nudity in front of her as she lay in her bed, trying desperately to sleep so that they would not come and touch her.

But she would open her eyes just wide enough to make sure they were keeping their distance.

With such memories of men's bodies, she smiled to think that none of them compared to Spotted Horse. One could tell that he was not a man who sat idly by. By the corded muscles in his shoulders, arms, chest, and legs, it was obvious that he was a man who loved physical activity. And she loved the way his flat belly seemed to flow so easily down to that part of him that was *definitely* larger than that of any other man she had ever seen. It was long, thick, and obviously ready to please a lady.

Marjorie's heart raced to think that she would soon be pleasured by such a manhood as that.

And she knew that a man must give a woman *much* pleasure with that part of his anatomy. She had listened long hours to her mother's sensual moans. She had listened to the men as they received pleasure from her mother. From as far back as Marjorie could remember, she had hoped to find a man who would make her have such wonderful feelings.

But until she had met Spotted Horse, she had not seen any man she wished to go to bed with, for she had felt nothing special for any of them.

And her mother had explained to her that when the right man came along, she would know it. Her stomach would flutter strangely. Her heart would beat so nervously she might at first think she was going to have a heart attack! And she would feel giddy and foolish in his presence. At night she would dream of nothing else.

Marjorie had felt all of these things for Spotted Horse, and even more.

Spotted Horse reached his hands for hers and entwined her fingers with his. Gently holding her hands above her head, he pressed his body against hers and guided her down on his bed.

Then he knelt down over her, his hands now roaming slowly over her body, his lips following their path with soft, sensual kisses and flicks of his tongue.

When his lips and tongue fell over one of her breasts, licking, sucking, and flicking, Marjorie almost went mindless with ecstasy. She couldn't imagine how anything could feel so wonderful.

Not until one of his hands went lower and found the soft, sweet place between her legs. She gasped with pleasure as he began to stroke her there. She swallowed hard and inhaled a quavering breath as the ecstasy mounted.

Then his lips slid upward and his mouth closed hard upon hers. He silenced her moans and gasps of pleasure with a fiery kiss. She was only scarcely aware of him positioning himself over her, his thick manhood now probing where his fingers had created such heat.

When he slid himself into her, slowly at first, and then with one insistent thrust that broke through her virginal, protective wall, she winced with pain and cried out against his lips.

The press of his lips on her mouth, so soft, yet demanding, and the rhythmic strokes he was making within her, made her soon forget the pain. Her alarm quickly changed to pleasure again. She twined her arms around his neck and lifted her body to meet each of his strokes within her. She felt as though she were floating on the pulsing crest of her passion.

Over and over again he plunged deeply within her, the fires of his desire burning higher through him, like molten lava spreading within his veins. He molded her closer to the contours of his lean, hard body. He held her tightly against him as he shoved even more deeply into her warm, velvet tightness.

Again his hands searched her pleasure points, tantalizing her with his fingers, his mouth now resting against the long, sweet column of her throat. He shuddered with desire when she wrapped her legs around his waist and drew him even closer to her. His lips moved again to her breasts and teased her taut nipples.

He kissed her again, then placed his mouth to her ear. "Your lips are so soft and passionate," he whispered huskily. "Your body is so pliant and sweet next to mine. My *mitawin*, I am dissolving into a tingling heat. It's spreading to my very soul."

His words drugged her. She kissed his eyelids closed, then whispered into his ear. "My darling Dakota chief, your heat is deliciously searing my heart," she murmured. "A madness seems to have engulfed me. Love me for eternity, my beloved, for that is how long I shall love you."

His hands cupped the soft flesh of her bottom. He held her tightly to him as he thrust rhythmically within her.

"Now," he whispered to her. "Come with me now to where the eagles fly! Soar with me, my love!"

His lips covered hers in a frenzy of kisses as he gave one last thrust that took them to the final throes of ecstasy.

Marjorie moaned as the most incredible sweetness swept through her.

She clung to him as her body quivered while his body quaked and spilled its seed deeply into her.

Afterward, as they lay together, breathless and snuggling, Spotted Horse was the first to come out of the reverie. He leaned on an elbow and gazed at Marjorie.

When he saw how she scarcely stirred, her eyes closed as though she might have fainted, panic seized him.

Had he made love to her too soon after her

illness? Had it been too much for her?

"White Bird," he said thickly. He placed a hand to her cheek. "Are you all right? Speak to me."

Marjorie heard the panic in his voice. She opened her eyes, then smiled when she saw the relief in his eyes. "Did you think I had died and gone to heaven from the pleasure of what we just shared?" she asked. She giggled. "*I* truly thought that I had."

"It gave me concern when I saw you so . . . so . . . lifeless," Spotted Horse said, not finding his alarm amusing.

"I was just lying there thinking about it, in awe of what we had shared," Marjorie murmured, cuddling next to him. "In my mind I was reliving it."

"You do not have to relive it in your mind when I am here ready to do it for real again," Spotted Horse said, forgetting his alarm in the wonder of their togetherness.

Marjorie gazed up at him. "Well, now, I didn't quite say that I was ready to, so *soon*," she said, her eyes dancing. "Lovemaking is wonderful, but for me it was exhausting. I would just like to lie here like this in your arms. Being here with you is like having a small piece of heaven on earth."

"The pain?" Spotted Horse said, slowly sliding his hands over her soft back. "Was it too much?"

"For a moment I thought I might die," Marjorie said, then leaned on an elbow and giggled when she heard him gasp. "I was only jesting.

The truth? Yes, it hurt. But it didn't take long for you to teach me how pain can soon turn to pleasure."

"That is good," he said, placing his arm around her and drawing her to him. He held her gently in his embrace. "There will be no more pain. Just pleasure."

She remembered something. "Again you called me White Bird," she murmured. "You truly wish for me to go by that name?"

"*Ho*, that is if you agree that it is a pretty enough name for you," Spotted Horse said, searching her eyes for the truth of her feelings.

"I love the name," Marjorie said softly. "And don't most Indian names have meaning?"

"*Ho*, your name White Bird means 'pure,' " he said, placing a gentle hand on her cheek. "I have never met anyone as pure as you, my *mitawin*."

She was touched deeply by this, but she could not help remembering how her mother had been forced to make a living. Her mother had been anything but pure.

Marjorie gave a silent prayer of thanks to God that she had not been thrown into the same circumstances as her mother. Marjorie was far more lucky than her mother had been. Marjorie had a man who would never let her down . . . who would never desert her!

"Thank you for everything," she whispered as she pressed her body closer to Spotted Horse's. "My darling, oh, my darling, you just don't know how blessed I feel for having found you."

"I am the blessed one," Spotted Horse said, then drew her lips to his and kissed her slowly, then more deeply, then with a fevered passion.

Marjorie quickly decided that she was not all that tired after all. She slid beneath him and shuddered with ecstasy when he thrust himself into her again.

This time he gave her a long and leisurely loving.

Chapter Twenty-four

The coughing sickness and deaths were now behind them, and the tears had dried in the Dakota village. Everything now proceeded in proper order, with real dignity. Peace had resumed between the Dakota and the white pony soldiers. The very air seemed exciting and different.

Inside the council house tom-tom beats sounded in quick rhythm, fires burned in four firepits, their smoke rising through smoke holes in the ceiling. Large slabs of meat cooked over the dancing flames. Huge platters of other foodstuffs lay beside the pits.

The whole village had crowded into the large, dome-shaped lodge to celebrate the marriage between their chief and the white woman whom they had grown to love and respect as though she were their blood kin. The private pledges between Marjorie and Spotted Horse would come later when they were alone in Spotted Horse's lodge.

Now was a time of fun and sharing for everyone.

Spotted Horse and Marjorie sat on a platform of soft pelts and blankets while everyone else sat on the floor in a wide circle as young braves played a hoop-and-spear game in the center of the lodge.

Marjorie felt as though she were floating on air, she was so happy. She felt like a princess. She glanced down at herself and ran a hand over the softness of her Indian dress. It was made of tanned deerskin and reached about halfway between her knees and her ankles.

Midway between the waist belt and the border of the dress was a fringe about four inches wide. Two rows of blue beads ran across the front above the belt, with ornaments of porcupine quills hanging down from them. Her leggings were painted yellow and fringed at the bottom and up the sides, marked with horizontal black cross-lines around the legs.

Marjorie had never worn anything on her feet as soft as the beaded moccasins that now warmly hugged them.

She reached a hand up and touched one of her braids. Little fringed rolls of deerskin were tied to the outside of the braids, close to the head. On the outer side of the deerskin rolls were tied sprigs of sage.

She gazed over at Spotted Horse. Sitting so

straight-backed and square-shouldered, he was handsome in his buckskin attire, heavily fringed and beaded. His long black hair, held back with a beaded headband, hung free of braids across his shoulder to his waist. His copper skin shone in the soft gleam of the lodge fires. In his eyes there was a gentle peace.

The beats of the tom-toms suddenly grew faster and louder, drawing Marjorie's eyes back to the hoop-and-spear game in which Sun Bear participated. She felt a warmth encircle her heart to see him so healthy now, his strength having totally returned.

She reached over and took Spotted Horse's hand and proudly continued watching Sun Bear laugh and play the game with his friends. She did not understand much about it, but Spotted Horse had told her that the hoops had been formed from small limbs or young tree shoots bent into a circle, then secured with leather thongs. Across the hoops, additional thongs were loosely woven which left openings for the long, straight sticks thrown by the players.

Before the game had started, two teams had been chosen. Now, as they played in teams, a player on one side threw the hoop sharply downward in front of himself so that it rolled swiftly toward the other team, who ran alongside it, throwing their spears, trying to get one through the hoop. Marjorie noticed that it was a surprisingly fast-moving game, for the young braves were agile and quick.

Marjorie's attention wandered as she became

distracted by thoughts of her stepfather and Snow. Six weeks had passed and neither man had been seen. She had to assume that both were long gone from the area. They surely knew that if they had stayed, their lives would be in jeopardy, not only from the Dakota, but also from the colonel at Fort Snelling. Both Snow and Albert had broken the law. Warrants for their arrests had been issued.

Nevertheless, Marjorie could not totally relax, knowing that her stepfather was out there somewhere, always a threat to her. Should he decide to return to the area, she knew it would be only because he felt he still had a score to settle with her.

As for Snow? She felt no real threat from him. He was a harmless weasel.

Thinking of more pleasant things, she turned and gazed at Louis Eckert and Doc Rose who sat together enjoying the merriment of the celebration.

When Louis seemed to sense that she was looking at him, he turned a soft smile her way. During these past weeks, he had come often to the village, not only to bring Marjorie supplies for making her paper dolls but just to be with her, as a father might want to be with a daughter. She felt a bonding with him, also, as though he were her true father.

Since Marjorie had never known her real father, and had never felt anything but silent loathing for all of her stepfathers, this was new for her—this closeness, this special love.

She returned Louis's smile, then glanced over

at Doc Rose. He was a jolly man whose generous heart had touched so many of the Dakota people's lives. He was treated with great respect by everyone in the village, except for the Medicine Man, who had even refused to attend the celebration today since the white doctor was there.

Learning of the Medicine Man's attitude, and not wanting to be the cause of trouble on this special day, Doc Rose had started to leave.

Marjorie had stopped him and encouraged him to stay. And she was glad that she had. She could see how much he was enjoying the celebration. He needed something in his life since his wife had passed away only three weeks ago, her heart having failed her at the age of thirty-five.

Marjorie was shaken from her reverie when Brown Hair made a sudden appearance in the lodge, rushing and roaring like a buffalo, and wearing the headdress and robe of the Buffalo Dreamer.

Everyone watched as he danced here and there among the crowd, bellowing like a buffalo. As he ran, the people parted and let him pass to avoid being hit with the horns on his head, which he tossed about like an angry buffalo.

He did this dance for some time, then left as quickly as he had appeared.

Spotted Horse stood and swept Marjorie into his arms. He gazed down at her, smiling. "Brown Hair's anger is now appeased," he said. "His demonstration was well received. He knows it. He will move onward as our Medicine Man and not look back to the time when his magic was doubted."

He brushed a soft kiss across Marjorie's lips, then whispered in her ear, "The games are over. It is time for you and I to continue the marriage celebration, but not with an audience. The vows spoken between us will be private pledges."

Feeling delighted to know that the rest of the evening would be spent alone with Spotted Horse, Marjorie clung to his hand as he led her outside.

Night had fallen. Snow covered everything in a white velvet sheen. The night itself was like infinity, the stars glittering in the heavens.

"This is a night we shall always remember," Spotted Horse said as he lifted Marjorie into his arms and carried her to their large tepee.

Once inside, he stopped and gave her a long, deep kiss, then placed her on her feet.

The fire's glow revealed much to Marjorie that made her gasp with surprise. She looked at all the things that lay on the floor of the tepee. She was stunned by the huge stacks of valuable pelts that lay around her.

She gave Spotted Horse a questioning stare.

"It is all yours," Spotted Horse said, gesturing with a hand toward everything. "In the Dakota culture, wives are purchased. The women do not consider it a disgrace to be bought and sold. The higher the price paid for them, the better they are pleased, for the payment of a great price proves that the woman is deemed valuable. All that you see are gifts from Spotted Horse to you, as payment for you."

"Payment . . . for . . . me . . . ?" Marjorie gasped out.

She marveled over the gifts of eagle feathers and elk teeth, the well-woven blankets richly adorned with Dakota legends, and piles of dresses, leggings, and moccasins, as well as the valuable pelts. She smiled, knowing that her stepfather would kill to have such pelts as those to sell at the trading post.

"And there is something else I wish to give to you," Spotted Horse said. He went to the rear of the tepee and lifted a small buckskin bundle from his storage bags.

He took the buckskin bundle back to Marjorie, and as she watched, he opened it and let something beautiful fall from inside it into the palm of his hand.

Marjorie gazed at the necklace, breathless over its loveliness. It was a circular piece of rawhide, decorated with a painted design, with small triangular indentations cut around its circumference.

"Let me place this around your neck," Spotted Horse said, stepping behind her.

She lifted her braids and listened to his explanation about the necklace as he fastened it.

"This is called 'the daybreak star' necklace," he said softly. "It is said that anyone who sees the daybreak star shall have wisdom, and from that wisdom, the peace that comes only from understanding."

When the necklace lay gracefully around her

neck, Spotted Horse slowly turned her to face him. He pointed out a piece of fur on the neck-lace. "The fur represents Mother Earth and all the good things of this life—food, clothing, and a place to live."

Reverently he touched a feather that also hung from the necklace. "The eagle feather means that our thoughts should rise high as the eagle," he said thickly.

"It is all so beautiful . . . the necklace, and your description of it," Marjorie said, tears fill-ing her eyes. Her happiness was so deep and complete. She now knew the Dakota way to say thank you and used it. "*Pila maye*, thank you for everything."

She laughed softly. "I had no idea I was worth so much," she murmured.

"*Mitawin*, my woman, you are worth every-thing to me," Spotted Horse said.

He placed his hands at her waist and drew her close in his embrace. He gently kissed her, then held her away from him again.

She watched him go and get something else from his belongings. When he brought back a fluffy white eagle feather, she watched wide-eyed as he tied it to a lock of her hair.

"This fluffy plume symbolizes a prayer for our happiness," he said softly. He then held her hands. "My love, our hearts were bound to-gether from the first moment we saw one an-other. I am yours as long as the grass shall grow and the snows shall fall. With these words, *mi-tawicu*, I take you as my *tawicu*, wife."

Finding the marriage ceremony so simple, yet

so beautiful because their pledges came from their hearts, Marjorie gazed up at Spotted Horse and spoke her heart to him. "My love, today, as we enter a marriage that will last a lifetime of laughter, I wish to tell you that my love for you is as wide as the sky, and as beautiful as a dove on the wing. I shall forever love you."

Delicious shivers of desire raced through her when he lowered his mouth over hers in a fiery kiss as he disrobed her.

She also disrobed him, and after they were both nude, he placed his hands to her waist and slowly lowered her to the thick pelts beside the fire. They felt free to make love in the open without being disturbed, for Sun Bear had made plans to stay with friends so that the newlyweds would be assured of privacy for an entire night.

As Spotted Horse blanketed Marjorie with his body, she was keenly aware of his strong thighs against her legs. His mouth seared into hers with intensity, leaving her breathless, trembling, and wanting.

She moaned when he slid his mouth away and his tongue flicked and licked the nipple of one of her breasts.

She closed her eyes in joyous agony as his tongue danced along her creamy skin, licking and nipping at her most sensual pleasure points.

His hands cupped her breasts. They pulsed warmly beneath his fingers as his hot breath raced across her flesh.

She felt the nerves in her body tensing when

she felt his hot and hungry mouth venture lower on her body, stopping where her sensual feelings seemed to be centered.

Desire gripped her when he touched her throbbing woman's center with the tip of his tongue.

When he dipped lower and gave her a wide, stroking caress, then nibbled at her womanhood with first his teeth and then his lips, tasting her sweetness, she almost went wild with pleasure.

Hardly able to stand the ecstasy, Marjorie reached her hands out for him.

"Please?" she whispered. "I need you."

Seeing the passion in her eyes, and having felt it in her reaction to this way of arousing her, Spotted Horse smiled at her and positioned himself over her again.

As he held her in a torrid embrace, he came to her, rhythmically thrusting deeply. His mouth covered hers in a fiery, deep kiss, his tongue surging between her lips, touching hers.

A delicious liquid languor stole over Marjorie as her body moved with his, her hips lifting to meet his each and every thrust.

They moaned and groaned throatily as the silent explosion of their needs was fulfilled on this, their wedding night.

Filled with such splendid joy, Marjorie clung to Spotted Horse.

His continued kisses enflamed her heart.

Exquisite sensations spiraled through her body.

Enfolding Marjorie in his solid strenth, Spotted Horse couldn't get enough of her slim, sensuous body as he pressed himself harder against her. His hands ran up and down her yielding flesh.

Then he eased a hand between them and enfolded a breast within it, his thumb tweaking the nipple. He felt the curl of heat growing in his loins. His world melted away as Marjorie's groans of pleasure fired his passion.

Then a searing, scorching flame shot through him. He held Marjorie more tightly as his body shook and quaked against hers and hers answered in kind as the spasms of pleasure overtook her.

The climax was violent, shattering, complete.

Afterward, they lay quietly together.

Spotted Horse kissed the softness of Marjorie's neck.

She kissed his eyelids closed.

"My *Zit-kay-lah-skah*, White Bird," he whispered into her ear. "My sweet White Bird."

"I do love the name so much," Marjorie murmured. "I love *you*."

She cuddled closer to him and they fell asleep, clinging to one another.

Chapter Twenty-five

On this, her first full day of marriage, Marjorie was learning much about her husband's customs that amazed her. One practice was especially surprising to her—how a Dakota husband doted on his wife. She could hardly believe it, for her mother had worked like a slave for her husbands, and earned no respect whatsoever.

And here Marjorie was . . . being treated like a princess!

The fire was warm and cozy as she sat beside it. She felt bubbly inside from her contentment, yet somewhat sad that her mother had never experienced the genuine sort of love that Spotted Horse felt for Marjorie.

She felt, ah, so blessed.

And not only to have Spotted Horse for a husband, but also to have Sun Bear as a son. Sun Bear had returned home long enough this morning from his overnight stay at his best friend's lodge to share breakfast with them. He had then left to sit in council with the young braves and older warriors to have a "talk fest."

Marjorie smiled as Spotted Horse even now worked with her hair, feeling deliciously pampered by him. He had gone to the lake, broken through the ice, and brought water back to the lodge. It was used not only for drinking, but also for sponge baths, which they took after warming the water in a large kettle over the fire.

"The first thing a dutiful husband does in the morning after baths and breakfast is arrange his wife's hair and paint her face," Spotted Horse said, resting on his haunches behind her.

With deft fingers he parted Marjorie's hair and then carefully brushed and plaited it into two braids, which he tied at the ends with strings of buckskin.

Marjorie lifted one of her braids and gazed at it. Wrapped with brightly colored porcupine quills and fluffs of eagle feathers, it was a work of art.

All of these little extras made her feel even more special. She knew already that she was going to enjoy being a part of the Dakota's lives.

"Now I will paint the part of your hair with yellow paint," Spotted Horse said, dipping his fingers into a small vial of paint, then gently smoothing the paint across the part of her hair.

He then moved around to face her and

smoothed red paint into her cheeks, and then gently across her lips.

When this was done and he had wiped the paint from his fingers, he sat back from her and gazed at her, warm admiration in his eyes.

"Now, except for your skin and eye color you look Dakota," he said proudly. He lifted a mirror from the floor and handed it to Marjorie. "Look. See. Tell me if you do not think you are beautiful."

Marjorie took the mirror and gazed into it. She could not believe it, for the paint on her face and in her hair, and the way her hair was braided with its beautiful hair strings, *had* made her into someone even she thought was beautiful.

Her painted cheeks seemed to make her eyes brighter.

Her hair drawn back into braids seemed to make her face look more oval and delicate.

And even though the paint on her lips had somewhat of a bitter taste, it enhanced her appearance. Her lips looked like a red cherry, ready to be plucked . . . or kissed.

"You do like it," Spotted Horse said, nodding. "You do see how beautiful you are."

He reached out and touched her skirt. "And do you also enjoy wearing the clothes of the Dakota?" he asked softly.

She gazed down at what she wore today. It was different from anything she had worn before. The outfit consisted of leggings, skirt and blouse, and a coat made of two yards of printed cloth. Its sleeves were tight and fitted closely to the body, but the neck was left bare.

The skirt was made of a single piece of blue broadcloth, the ends lapped and sewed together. It was worn smooth in front and behind, but was gathered at the sides by a girdle.

The leggings were made of red broadcloth, reaching from her knees to her ankles, and fastened at the upper end with garters.

"Yes, I love it all," she murmured, giving Spotted Horse a wondrous smile. She gazed slowly over him. He wore only a breechclout, and his hair was not yet brushed. "And now let me brush your hair. Can I even braid it? I have never seen your hair braided."

"As I told you before, braids are for women," Spotted Horse said, sitting down beside her. "And no, the duty of a wife does not include brushing her husband's hair. I shall brush it, myself. You sit and watch. Let us share morning talk before we begin our chores for the day."

Marjorie was eager to please, and to learn the daily activities of a wife of a Dakota chief. She wished to please him in every respect. She never wanted him to have cause to send her away, or abandon her, as she knew men were wont to do after being married for only a short while!

"Tell me about Sun Bear," Marjorie quickly said, wanting to block from her mind all troubling thoughts of her past. "Tell me about the talk fest that he was so eager to be a part of today at the council house."

Spotted Horse slowly brushed his hair as he gazed into the leaping flames of the lodge fire. "The talk fests are held so that the young braves can hear the *wilo-oyake*, the history of the Dakota tribe," he said, himself recalling the long talk fests of his youth, and how he had eagerly listened and learned so much about his people that made him proud to be Dakota.

He looked over at Marjorie as he laid the brush aside and began smoothing his hair with deer's marrow. "The stories are told by the elders of our tribe," he said. "These stories teach the braves virtue, kindness, obedience, thrift, and the rewards of right living."

He laughed softly. "And some stories are those of pure fancy," he said.

He grew serious again. "But most of all, great pains are taken to educate our young in the hunter's craft," he said. "The old warriors tell stories that have become tribal history. As they grow older, they live over their lives through the retelling of great events."

"I would love to sit in on one of the talk fests some day," Marjorie said, moving to her knees. She clasped her hands on her lap. "Could I? I want to know everything about your people."

"Talk fests are for boys and men, not girls and women," Spotted Horse said, wiping the grease from his hands onto a buckskin cloth. "But *I* will, in time, teach you everything you will ever need to know about my people." He reached a hand to her cheek. "About *our* people, yours and mine, for you are now also Dakota since you are married to a Dakota chief."

She reached up and took his hand and drew him into her embrace. "I am eager to know everything," she murmured, brushing her lips against his. She giggled. "You have already taught me so much in bed."

"There is much more to learn there, also," Spotted Horse said, chuckling. He framed her face between his hands and brushed soft kisses across her brow, her cheeks, and then gave her a deep, long kiss that left her weak.

When he drew away from her and rose to his feet, holding a hand out for her, she thought he might lead her to the bed.

She took his hand, her heartbeat rapid at the thought of making love again this morning. They had awakened before sunrise to share lovemaking before Sun Bear returned home.

He took her hand and led her to the rear of the tepee, but not toward their bed.

"*Ho*, yes, much time will be spent in bed, teaching each other our favorite ways of making love, but not this morning," Spotted Horse said. "We have chores to do before Sun Bear returns. When he does come back, I have promised to teach him how to make shot for the firearm I plan to give him on his next birthday."

"I *think* I can wait until tonight for our lovemaking," Marjorie said, giving him a sly grin. "But if I were you, I would not kiss me again . . . until tonight. My darling, I think you have turned me into a vixen."

He turned suddenly to her and yanked her against his hard body and wrapped his arms around her. His lips took hers by storm, his hands eager as they tried to find a place in her clothes for entry to her breasts.

But finding no way to reach her flesh, except

249

to tear the clothes from her, he stepped away and gazed down at her with a slow, teasing smile. "I am not certain now if I like the woman clothes of my people," he said, chuckling. "They are like a prison, locking me away from the body I wish to caress."

She slinked up next to him. She felt brazen as she slid a hand down the front of his breech-clout and clasped her fingers around his manhood. "I like the breechclouts the men wear," she murmured, seeing his eyes take on a haziness as she squeezed and stroked him. "Darling . . ."

The sound of children's laughter outside the lodge drew Marjorie and Spotted Horse away from each other.

They gazed with longing at one another, then turned and smiled somewhat awkwardly at Sun Bear as he rushed into the lodge, brushing snow from his buckskin coat.

"It is snowing again, but it is only a dusting today," Sun Bear said, stopping short to stare from Spotted Horse back to Marjorie. "Did . . . I . . . interrupt something? Should I leave and come back later?"

"No, you disturbed nothing but lovers at play and you will get used to that since your father and his wife are so much in love," Spotted Horse said. He took Marjorie's hand. "Son, sit by the fire and warm yourself. I will teach White Bird how to fill pillows with fresh cottonwood floss, and then I shall teach you how to make shot."

"And while your father teaches you, I shall

resume making paper dolls," Marjorie said, smiling when she saw quick interest leap into Sun Bear's eyes.

"I wish to watch you make paper dolls," Sun Bear said, then looked quickly at his father with a silent apology in his eyes when he saw his father's jaw tighten at the thought that a son might prefer girl things to young men's.

"But I would rather learn to make shot," he was quick to add. "When I travel to Deer Run to bring home many deer, I hope to down the animal with shot made by my own hands, not someone else's."

"Deer Run?" Marjorie asked. "Where is that?"

"I am certain, while horseback riding, you have been at the Dakota Deer Run," Spotted Horse said. "The Deer Run is the place that the Deer Dreamer, with his mysterious powers and medicine, sends the deer when meat and skins grow scarce in camp. There the hunters can easily kill all that are needed."

"Where is it?" Marjorie asked, her eyes wide.

"It is where the bank along the Mississippi River is high and steep, and at its foot the river runs dark and deep," Spotted Horse explained. "No deer would leap from this bank. A narrow path has been cleared through the woods up to the space on the bank of the river. On either side of the path the woods are thick, and the limbs and boughs have been laced and interlaced to form an unbreakable fence through which the deer cannot go. This leaves but one entrance to the deer enclosure."

"And, Marjorie," Sun Bear quickly interjected. "The day before the deer are to be run into the Deer Run, the Deer Dreamer purifies himself in the sweat lodge. He then asks the *Big Holy* to send the deer to the people. Early in the morning, the Deer Dreamer sends out two scouts, each carrying the magic medicine. The scouts walk in a great circle, and all the deer within this circle are driven toward the path that leads to the enclosure. If a deer approaches the footprints made by the scouts, it will not be able to cross and get outside of the circle because of the magic medicine."

Spotted Horse smiled at Sun Bear, then reached a hand out for Marjorie. "Sit down beside me," he said as he took a large buckskin bag from the stack where he stored supplies for the long winter months. "It is now time for your lesson. We will talk again later about the Deer Run, and my son's anxiousness for the hunt."

Marjorie sat down on the soft mats on the floor beside Spotted Horse.

"I have here several fresh buckskin pillowcases that were made for my lodge by the village women," he said, spreading them out between himself and Marjorie. He lifted a large buckskin bag that was fat with cottonwood floss he had saved from the past summer. "Take the cottonwood floss. Stuff each pillowcase with as much as you can get in it."

He then pointed out sinew that was to be woven by hand through the holes in the pillow cases. "Once the pillows are stuffed, you will close them at the ends with sinew," he instructed.

She busied herself stuffing the pillowcases as he also joined in the simple chore. "Tomorrow, when I do not have teachings for my son, it will be cleaning day in our lodge. I will use *hai-pajaja*, a soap and suds made from *hupestula*, the root of the yucca plant, for scrubbing and cleaning."

"You said that *you* will use the soap and suds for scrubbing," Marjorie said, looking up at him as she pressed cottonwood floss into a bag. "Surely I am expected to do the cleaning. I am your *tawicu*, wife."

"Cleaning is not a Dakota wife's duty," he said, smiling over at her. "It is the man's."

"But you are a chief." she said guardedly.

"I am also a man," he said matter-of-factly.

Marjorie was stunned to know that as a wife not all that much would be required of her, except for such things as stuffing pillows and cooking. Surely in the spring she would be required to prepare the garden for planting. She wanted to feel useful, *some*how!

"My mother almost killed herself doing household chores," she blurted out.

"Your mother married the wrong men," Spotted Horse said, his eyes twinkling as he gazed at Marjorie.

Once the pillows were filled and ready for their beds, Marjorie got the large box containing her paper doll equipment, which Louis had been so kind to bring to her, then went and sat down beside the warmth of the fire. She had already been told that for this first week of her marriage to the people's chief, she was not to

253

cook. All of their meals were to be brought to them.

Yes, she felt pampered, all right. She had never expected life to be easier living as an Indian than as a white.

Adoring Spotted Horse, she laid her paper doll material aside and watched him teach Sun Bear how to make shot, yet as she watched, her mind wandered. She could not help thinking about all of her mother's precious things, and also her own belongings, which had been left at the cabin. With Albert now gone, surely she could go and get what she wished from the cabin before some other family came along and saw that the cabin was deserted and claimed everything as theirs.

"Spotted Horse," she blurted out, drawing his eyes quickly her way. "Is the snow too deep for us to return to my cabin? Albert is no longer there. I would love to take what is mine or my mother's. Do you think you can take me there? Or is the weather too bad for traveling?"

"The snow that fell before today was a hard snow and is now packed solid on the ground," Spotted Horse said. "It is the sort that makes traveling easy. Yes, today, after I finish with Sun Bear's lessons, I shall take you to the cabin."

"Oh, thank you," Marjorie said, her pulse racing at the thought of being able to reclaim so much that was dear to her heart.

She resumed making paper dolls, but stopped long enough to follow Spotted Horse's teachings about making ammunition for the smooth-bore gun that sat back in the corner with Spotted Horse's cache of weapons.

"You manufacture shot from bar lead by melting and pouring it through a sieve of perforated bark held over water," he said as Sun Bear attentively watched and listened.

"Shake the sieve while the lead is running, so that it falls into the water in drops," he further instructed, doing it as he explained.

Marjorie had noticed that the Dakota used smooth-bore guns as well as rifles. The warriors occasionally carried bows and arrows, but mainly for show.

Spotted Horse had shown her his otter-skin quiver and told her that of all his belongings, he prized it the most. Whenever he wore it at the big feasts and ceremonies, he was envied by all of the other warriors, for his was the finest quiver of them all.

It had been his father's, and his father's before him.

"I think the lessons are complete for today," Spotted Horse said, resting a hand on Sun Bear's shoulder. "Now, do you wish to travel with me and White Bird? Or would you rather go and join the other young braves at play in the snow?"

"I wish to go and tell my friends about my lesson today," Sun Bear said, his eyes wide and anxious.

"Then go, *micinksi*. We shall not be gone for long," Spotted Horse said.

After Sun Bear gave both Spotted Horse and Marjorie a hug and left, Spotted Horse went to the back of the tepee and changed from his breechclout to a warm, fringed buckskin suit and moccasins.

He brought a warm cloak made of a bear pelt to Marjorie. He slid it over her shoulders, then gave her gloves made from a smaller forest animal.

He then put on a warm hooded robe and gloves.

They left the lodge and mounted their horses, with loaded rifles sheathed in both of their gunboots.

The ride to the cabin was not long, but the chill of the day made it seemed twice as far.

When they arrived and went inside, they welcomed the walls that protected them from the wind.

As Marjorie looked slowly around her, Spotted Horse knelt down before the fireplace and started a big enough fire to keep them warm while Marjorie went through her belongings.

"I can feel Albert everywhere inside this cabin," Marjorie said, sliding the cloak off and laying it across a chair. She slowly removed one glove and then the other as she gazed overhead at the loft, where Albert had always slept. She could not help imagining him there, ready to jump down and strangle her.

She shook this thought from her mind. She was safe while with Spotted Horse. She did hope that she was right to think that Albert had gone far away where she would never be bothered by him again.

She went slowly through the cabin until she

had stuffed many of her belongings into a large parfleche bag that Spotted Horse had brought.

She then went through her mother's things. She picked up her mother's Bible and flipped the pages to certain passages. She shivered inside to see which ones her mother had underlined.

The passages were about sin and forgiveness and about whoring. Marjorie wondered if her mother had ever gotten comfort from the scriptures. Or had she gone to her grave feeling guilty for all of her transgressions?

Knowing that this Bible was one thing her mother had depended on during her last months of life, Marjorie slid it into her bag.

Then she picked up a bottle of perfume that her mother had worn during her days in the brothel. Marjorie took a whiff of the perfume, and the scent brought a vivid image of her mother.

But she couldn't keep it. It was too much a reminder of the bitter, ugly past, when Marjorie had no roots, or pride.

She set the bottle down on the table and turned to Spotted Horse. "I'm ready to leave," she murmured, the bag bulging with not only her paper doll equipment, but many other things that she had always cherished, among them a diary.

"You have everything that is special to you?" Spotted Horse said, going to take the heavy bag from her.

"Yes," Marjorie said, turning to take a slow look around the dingy, ugly room.

Then she turned quick eyes to Spotted Horse again. "Unless you wish to take some of the pots and pans, or dishes."

"No, none of those things are important to Spotted Horse," he said thickly. "What Spotted Horse wants for his lodge, which is now also yours, he will get in his own way."

"Yes, I understand," Marjorie said. She knew that he was thinking about Albert and, hating the man so much, wanted nothing to do with anything that had belonged to him.

Snuggled warmly again in their cloaks and gloves, Marjorie and Spotted Horse went outside to their mounts.

After Spotted Horse secured the heavy bag to the side of his saddle, he looked over at Marjorie, who had yet to mount her horse. She was peering intensely into the forest.

He went to her and placed a finger beneath her chin and turned her eyes to him. "What is wrong?" he asked.

"I feel a presence," she said, an uncontrollable shiver racing across her flesh. "Do . . . you . . . think Albert is out there watching us?"

"I think it is your imagination," Spotted Horse said, smiling down at her. "Now, *tawicu*, let us go home and never think of this place or that man again."

"It will be my pleasure," Marjorie said, laughing softly.

He helped her into her saddle, then swung himself into his. They rode off together, confident of their safety, their future, their happiness.

Behind them, hooves stirred the snow as a horse moved from behind a thick stand of trees. Albert laughed to himself to think that Marjorie was so damned smug with the Injun. He'd show her soon how wrong she'd been to double-cross Albert Zimmerman!

His eyes two points of hate, he followed them, but kept far enough back to remain invisible.

"Soon, Marjorie, soon . . ." he whispered.

Chapter Twenty-six

A fresh snow had fallen, and the forest was like a fairyland. Marjorie was warm and content as she snuggled beneath a heavy bear pelt where she sat across from Spotted Horse beside a small hole in the ice at the edge of the Mississippi River.

"I've never been ice fishing before," she said, smiling at Spotted Horse. "Spotted Horse, do you truly believe we will catch any today?"

"Today we are in luck," Spotted Horse said, smiling at her as he prepared himself for fishing. He would be using a bow and arrow today. He was attaching a heavy string to the arrow so that it could be drawn back again after spearing the fish.

"The recent heavy snowfalls have closed up cracks in the ice where the fish usually breathe in their air," he said. "To avoid suffocation to-day, they have crowded together beneath the ice. They will be easily taken in."

He nodded. "In the spring, after so many fish have smothered beneath the ice, and the ice thaws, the fish are thrown upon the shore by the waves," he said. "My people gather them up and eat them if they are found before they have spoiled."

He gestured with a free hand toward a large blanket that he had left on the ice beside Marjorie. "It is time now to cover ourselves with the blanket," he said, taking one edge of the blanket as she handed it to him. "The blanket will help block out the light so that the fish will not see our shadows and be too frightened to come close enough for us spear them."

"I'll make sure the blanket is held up far enough to give you room to shoot the arrow through the hole," Marjorie said, crouching down on a layer of thick pelts that Spotted Horse had placed there for her after cutting the hole through the ice. She giggled. "This is so much fun."

"It is days like this, when we are alone together, that I also enjoy . . . as you call it . . . fun," Spotted Horse said softly. "You will soon discover that because of my duties I must leave you alone in our lodge perhaps too often."

"I have my paper dolls to fill my lonely hours," Marjorie said. "And my daily chores, for, Spotted Horse, I cannot just sit by and watch you do the chores that I feel are meant to be a woman's.

Cassie Edwards

I hope you will understand my need to do these things for you."

She paused, then said, "And, darling, *I* want to cook whatever fish we catch today. I truly love to cook. Why must I sit by like a nincompoop as the women of your village bring us our meals?"

"Nin . . . com . . . poop?" he said, his eyebrows raising. "That is a word I am unfamiliar with. What sort of word is it? What does it mean?"

Marjorie laughed softly. "It's a word used to describe a foolish person," she said. "You wouldn't want me to be labeled a nincompoop, now would you?"

"No," he said, also laughing. "You do not fit the description of a nin . . . compoop. But it *is* the custom of our people that a wife does not cook for a husband for a full week after marrying. This is time best spent relaxing together, not working over a cook fire."

Even though the blanket was meant to block out the light, Marjorie could see well enough to make out the gleam in his eyes as he peered over at her. She wondered what he was thinking about. Surely it was not food!

"The time a wife spends with her husband is time spent making a baby," Spotted Horse then said, making Marjorie understand why he had given her that teasing, wicked look.

"That is a roundabout way of saying that this is time spent making love," Marjorie said, a sensual shiver coursing through her at the memory of their lovemaking only this morning.

262

"Yes, making love is the prime reason for giving the woman nothing to do or think about but her husband," Spotted Horse said, nodding. "But, my wife, this warrior, this *chief*, also thinks of children. Would it not be a good thing to give Sun Bear a brother, or *wiyanna*, a girl child . . . a sister?"

Marjorie paused for a moment without answering. She had never thought about having children. Her troubled past had excluded such thoughts from her mind, for she would never have wanted to bring a child into such a world as she had known before meeting Spotted Horse. She would not have wished her life as a child on anyone!

But now?

Now that she had a wonderful man and roots, why couldn't children be a possibility?

And wouldn't it be wonderful to see Sun Bear with a child? He was such a gentle young man with a big heart and much love to give a brother or sister.

"Yes, I would love to have a child," she blurted out. "For Sun Bear, but, my darling, mainly for *you*. I would adore having your baby. You are such a wonderful father to Sun Bear, and he is not even your blood kin. I can just imagine how you would dote on a child born of our love."

"I have been known to dote on Sun Bear," Spotted Horse said, chuckling.

"Yes, I know," Marjorie said, laughing softly. "I have seen it. I have loved seeing it. Had I only known such love from my father . . ."

"You have many people now who love you," Spotted Horse said thickly. "Never will you have to feel alone again. I will see that your life is filled with much happiness. You will have the satisfying feeling of belonging."

"I already do," Marjorie said, sighing with contentment. "Because of *you*, I do."

Their eyes held for a moment longer.

Then Spotted Horse nocked his arrow to his bow. "If we are to catch fish today we had best grow silent and wait," he said. He watched and listened for the splash of the fish, a bag ready at his side for those he would catch.

Marjorie was fascinated by how ice fishing was actually done. She had heard Albert speak of it many times, but he had never allowed her to go with him on such ventures.

Of course, she thought sarcastically, Albert had given her the fish that he had caught and made her clean them.

Yet she did enjoy cooking them. She knew how to make them extra crispy. Today, she had asked one of the warriors who had planned to go to the trading post to get some special cooking supplies for her.

She had asked him to get a can of lard, flour, cornmeal, and small bags of salt and pepper. She had also asked him to buy a cast iron skillet.

She had done this while Spotted Horse had been in a short council with some of his braves. She hadn't done it in this roundabout way to go behind his back. It was a surprise that she had planned for him. She was going to prepare him the best fish he had ever eaten!

"I *will* be able to cook the fish we catch today, won't I?" she whispered to him.

"*Ho*, if that makes you happy, yes, you can cook the fish," he whispered back. "Now sit quiet and say no more words." He laughed quietly. "If it were possible, I would say do not even breathe. I sense the fish are near. We do not want to frighten them away."

"I'm sorry if my chattering has delayed them coming to the hole," Marjorie whispered back to him, then became stone quiet as she waited again for the exciting moment of their first catch.

And then it all seemed to happen at once. Spotted Horse speared first one fish and then one after another until their bag was overflowing.

Marjorie felt that it was safe to speak now, for if she did scare the fish away, they had most certainly caught enough.

"We will be eating fish until they come out of our ears," she said, laughing.

"Out . . . of . . . our ears?" Spotted Horse said, raising his eyebrows. He laughed then. "Oh, of course what you said is only a way of jesting, is it not?"

"Yes, I do sometimes enjoy 'jesting,'" Marjorie said, her heart soaring in her happiness. "Being with you makes me light-hearted and gay. I don't want to ever have cause to be so serious again that I don't feel like fooling around and making jokes."

"I will make it my life's goal never to give you cause to frown again," Spotted Horse said, laying his bow and arrow aside. He nodded toward the blanket. "Lay the blanket aside. Give me your widest smile."

"Do you truly wish for me to remove the blanket?" she asked, not sure if *he* was jesting or not.

He shoved his end away from himself, then drew the blanket away from her. "We no longer need the blanket," he said. "It is time to take our catch home."

She laughed softly.

She then stared somberly down at the bag, which was overflowing with the fish, and sent a slow, questioning look at Spotted Horse as he folded the blanket and slid it into a large parfleche bag.

"Who is going to clean the fish?" she asked warily.

"Since you are so adamant about cooking the fish, I will gladly give you the chore of cleaning them," Spotted Horse said, his eyes dancing as he watched her reaction. He knew that no woman enjoyed cleaning fish. He did not think that his wife was an exception. He just found it too tempting to tease her this morning. He could see the immediate look of horror in her wide eyes. He could even see her shiver slightly at the thought of the chore.

Marjorie felt trapped. She wasn't sure what he really wanted her to say. Did he truly want her to clean the fish? If so, she would. But if he did not feel all that strongly about it, then she would beg him to tackle the messy job.

She gazed intensely at him, then saw that

twinkle in his eyes that came when he was only playing with her.

"I shall gladly hand over the unpleasant chore to you," Marjorie said as she stood up.

"Careful," Spotted Horse said, reaching a quick hand out for her when he saw her feet slipping on the ice. He drew her into his arms. He lifted her chin with a finger. "Can you ignore my fishy smell if I kiss you?"

"You could smell like a skunk and I still would want you to kiss me," she said, giggling when he chuckled at her comment.

Then he encircled her with his arms and held her close as his mouth covered hers in a soft, sweet kiss.

But a howling of the wind, causing the bare limbs of the old oak trees above them to creak and sway, drew them apart. Marjorie looked toward the sky just as snow started falling from the low, gray clouds. "As though we don't have enough snow," she said, groaning.

She stepped gingerly from the ice, then loaded the sleigh with their equipment as Spotted Horse handed it to her. The horse neighed and flicked its ears as the snow began falling thicker, soon covering the hole that had been cut in the ice.

"We'd best head quickly for home," Spotted Horse said.

He helped Marjorie into the sleigh and covered her with pelts. He studied the path they had followed to get to the river. It was quickly being covered by snow.

"I think it's best to follow the river for a while,

then when we come closer to Lake Calhoun, I shall go across country," Spotted Horse said, snapping the reins.

As they traveled along, the wind picked up, whipping the snow away from the frozen edges of the river, leaving the ice bare in spots.

Marjorie paled and gasped when she saw something beneath the frozen water. To make sure of what she had seen, hoping it was only a mirage caused by the sheen of the ice and the snow flitting across it, she blinked her eyes.

When she knew that what she had seen was true, oh, so grotesque and real, she grabbed Spotted Horse by the arm. "Stop!" she cried.

She looked over her shoulder. The horse had taken them quickly past the spot where she had seen a man frozen just beneath the surface of the river.

"What is wrong?" Spotted Horse asked, drawing a tight rein. He looked over at Marjorie. He had heard the panic in her voice. Now he could see her expression, as though she had seen a ghost.

Marjorie threw the pelts aside. "Come with me," she said, stepping down from the sleigh. She gave Spotted Horse a frightened look. "I saw a man!" She turned and pointed toward the ice. "There! In the ice! He's frozen in the ice!"

When Marjorie reached the spot where she had seen the man, she stopped and stared down at a sight that made shivers of horror shudder through her.

It was Snow, the casket maker.

His pink eyes were staring blankly up

through the ice, a look of stark terror on his face.

Marjorie gulped back a bitter taste in her mouth and gasped when she saw Snow's fingers red with blood from having tried to claw his way through the ice prison.

Chapter Twenty-seven

Spotted Horse drew a tight rein and stopped the horse. He jumped from the sleigh and went back to Snow. Marjorie watched as Spotted Horse considered how he might remove Snow from the frozen river.

"I will have to send warriors later to get Snow out of the ice," Spotted Horse said, giving Marjorie a sideways glance. "One man can't do it."

"I can't say that makes me unhappy," Marjorie said. "I don't think I could stand having . . . that . . . body . . . in the sleigh with us. It's been terrible enough seeing him, much less being near him."

Then a thought came to her that sent chills up and down her spine. Until now, she had not thought to wonder how he might have gotten there. Had he fallen in and been trapped beneath the water? Or had someone purposely cut a hole through the ice, then shoved Snow in the water and held him there until he drowned?

"I'm suddenly afraid," Marjorie blurted out, glad when Spotted Horse drew her into his arms. "Snow may have been murdered. Who . . . ?"

Then she jerked away from Spotted Horse and gazed wild-eyed up at him. "Albert!" she cried. "Surely it was Albert! Who else could have cause to hate him enough to kill him?"

Spotted Horse sighed. He bowed his head in deep thought and kneaded his brow.

Then he looked at Marjorie again and took her hand. "*Ho*, I, too, see how your stepfather might be at fault here," he said somberly. "I guess it was false hope that made me think he'd left the area."

"But if he *did* commit this crime, surely he has left now," Marjorie said, her words rushed and nervous.

"He could not have done this too long ago, for the ice has only recently thickened over the lakes and rivers," Spotted Horse said.

When he saw the despair and worry in Marjorie's eyes, he placed a gentle hand on her cheek. "Do not worry so," he tried to soothe. "Albert is gone. And if not, you have a husband who now protects you."

He placed a finger beneath her chin. He smiled at her, hoping she couldn't tell that it was forced, for he truly had no reason to smile. He really felt that the white man *was* still in the area. Like Marjorie, he had sensed Albert's presence when they'd left her cabin the other day.

"Let me see a smile," he said softly. "You have so much to make you smile. Albert is only one man. Do not let him take the joy from your life. Did he not do that enough while you lived with him? He would be proud if he knew that he caused you unhappiness now even in his absence."

"Yes, you're right," Marjorie said, straightening her back and lifting her chin. "I won't let him have the satisfaction of even *suspecting* that he is still causing me grief."

She looked slowly over her shoulder at Snow, then tightened her jaw as she again gazed into her husband's eyes. "I won't even allow myself to think that he may have killed Snow as some sort of warning to me, a threat," she said.

"If he is still anywhere near here, Albert is the one who should feel threatened," Spotted Horse said. He walked Marjorie back to the sleigh and arranged the pelts on her lap, then placed a blanket around her shoulders. "If he is found, and it is discovered that he means to harm you, I will not take him to the white man's court for punishment. He will be punished by the Dakota's code of law!"

Marjorie heard the conviction in her husband's voice. Also the bitterness.

A deep sadness overcame her to know that she was causing Spotted Horse such tumultuous emotions, when all she ever wished to bring into his life was love!

She silently prayed that they were both jumping to conclusions, that Albert had had nothing to do with Snow's death.

She hoped that he was miles away from here, perhaps even as far as Canada, starting a new life. He had talked often of wishing to live in Canada one day. What better time to go than now?

"I'm not going to think about Albert anymore," she said, settling into the warmth of the blankets and pelts as Spotted Horse snapped the reins and the horse moved onward through the deepening snow. "I'm going to consider him the same as dead."

She didn't voice aloud what she truly wished—that it had been Albert imprisoned in the ice instead of Snow! Then her worries about her stepfather would be finally over, for no matter how much she tried to convince herself and Spotted Horse that she wasn't going to worry about him, she would. She knew how much Albert hated and resented her. Such hate festered inside one's mind. It could cause a man to perform ungodly acts.

"We will be home soon beside the warm lodge fire," Spotted Horse said, giving her a sideways glance. He held the reins with one hand and held his free hand out for Marjorie. "Come and sit closer."

Smiling, she scooted over and eased her body up next to his. She sighed with pleasure as he slid his arm around her waist and held her even closer.

"Now this is how it should be," Spotted Horse said, smiling down at her as she gazed up at him with adoration. "Man and wife warming each other beneath blankets."

"Yes, my darling, this is how it should be," Marjorie said, snuggling closer. "For always."

As they rode onward, she listened to the creak of the snow-laden branches overhead. She gazed up at the white sky over the hemlocks bowed with snow.

Her attention was drawn quickly elsewhere when an antlered buck and his doe suddenly fled, with tails up, in long leaps, lovely and slow, through the snow.

But Marjorie was becoming aware of something else. The snow that covered everything with its white glaze was causing a glare that was suddenly making her eyes ache. She rubbed first one eye and then the other with the back of her gloved hands.

And when that didn't relieve the ache, she momentarily closed them.

As she opened them again, she gasped with horror when she discovered that she couldn't see anything!

No white glare!

No snow!

Not even her husband sitting so close at her side!

And the sudden pain that was suddenly in her eyes, like a stabbing knife, caused her to grab at them and scream.

Taken off guard by the sudden screaming, Spotted Horse froze. He drew a tight rein and stopped his horse as he looked quickly over at Marjorie.

When he saw her wiping at her eyes and moaning, he immediately knew what was wrong.

She had been stricken with snow blindness!

Understanding a great deal about snow blindness, because his people had often been afflicted with it during the long, snow-filled days of winter, Spotted Horse knew what to do.

He reached his hands out for Marjorie and gently gripped her shoulders. "White Bird, I'm lowering you onto your back," he said thickly.

When she winced and cried out, he felt her pain as though it were his own. He made sure that she was comfortable on blankets, then slid a pelt over her up to her chin.

"Bear with me," he softly encouraged. "I know of ways to help relieve the pain."

"It hurts so," Marjorie cried, again rubbing her eyes.

"Do not rub your eyes," Spotted Horse said, gently taking her wrists and bringing her hands down to her sides beneath the blankets. "Lie there as I get some snow. The snow on your eyes will help with the pain."

Her heart pounding, she tried to fight off the pain, afraid that she had already shown herself to be a baby in the eyes of her husband. She forced herself to lie quietly beneath the pelts.

And when she felt the cold snow on her eyes as Spotted Horse placed it there, she sighed with relief. The snow *was* relieving her of some of the pain.

"Let it stay on your eyes for a moment

longer," Spotted Horse said, kneeling beside her, watching her.

Then he carefully slid the snow away. "Now open your eyes slowly and see if your sight has returned," he said warily. He could recall some cases when snow blindness lasted for several weeks! The pain sometimes lasted that long too. He was not sure if he could bear watching his wife suffer for so long!

Scarcely breathing, hoping that this would all soon be behind her, Marjorie slowly opened her eyes.

Disappointment and grief overwhelmed her when she still saw nothing. Everything was a blank. A white, strange sort of blank.

Seeing her grimace, and then seeing a slow trickle of tears coming from the corners of her eyes, Spotted Horse realized that his wife still could not see.

Gently he placed an arm around her waist and drew her up into his embrace. As she clung to him, softly crying, he slowly rocked her back and forth, as though she were a child and he the parent.

Realizing that she was causing her husband much concern, Marjorie fought back her tears. "How long will this last?" she murmured. "Please tell me that it isn't something that might never be reversed."

"The time varies for each person who is stricken with snow blindness," Spotted Horse said. "But you *will* get over it. You *will* see again."

She clung to him as he kissed her.

Then she welcomed the warmth of another pelt over her as he made sure she was warm before resuming the trip back to their home.

"We will be beside our lodge fire soon," Spotted Horse said, brushing a kiss across her brow.

He took one more lingering look at her huddled beneath the blankets and pelts. Tears came to his eyes to see her lying there so meek, so helpless.

Then he hurried and grabbed up the reins.

He sent the horse into a faster lope along the river, then made a wide swing away from the ice and headed toward his village.

Once there, he ignored the rush of his people from their lodges when they saw that Marjorie was lying down instead of sitting beside him. Spotted Horse answered everyone as briefly as possible when they asked what was wrong.

He soon had her inside their lodge and on a thick, warm pallet of blankets beside the fire.

"It seems you have managed to get out of cleaning the fish," Spotted Horse said, laughing softly as he took her hand. Just then one of the women brought in a kettle of stew and hung it over their fire.

Understanding that Spotted Horse was trying to lighten her mood, Marjorie laughed along with him. "Quite clever of me, wouldn't you say?" she said, twining her fingers through his. "Oh, how I do hate cleaning stinky fish."

Then she grew solemn again. "Do you see anywhere the supplies that I asked Pleasant Moon to purchase at the trading post for me?" she asked softly. She had so looked forward to preparing the fish for Spotted Horse.

Spotted Horse nodded a thank you to the woman who had brought the stew as she walked toward the entranceway. When she was gone, he looked around the tepee and saw a large parfleche bag lying with the other cooking supplies.

"Yes, the supplies are here," he said. "I shall get them for you. At least you can touch them to see if he brought everything you asked for."

She grabbed his arm. "No," she said quickly. "Do not get them. I can't use them now anyway." She still wanted to surprise him. And if he saw the supplies, he might guess what she had planned.

Now it would just have to be another time.

Sun Bear rushed into the lodge, his eyes wide and worried as he fell to his knees beside Marjorie. "I was out sledding with friends when word was brought of your illness," he said, breathless. His hand was cold as he lifted it to Marjorie's cheek. "Is it true? You cannot see? You have snow blindness?"

"Yes, but I will soon be all right," Marjorie reassured, taking his hand, affectionately squeezing it to warm it. "My oh my, but aren't you cold. Didn't you wear your gloves?"

"Yes, but the cold penetrates them too easily for my flesh to stay warm for long," Sun Bear said.

"I think you should stay in our tepee by the fire," Marjorie said softly. "I . . . think . . . you should stay out of the glare of the snow."

"I am used to snow," Sun Bear said. "I have

played in it since I first walked. My eyes are used to it. It affected you in such a way because you are used to staying inside."

He gave her a quick hug, then leaned away from her. "My friends are waiting," he said. "Is it all right if I leave you and resume playing with them? Or would you rather I stay with you?"

Spotted Horse patted Sun Bear on the shoulder. "Son, you go and play," he said, ushering him by an elbow toward the entranceway. "I believe your mother needs some rest."

"I will come home soon if you need me," Sun Bear said over his shoulder, then ran outside.

Spotted Horse went to the back of the lodge and got a ladle, wooden bowl, and spoon. He took these back and filled a bowl with stew.

"I think you will be much warmer and more comfortable for your nap if you have some food in your stomach," he said, setting the bowl aside so that he could help Marjorie to a sitting position. "I shall feed you."

Marjorie sighed. "I can't even feed myself," she said, her voice breaking. "And not only that! While I am unable to see, there are many things I won't be able to do for myself. I will be totally helpless!"

"I will be your eyes," Spotted Horse said, leaning over to kiss her brow. "Now just sit there and forget why I am feeding you. Just enjoy it. It smells delicious, would you not agree?"

"Very," Marjorie murmured. She was not truly hungry, but she would eat to please him.

He slowly fed her the stew, then when the bowl was empty, he eased her back down onto the blankets. "While you are resting, I will go to council with my warriors to decide what should be done about Snow, whose frozen body now awaits burial," he said thickly. "If I take the body to the fort, some soldier who looks for any reason to condemn a redskin might take advantage of this situation and make it look as though the Dakota are responsible for the man's death. It will be hard to explain his death."

"I truly believe it is best just to bury him and be done with it," Marjorie said, fearing that what Spotted Horse suspected might be true. The soldiers *might* blame him and his people for Snow's death. Spotted Horse, himself, might be arrested. "Ironic as it might seem, you will be burying him in one of his own pine boxes that he brought to the village for your children's burial."

"Burials do not come easy during the winter months when the ground is frozen," Spotted Horse said gloomily. "And the colonel at Fort Snelling forbids burial on scaffolds in trees. I most certainly will not place this man's body with those of my people who are buried in the burial cave that sits far in the forest from Lake Calhoun and the Dakota village."

He kissed her brow. "I will do what must be done," he said. "Rest. I will try not to be gone too long."

Sorely tired, Marjorie drifted into a troubled sleep, then awakened with a start at a noise in the lodge. "Spotted Horse?" she said, leaning on an elbow. "Have you returned from council?

How did it go? What are you going to do about Snow?"

When she felt a rough, callused hand cover her mouth, and she recognized the voice that whispered to her, a quick panic filled her. Albert! She grabbed at his hand trying to get it away from her mouth. But his grip was too tight and he was too quick in slipping a gag around her mouth for her to yell for help.

She fought against his hold when he struggled to tie her hands together behind her. But again he was too strong. Soon she was rendered totally helpless.

"You'd best stop wriggling or I'll take you out in the cold without a blanket around you," Albert whispered as he slid a blanket around her shoulders, tying the ends together beneath her chin.

He paused a moment longer when he gazed at her feet.

He slid moccasins on them and tied her ankles together.

"I don't think you're going anywhere now," Albert whispered in her ear, chuckling. "So just wait here like a good girl for your daddy while I check through the slit I made at the back of the tepee so I can see if anyone is there to catch me when I take you through it."

Feeling trapped, and uncertain of Albert's plans for her once he got her away from the village, Marjorie was so afraid, her knees were weak.

She silently cursed her blindness. If she could at least see, surely she could find a way to escape the clutches of this man she hated with a vengeance.

But she couldn't see. And the pain in her eyes was so bad, it was one massive throbbing.

Yet when Albert came back for her and grabbed her up into his arms, she still tried to wriggle herself free. But without luck. He carried her outside and took her quickly into the forest.

"We'll get away quickly enough on this sled," Albert said, chuckling as he placed her on a sled and tucked blankets warmly around her.

He sat down beside her and slapped the reins, sending the dog team into a fast race through the forest.

"I have the perfect hiding place for my little darling daughter," Albert said, sarcasm thick in his voice. "Have you missed Daddy, Marjorie?"

Of course Marjorie couldn't tell him how she felt. The damnable gag was still in place.

And she again silently cursed her blindness, for she could not tell where he was taking her.

Where would he feel safe from the Dakota, she wondered to herself.

She couldn't think of any place, for surely Spotted Horse and his people knew every nook and cranny of this forest.

She waited with bated breath as Albert continued onward, the breeze icy against her cheeks.

"And so you and Spotted Horse found Snow, did you?" Albert said, laughing into the wind. "I guess you have to know that I placed him there. I am betrayed by someone only once. They never get a second chance. He'll never betray anyone again, *ever.*"

Marjorie cringed to hear his glee over the death of Snow. Fear filled her heart over how he bragged about no one being able to betray him more than once. In a sense she had betrayed him. She could not help thinking that he had abducted her to kill her.

But when?

How?

"Yep, several people have hell to pay for treating me so badly," Albert grumbled. "Snow is dead. I've abducted you. You will soon know why. Then I plan to kill Spotted Horse and Sun Bear!"

Terror gripped Marjorie's heart even more now, for she knew that she was in the company of an insane man. To actually know that he planned to kill Spotted Horse and Sun Bear made her sick to her stomach.

And she was helpless to do anything about any of his threats.

She felt doomed, yet surely when Spotted Horse found her gone, Albert would be the first person on his mind to blame.

She prayed to herself that Spotted Horse would discover her absence soon, and that when he went searching for her, he would bring many warriors with him. Albert's threats against Spotted Horse's life were all too real!

Another thought came to her that sickened her. Sun Bear! What if Albert came across Sun Bear and his friends sledding in the forest?

It made her grow cold inside to think of how

quickly Albert might snuff out Sun Bear's life, and laugh while doing it!

She would never forget the thrill that Albert had gotten by skinning the poor fox alive.

Killing seemed something that gave him more pleasure than perhaps even women.

No, she had no idea what to expect of him, not now that she was his prisoner, and completely at his mercy.

Chapter Twenty-eight

Tired from his long day of sledding, his fingers aching from the cold, Sun Bear hurried into his lodge and over to the fire.

He stopped short when he noticed that Marjorie wasn't there resting on her pallet of furs beside the fire. His eyebrows rose when he noticed how her blankets and pelts were tossed around.

As he slid off his rabbit-fur coat, he searched the large tepee for Marjorie and saw her nowhere. He gasped when he saw the large tear in the lodge covering. It didn't take long for him to realize that someone had been there.

They had taken Marjorie away by force!

His coat half on, half off, Sun Bear ran from the tepee and breathlessly went inside his father's large council house.

Not caring that he was disturbing a council between his father and the warriors, he ran up to Spotted Horse and grabbed his hand.

"Come, *ahte!*" he cried. "Something has happened to White Bird! She is gone! The back of our lodge has been cut with a knife!"

Spotted Horse stared at Sun Bear disbelievingly for a moment, his heart racing. Then he broke into a run. As soon as he entered his lodge, he saw for himself the disarray and the opening at the back.

His heart aching, Spotted Horse hurried to the opening and stepped outside. He studied the two sets of footprints in the snow. He could tell by the drag marks that his wife's assailant had half dragged her away from her home. He also noticed that, as before when she had been abducted, the one who took her away was a white man. He wore white man's shoes! Not moccasins!

"*A-i-i-i*," Spotted Horse cried, lifting his eyes to the heavens. "Why, *Big Holy*? Why would you allow this to happen to my woman again? Why?"

With Sun Bear close beside him, Spotted Horse followed the tracks in the snow, which led to tracks made by a sled and dog team.

"This is how she was taken away," Spotted Horse said, his thoughts clear now. He was certain who was responsible for Snow's death. Albert!

"If it is he, and he has harmed her—" Spotted Horse shouted into the wind, a fist raised in the air.

"Who, Father?" Sun Bear asked. "Who do you think did this?"

"I do not think, I *know*," Spotted Horse ground out, never hating any man in his life as much as he now hated Marjorie's stepfather.

"Marjorie's stepfather?" Sun Bear asked softly.

"*Ho*, he is the only one who could hate me and my wife enough to take this cowardly action against a helpless woman," Spotted Horse said, his eyes flashing angrily as he turned and ran back toward his lodge. "And . . . he . . . will pay."

He rushed inside his tepee, Sun Bear close at his heels. His jaw tight, his heart hammering inside his chest, Spotted Horse threw on his warmest robe and yanked his rifle from his cache of weapons.

"*Ahte*, can I go with you to search for her?" Sun Bear cried. "Please?"

Spotted Horse turned to him and placed a hand on his shoulder. "You will best serve your father if you stay here," he said thickly. "If, by chance, your mother gets free—"

"But, *ahte*, her eyes!" Sun Bear cried. "She is blind! Even if she does manage to get free of her abductor, how could she find her way home? Please let me go! Let me help search for her."

Sun Bear's reminder of Marjorie's blindness was like a knife thrust into Spotted Horse's gut. His wife had no way to defend herself, to find ways to escape, as she would normally.

"You are right, my *micinksi*," Spotted Horse

said, his voice low and filled with remorse. "My wife will not return unless we go and find her and bring her home. Yes, you can accompany me on my search for her. While I go and gather together many warriors for the search, you prepare my dogs and sled."

Sun Bear nodded.

Gratified that his father trusted him enough to allow him to go with him, Sun Bear hurried in one direction outside and started rounding up the dogs, while his father hurried in another, toward the council house, where the warriors had been abandoned by their chief.

The shocking news of what had happened to their chief's wife spread quickly through the village. Everyone came and stood silently watching as the many dogs and sleds left in a frenzy, snow flying beneath their wooden runners.

Spotted Horse went to where he had seen the tracks of the dogs and sled. Thankful that the snow had ceased falling, he began following the tracks. In his mind he was planning how he would make Albert pay for placing his wife in danger a second time.

For certain, his death would not come quickly! And Spotted Horse would be sure that the soldiers at Fort Snelling never knew that a white man had been killed by the Dakota. The man's body would be hidden so well, no one would ever find it.

His thoughts returned to Snow. At this very moment Snow's body was being taken to a cave, where it would stay until spring arrived and it could be buried in the ground.

Spotted Horse would not be so kind to Albert. He would be taken to a wolves' den that Spotted Horse knew about. In time, the wolves would remove all traces of the white man! He smiled at the thought, for the white man deserved no mercy.

He centered his thoughts again only on the search. Finding his woman was of utmost importance now. How her assailant would die was of secondary importance.

His eyes aching from watching the trail so closely, he pressed on. He would find his wife, or his life would not be worth living!

Chapter Twenty-nine

Knowing that Spotted Horse and his warriors would soon be following him, Albert had devised a plan. He had prepared a hiding place for himself and Marjorie. They would stay there until enough days had passed for him to feel safe to travel onward.

"Canada!" he thought to himself as he sent his dogs and sled on through the crunching snow. "Ah, Canada."

It had been his dream for so long to live in Canada, where the land was wide and free, perfect for such a man as he, whose spirit was wild and unsettled.

Yes, he would eventually go there.

But for now, he had only one thing on his mind. To get Marjorie hidden so that he could be assured of having her with him when he fi-

290

nally saw the fulfillment of his dreams.

When the ice melted in the rivers, and the air warmed with the freshness of spring, he and Marjorie would travel safely out of the Minnesota Territory on a riverboat, and then acquire horses and pack mules for their final journey north.

With Marjorie with him, his life would begin anew. She would be his wife. She was the first woman, ever, to really stir him. Never had he hungered for a woman as much as he had wanted her!

His thoughts were brought back to the present when he saw the Minnehaha Falls, known to the Dakota as "Little Waterfall."

He sent a quick look over his shoulder to make sure that no one was present to see where he was taking Marjorie.

Smiling wickedly, he could hardly wait for total privacy with the woman he had loved since he had first seen her. It had been hard, these past months, not to reveal his feelings for her. He had hoped that, in time, she would soften toward him, but to no avail. It was obvious that she loathed the very ground he walked on.

But now? She had no choice but to accept him into her life. He would forbid anyone else to go near her until he had her big and pregnant with his child. Even she would have no choice but to accept him then. She would have no choice but to forget Spotted Horse! She would want to stay with the father of her child . . . *Albert*.

When they reached the waterfall, Albert drew a tight rein and stopped the dogs.

Marjorie tensed as she felt the sled stopping. She tried desperately to see, yet her sight was still dim. She was now able to make out at least shadows and movements as Albert left the sled and reached his arms out for her.

"Come to Papa," Albert said, chuckling as he lifted her into his arms. "I have made a place safe and warm for you."

Desperation filling her, not knowing what the crazy, vile man had planned for her, Marjorie tried to wriggle herself free, but she only succeeded in making him strengthen his hold on her.

"You'd just better settle down,'cause if I drop you once I start takin' you downhill, you won't live long enough to tell about it," Albert said, holding her tightly as he stepped away from the dogs and sled.

Marjorie flinched, wondering why he shouted at the dogs and sent them away. She listened as their yapping got fainter and fainter.

Then she became aware of something else. The sound of water falling and plunging across rocks, and the splash when it fell into pools of half-frozen water below.

She suddenly realized where he had brought her. To the Minnehaha Falls! But why? she wondered desperately to herself. Why had he sent the dogs and sled away?

"This can be a mite bit tricky. I've got to carry you down the side of the slippery rocks to get you behind the falls," Albert said, gingerly carrying her slowly down the side of the hill. "I felt you tense when you heard my mention of the falls. Yes, Marjorie. I've prepared us a hiding place behind the falls. A warm fire and food awaits us there even now. And many warm blankets and pelts for our beds. I now realize you've got snow blindness. But soon that'll pass and you'll be able to see our little hideaway."

Marjorie was aghast to realize how long he must have planned this. Now she understood why he had sent the dogs and sled away. He didn't plan to use them again, since they were going to wait out the worst weather in the safety of the cave. He would also fool Spotted Horse into following the sled tracks away from the falls.

Yes, Albert had thought of everything, but he had not taken into account two truths: Spotted Horse's love for her, which would keep him searching high and low until he found his wife, and *her* hatred for Albert, which would drive her to escape him once her eyesight returned and she was capable of fending for herself again.

Until then, she had no choice but to play along with him.

Afraid of the dangerous descent to the small river at the foot of the waterfall, she clung to Albert's neck and said a silent prayer.

She breathed a heavy sigh of relief when she felt him step out on solid land at the foot of the falls. At least that danger was behind her.

She grew wary as Albert carried her behind the half-frozen falls into the cave. The icy sprays of water sent a chill clean through to her bones.

The warmth of the fire was welcome as Albert put her on a thick pallet of blankets beside it. She was glad when he removed the damp blankets from around her shoulders and replaced them with dry blankets warmed by the fire.

She inhaled a quavering breath when Albert finally removed the gag from her mouth and she could breathe normally again, and speak.

"Albert, you know you won't get away with this," she said, wishing she could see him and watch his every move. She had no idea what his true motives were for bringing her there. "My husband will find you. Can you imagine what he's going to do to you for abducting me?"

Albert took a quick, unsteady step away from her. "Your husband?" he gasped out. "Did you do a fool thing like marry an Injun? Did you do it willingly?"

He laughed throatily as he tossed his coat aside and knelt down in front of her, his eyes level with hers. "Naw, you wouldn't marry a redskin willingly," he said, chuckling. "You wouldn't allow your infatuation with him to go that far. You were forced into it, weren't you?"

He reached out and grabbed a thick handful of hair at the nape of her neck and gave it a hard yank. "Tell me that he forced you into it," he said, his voice low and threatening.

Suddenly afraid for her life, Marjorie felt no choice but to lie. Later, when she got the best of him, she would shout the truth at him.

For now, the important thing was to get through this horrible ordeal alive.

"Yes, he made me do it," Marjorie said, wincing when he gave another yank on her hair. "Please, Albert. Just let go of my hair. My eyes are hurting me so. Why must you add to my misery?"

Albert slowly eased his fingers from around her hair, and then jerked his hand away from her. "I'll go out and get some snow for your eyes," he said thickly. "It'll make them feel better."

"Yes, I'd appreciate that," Marjorie said, breathing easier when she heard him leave.

She searched around behind her with her tied hands for a rock that might have a sharp edge to cut the ropes at her wrists.

But he was back too soon.

Her fingers went limp.

"Hold your head back," Albert said, his voice soft and caring. "Let me get the ice on your eyes. Surely by tomorrow you should be able to see things again. I've so much planned for us. I'd like to see the excitement in your eyes as I tell you."

Marjorie could not believe this man and how crazy he was. If he thought that anything he had planned would excite her, then he most certainly *was* insane!

"Oh, that snow feels so good," Marjorie said, playing along with him. "So refreshing. It does take some of the pain away. Thank you."

"Marjorie, I don't mean to do anything ever that hurts you," he said. "I'm sorry about yanking on your hair. But you just make me so damn angry sometimes I can hardly help myself."

"I'm sorry if I do anything, ever, to anger you," Marjorie said in a soft purr, finding it easy to lie to this madman. If only it would help her reach her goal of escaping.

When she tried to reposition her feet, she winced. The ropes around her ankles seemed to dig more deeply into her flesh each time she moved them.

"Albert, could you remove the ropes at my ankles and wrists?" she murmured. "They are so raw, they almost hurt worse than my eyes."

"Then we've got to get rid of those ropes, don't we?" Albert said, sliding a sharp knife from the sheath at his right side.

Marjorie held her breath, hardly believing that he was being taken in by her sweet talk. That was true proof of his insanity, for if he was thinking logically, he would know that once she was freed of her bonds, she would do everything and anything to escape.

Yet he knew there was one thing in his favor that might stop such an escape. Her snow blindness.

"Now; does that feel better?" Albert said, tossing the cut ropes aside. His fingers went over the rawness of one of her wrists. "Does it hurt real bad?"

"It stings," Marjorie said, hardly able to bear having his fingers touching the flesh of her wrist. "But in time it will heal."

"I'll get us some food," Albert said, moving away from her. "Are you hungry?"

"Very," Marjorie said, slowly rubbing her wrist.

As he prepared some of the food that he had stored in the cave, Marjorie became quiet. She was turning her plans over and over in her mind. Although she was snow blind, by damn, she would still find a way to escape from this madman. She only hoped that she could then find her way back to the Dakota village.

She grimaced at the thought of climbing back up from the foot of the falls, alone. One slip of the foot and she would plunge to a sure death!

Chapter Thirty

Spotted Horse frowned when snow began spitting from the sky again. If the tracks he was following were covered, chances were he might never find his woman!

Even now, there were only the faintest dog and sled tracks. The wind had blown a dusting of snow over them.

Sun Bear was on Spotted Horse's sled, standing beside him, his eyes watching the tracks that reached out before them. But as the snow began to fall thicker, he grimaced.

"*Ahte*, pray to the *Big Holy*!" he cried, looking up at Spotted Horse with frightened eyes. "Tell the *Big Holy* to stop the snow! We will never find White Bird!"

Hearing the desperation in Sun Bear's voice, Spotted Horse wondered what he could say to his son. He had begun praying the moment he had realized Marjorie was gone. How could he explain to his son that sometimes it took longer for some prayers to be answered than others? How could he tell his son that sometimes prayers were not answered at all, for if they were, there would have been no deaths at his village caused by the whooping cough disease!

"She will be found," was all that Spotted Horse could say.

But when he saw a puzzled look in his son's eyes, he quickly added, "But I will again say a prayer. A silent one."

He placed a gentle hand on his son's shoulder. "You say one, also, in your own silent way."

Sun Bear nodded and turned his eyes away.

A knot formed in Spotted Horse's throat when he saw his son lift his eyes to the white heavens. Tears burned at the corners of his eyes when he saw his son's lips move in a silent prayer.

The barking of his team of dogs, and that of another team answering from somewhere ahead, drew Spotted Horse's eyes away from Sun Bear.

His breath caught in his throat when he again heard the barking of dogs somewhere up ahead through the swirling, thick snow. The tracks were no longer visible. Yet the barking dogs were like a beacon through the snow, calling him onward. He had to believe it was the very dogs that had carried his woman away from the safety of her lodge!

He slapped the reins and shouted at his team

Cassie Edwards

of dogs. They barked and howled as they fought against the thickening snow at their feet.

Yet they dutifully went onward.

When Spotted Horse was finally able to see a team of dogs only a short distance away, and a sled that had overturned and was stuck in a snowdrift, his heart skipped a nervous beat. Marjorie might be beneath the overturned sled, either injured . . . or dead.

Spotted Horse handed the reins to Sun Bear. "Take care of them for me," he cried. "Stop the dogs. Hold them steady."

Spotted Horse jumped from the sled before it stopped.

Breathless, his pulse racing, he trudged through the snow, then fell to his knees beside the overturned sled.

His fingers trembled as he gave a yank to right it.

His feelings were mixed when he saw that no one was beneath it. He was glad that Marjorie was not there, injured. But he was disappointed that he still had not found her.

As his warriors came to him and stood around him, he stood up again and turned a slow gaze their way. "She is not here," he said, his jaw tight.

He turned and gazed into the distance, then looked closely all around the sled. There were no traces of footsteps, yet had there been some, surely the snow would have covered them.

He looked from warrior to warrior. "Search in all directions, but do not go far," he said, despair filling him as his hopes of ever finding his

300

wife faded. "We want no casualties among us. Search only as far as you can still see the dog sleds where you have left them. If you go farther than that, you might not find your way back."

Everyone parted and went their separate ways.

Spotted Horse held onto Sun Bear's hand as they began their slow, yet determined search. He would take no chance of his son getting lost out there in the snowdrifts where anyone who was stranded could be the prey of any number of wild animals.

Spotted Horse did not want to think of the possibility that his wife might even now be at the mercy of animals, two- *or* four-legged!

One by one the warriors went back to their dogs and sleds and waited for Spotted Horse to return.

When he did, his shoulders slumped, his spirits so low he felt lifeless inside, Spotted Horse stood beside his sled for a moment, silent.

Then he lifted Sun Bear on the sled and covered him with warm pelts.

Slowly he turned to his warriors. "One of you tie this stranded dog team in with yours," he said. "There is no point in letting these dogs pay for the ignorance of the man who left them here to die in the cold."

"But White Bird!" Sun Bear cried. "What if the man is hiding with White Bird and wants the use of the sled once we are gone? Will she not be the one to pay for the man's ignorance?"

"If she was anywhere near, hiding with the man, do you not know that one of us would have found them?" Spotted Horse said thickly.

He turned and gazed down the long avenue from which they had traveled. "No, they are not here," he said somberly. "I now know what happened. White Bird and her abductor are somewhere back there. The dog team was set loose to fend for themselves to fool us into following them, to make us think we were still on their trail. Yes, they are back there somewhere but we cannot take any more time today to look for them. Night is falling. The temperatures are at the dangerous point. We will return to our lodges tonight and resume our search tomorrow. All of you pray for sunshine and clear skies!"

He raised a fist into the air. "*Ho*, my warriors, we must return home," he cried. "But tomorrow we will retrace our steps. We will go slowly and inspect all places where my woman might have been taken into hiding!"

He climbed aboard the sled, took the reins, and turned the team of dogs around.

He snapped the reins and rode off into the thickening snow. Night had come too soon for this proud Dakota chief.

"*Ahte*, she will be all right," Sun Bear said, reaching from beneath his blankets and pelts to place a gloved hand on his father's shoulder. "I am sorry I proved myself to be the child I am a while ago when I showed doubt of finding Mother. We cannot lose her after having just brought her into our lives! No. The *Big Holy* will not allow it."

Spotted Horse turned proud eyes down to his

son. "Also, you and I won't allow it," he said thickly. "We will find her soon and take her back home where I vow nothing will ever again be able to harm her."

"We must find her," Sun Bear sobbed, knowing that once again he was behaving like a child, but no longer caring. His heart was too sad over Marjorie to care about what it looked like for him to be crying over her absence!

Spotted Horse was touched to the core of his being by the intenseness of the feelings his son had for White Bird. He now knew for certain that nothing would keep him from finding her!

He rode onward, past Minnehaha Falls. . . .

Chapter Thirty-one

As the smell of cooked venison reached her nose, making Marjorie realize how hungry she was, she became aware of something else.

Her eyesight! She was slowly regaining her eyesight. She was now not only seeing movement and shadows. She could actually make out Albert as he knelt before the cook fire slowly turning the meat on a spit.

She could also see that he had a pot of food sitting in the coals of the fire. The smell of corn filled the dampness of the cave with its glorious aroma.

Her excitement building, Marjorie blinked her eyes. More and more was disclosed to her as each moment passed.

She could see piles of blankets and pelts laid against a far wall. She could see boxes of canned food, and more than one firearm leaning against the wall of the cave.

She gulped hard when she made out several bottles of whiskey sitting on one of the boxes. She knew that when Albert drank to excess, he got crazy. If he got crazier than he already was, she knew that she would be in great danger!

Her pulse raced as she gazed at the entrance of the cave and heard the splash of water outside where the waterfall spewed down over the rocks overhead and into the half-frozen river below.

She knew that her chances for escape increased the more she could see. If she had tried to walk along the shelf of rock that ran along beneath the falls without being able to see clearly, she might have lost her footing and plummeted to her death.

No. She would not try to escape just yet. She would eat first and then make her move!

She smiled at how well she could see things already.

And, thank God, the pain in her eyes was gone.

Again, while Albert concentrated on preparing their meal, Marjorie looked around her. Yes, from the amount of supplies in the cave, and the lived-in look of the place, she could tell that Albert had been hiding there behind the falls for some time. She could hardly believe how warm and cozy it was with the fire's glow and several kerosene lanterns sitting here and there.

She had to wonder how he had brought all of

this to the cave without being noticed. The Dakota village was not that far from the falls. And there was a small road only a few feet away, where settlers traveled from time to time.

"Ready to eat?" Albert asked, gazing at her over his shoulder.

When he caught her staring at him, his eyebrows rose and he turned to face her.

Slowly he crawled over to her. "Can you see?" he asked, suddenly waving a hand before her eyes.

The suddenness of the motion made Marjorie flinch.

Albert drew his hand away and laughed throatily. "By God, you *can* see," he said. "That makes things much better, now, don't it?"

"What do you mean?" Marjorie asked guardedly, inching away from him as he crawled closer toward her.

"A girl is much more fun if she can see what a man offers her," Albert said, reaching a sudden hand out and grabbing her breast.

Repelled, stunned, Marjorie slapped his hand away. "What do you think you are doing?" she gasped, paling. "Keep your hands off me."

Albert shrugged. "Sure," he said, then went back to the cook fire. "Come on. Sit down close to the fire. I think you'll be surprised that your pa knows how to cook so well."

"Don't call yourself my pa," Marjorie said, her hunger causing her to do as he asked. "Thank God you aren't any kin to me."

"Yes, there are advantages to that," Albert said, giving her a sly look as he handed her a plate of venison and parched corn. "Eat up. The food'll warm your insides. Also it'll help build up your strength."

Knowing that she was undeniably hungry, Marjorie tore into the food with her fingers and soon had the platter emptied.

"Have some more," Albert said, slapping another piece of meat on her plate. "It'll be some time before I cook again."

He smiled crookedly at her as she began eating the meat. "Admit it, Marjorie," he said, chuckling. "Tell me I'm almost as good a cook as you."

"I'll admit nothing," she said, wiping her mouth with the back of a hand. "I'm only eating what you cooked because there is nothing else."

Her insides tightened when he went and grabbed a bottle of whiskey. He brought it back and sat down again beside the fire.

She watched him with mounting fear inside her heart as he poured himself a tin cup of the liquor and quickly consumed it, and then a second, and then a third cup.

He belched and laughed boisterously at her disgusted reaction. He filled another cup with whiskey and shoved it toward her.

"Drink up," he said, his words slurred from the amount of whiskey he had consumed.

"No, I hate the stuff," Marjorie said, visibly shivering. She set her empty plate aside and scooted farther away from him. "I can't even stand the smell, much less the taste."

"You don't know what you're missin'," Albert said. He clumsily fell over to one side as he held the bottle out toward her. "Just a little, itsy bit of whiskey? For your pa?"

"I told you before to quit referring to yourself as my father, and damn it, Albert, I don't want *any* of that stuff," she said, shoving the bottle away.

"Have it your way," he said, belching again.

He took another deep swallow, and then set the bottle aside.

Marjorie stiffened when Albert looked at her again, but this time with a determination she had never seen before. There was something in his eyes that made her grow numb and cold inside. As his gaze roamed slowly over her he seemed to be mentally undressing her.

When Albert suddenly crawled over and cupped one of her breasts in his hand, his free arm moving clumsily around her waist to draw her closer to him, she was stunned speechless . . . especially when his lips came down on hers in a wet, demanding kiss.

Revolted, and feeling as though she might vomit, Marjorie gave him a shove that caused him to fall over backward.

Her heart pounding, she looked quickly at the cave entrance. Could she escape now, while he was drunk and disoriented?

But she knew too soon that he was not all that disabled, after all. He came back at her with a vengeance. He held her down while he tied her up again, his eyes narrowed as he glared at her.

"You think you're too good for me, huh?" he said, his shoulders swaying in his drunkenness. "All right. If it's because of the whiskey, I'll sleep it off. *Then* we'll see what your excuse will be."

He laughed. "No excuse will keep me from havin' you," he said. "I've had feelings for you for a long time, but didn't act on them. I've been waiting for you to soften toward me. But now I've waited long enough."

"You disgust me," Marjorie said in a low hiss. "No matter if you are drunk or sober, you'll never be able to lay your hands on me. Lord help me, once my hands are untied again, I'll kill you."

"You'll change your mind," Albert said, chuckling. "Even if I have to leave your hands tied for months to get you tamed into doing as I tell you, young miss prissie."

He leaned into her face. "Marjorie, how'd you like to spend Christmas in this cave?" he taunted, chuckling. "I'll cut us a beautiful tree. Will you decorate it with me?"

"You are absolutely insane," Marjorie said, now truly afraid that she would never see Spotted Horse again. Albert had thought of everything, it seemed.

The one thing that gave her some hope was the fact that Spotted Horse would not leave a stone unturned while looking for her.

In time, surely he would remember the cave behind the waterfall!

"Not too insane to know I've got to get some shut-eye," Albert said, plopping down on his blankets beside the fire. "I'd advise you to get some sleep, yourself. Or better yet, stay awake and think about what I said about us bein' to-gether. If you ever want those ropes removed again, you've got to cooperate with your papa."

Laughing throatily, he closed his eyes.

Marjorie trembled from a mixture of fear and disgust. But most of all, she was lonely for Spotted Horse. She could not believe that Albert had actually abducted her because he planned to keep her as his love slave!

A . . . love . . . slave, having to endure whatever he chose to do with her!

She winced as she wrestled with the ropes, only succeeding at making her raw skin even worse.

"I'm helpless," she whispered, tears splashing from her eyes. "I *can't* escape!"

Worn out from the ordeal, she drifted off into a restless sleep.

Chapter Thirty-two

Marjorie awakened to the smell of food cooking again over the fire and the aroma of coffee. A full night had passed and she was still a prisoner, but at least she was still alive!

As she slowly closed her eyes she envisioned herself back at the cabin, her mother puttering around in the kitchen before breakfast.

Her mother had risen with the sun each morning. The first thing she had always done was put coffee on her cook stove. She had enjoyed a cup alone before having to face Albert with his grumblings and complaints.

Just the thought of her mother gave Marjorie a strange sort of comfort, for it seemed as if she might be there right now, her soft hand touching Marjorie's cheek, saying that things would be all right, that *she* had escaped *her* sordid life.

Marjorie would also, but in a much better way. Marjorie's wonderful husband, who seemed not to know the meaning of the word "complain," would find her.

Marjorie's eyes flew open. She was trembling, her heart pounding, from what she had just experienced.

It had seemed that her mother was there.

It had seemed as though her mother's soft hand had touched her!

And the reassurances about Spotted Horse! Yes, Marjorie knew that he would keep searching for her until he found her.

"I see you're finally awake," Albert said, yanking a leg off the roasted rabbit on the spit.

Marjorie turned her eyes toward him just as he pulled a huge hunk of meat from the bone with his yellowed, crooked teeth. She shuddered with disgust at his appearance. He hadn't bathed. His clothes were filthy. His hair was tousled and greasy.

"I'll untie you and share breakfast with you if you promise to behave yourself," Albert said, holding the rabbit leg out toward her, teasing her with it. "Smell it? Don't it just smell so good you can't resist it?"

"How could you go hunting for venison and rabbit in this weather?" Marjorie said. "And how could you be daring enough to go out of this cave when you have to know that Spotted Horse is out there searching for me?"

"I collected all of these supplies, even hunted for meat, before I abducted you," Albert said, wiping grease from his mouth with the back of his shirt sleeve. "I stored the meat at the back of the cave where the temperatures are cold enough to keep meat for weeks without it spoiling."

He nodded toward the canned food. "I even went upriver, where no one knew me, and bought these supplies," he said, chuckling. "I have some canned peaches. Want some?"

"Where is your horse and wagon?" Marjorie asked guardedly.

She wanted to learn everything he had done since his disappearance, so that she could tell Colonel Dalton when Albert was caught and taken in for questioning. *She* would give the answers he refused to provide!

"I knew we'd be here for a spell, and not wanting to be bothered with a horse, especially a bulky wagon, I took them some distance from here and left them. I stole the sled and dog team," he said. He smiled crookedly. "Smart, huh?"

He took another bite of meat and eagerly chewed it, grease rolling out of the corner of his mouth.

"Then how do you expect to get far when spring comes and it's safe to travel again?" Marjorie asked, the blanket sliding from her shoulders as she slowly sat up.

"I'll steal my means of transportation when I need it again," Albert said, laughing boisterously. He leaned his face closer to Marjorie's. "Why, I might even sneak into that Dakota village and steal two horses from *them*. One for me and one for you."

"I wish you'd try," Marjorie said, her eyes gleaming. "You'd get caught. From now on, no one will be able to get near that village without sentries catching them."

"We'll see," Albert said, tossing the bone into the flames of the fire. "We'll see."

He crawled over and rested on his haunches before Marjorie. "Well? How is it to be?" he said, his eyes searching hers. "Will you be civil this morning if I untie you? Or will I have to keep you tied until spring?"

"I wish to be untied," Marjorie said, looking nervously from side to side. Her eyes wavered as she then looked at Albert. "I need to be untied so that I . . . so that I . . . can . . ."

"Eat? Or pee?" Albert said, howling with laughter.

Marjorie's jaw tightened. Her eyes flashed angrily. "You crude man," she said in a low hiss.

"Well, you'd not be human if you didn't have to take a leak now and then," Albert said, crawling behind her, slowly untying her hands. He then untied her ankles.

"Go on," he said, waving his hand toward the darker depths of the cave. "Scat. Go and do your business."

Marjorie's heart raced to know that he was going to allow her to move from his sight this easily. Surely there was. . . .

"And don't waste your time lookin' for a way to escape at the other end of the cave," he said, as though he had read her thoughts. "I inspected it before I brought you here. There ain't nothin' at the far end but a cold dampness."

Her heart sinking, Marjorie rose to her feet and walked slowly away from him.

"You'd best take this blanket," Albert said, throwing a blanket toward her. "It's mighty chilly away from the fire. We don't want you takin' pneumonie, now do we?"

Marjorie turned and gave him a glower, then picked up the blanket and clutched it around her shoulders as she went on into the darkness.

The smell of sour, mildewy dampness overwhelmed her.

Her feet slipped on rocks that had ice frozen over them.

The silence was so intense, she felt as though she had walked into the depths of hell.

Hating the aloneness and the freezing cold nipping at her nose and cheeks, she hurried with her job, then went back to the campfire and welcomed the warmth as she stood closer over it.

"Now let's get some food in you," Albert said, gently taking the blanket from around her shoulders.

"I'm not hungry," Marjorie said stubbornly, even though her stomach ached.

She watched the smoke from the fire being sucked slowly out toward the cave entrance. There seemed to be a strange sort of air depression outside today. Her pulse raced to think that perhaps the smoke might waft up to higher ground.

If Spotted Horse rode by just as it. . . .

"Eat, damn it," Albert said, interrupting her

thoughts as he forced a hunk of meat into her hand.

Knowing that she was foolish to refuse food since she would need her strength for her escape when she had the opportunity, she sank her teeth into the meat and ate it, although it seemed uncommonly salty.

She shivered as the salt seemed to make her tongue swell and pucker.

Her thirst came on her so quickly, she gagged and dropped the uneaten meat to the floor.

Out of the corner of her eye she saw Albert go to his cache of whiskey.

Her insides tightened when she saw him remove the cap from one of the bottles, then pour the vile liquid into two tin cups, not one. This had to mean that he was going to offer her one of the cups, even knowing that she had refused to drink the whiskey yesterday.

She could not deny being thirsty. But water was her preference, not whiskey!

"Thirsty?" Albert said, going to her, taunting her as he held the cup out toward her, then suddenly pulled it away.

"Yes, I'm thirsty, but not for that rot-gut," Marjorie said, looking past him for jugs of water.

"Whiskey is all I'm offerin' you," Albert said, again holding the cup out toward her. "Here. I'll quit playin' with you. Take it. Drink up."

"I . . . don't . . . want your whiskey," Marjorie hissed out, her lips and throat so dry she could hardly speak. She placed her hands to her throat. "What in God's name did you do to that meat?"

His eyes danced as a mocking smile quivered across his lips. "I purposely salted it too much so that you would have no choice but to drink whiskey to quench your thirst," he said, laughing throatily.

"You what?" Marjorie gasped, paling. "Why are you so adamant about me drinking that vile stuff?"

"One loses one's inhibitions after drinking enough whiskey, that's why," Albert said, his smile having faded into a dark, leering grimace.

"Inhibitions?" Marjorie said warily. "You want me to lose my inhibitions? You vile, disgusting man, why are you doing this to me? Why?"

"I've already told you why," Albert grumbled. "So quit fightin' it. I the same as bought and paid for you when I married your ma. Didn't I always keep food on the table for you? Didn't I offer you a roof over your head and clothes to wear? Didn't I even put up with your nonsense of making paper dolls without yelping at you?"

"Just because you did those things does not give you any rights to me," Marjorie said, knowing that was exactly what he meant. "I am married. And even if I wasn't, I would never allow you to touch me."

"Well, now, I don't think you have much say in the matter, do you?" Albert said, making a quick lunge for her. He grabbed her by the back of her hair and yanked her around to face him.

"You're mine now," he hissed into her face.

"Not the damn fool Injun's. Don't you know that it ain't respectable to consort with Injuns? Their smell rubs off on a body. Do you want to stink like a savage the rest of your life? Do you?"

Uncontrollable tears rolled from Marjorie's eyes as he gave another yank to her hair.

She knew that arguing with this madman would be in vain. She *had* to find a way to get away! She knew that his intentions were to take her sexually!

Albert raised the tin cup of whiskey to her lips. "Drink," he growled, tipping it against her lips.

When she refused to open her lips, he gave an even harder yank on her hair.

"Let me go and I will," she finally said, sobbing. "Just please don't force it down my throat."

Although she dreaded the taste of the alcohol, her thirst was so deep that even she could not help welcoming the liquid as she slowly drank it.

But her thirst was still not quenched. She could not deny needing another drink.

She watched with eager eyes as he filled her cup again with more whiskey.

"You see? It ain't all that bad, is it?" he said, enjoying his own cup of whiskey. "Drink up. There's plenty where this came from."

After drinking the two cups of whiskey, Marjorie felt giddy. She giggled as she held out the cup for its third filling.

The heat rising in his loins, Albert watched as Marjorie now willingly drank the whiskey. He poured more into the cup, then sipped his own, his eyes never leaving Marjorie as he slid his gaze slowly down, stopping at her heaving breasts.

He had wanted her for so long, and by God, he was going to finally have her!

Chapter Thirty-three

The sun was bright, the sky blue as Spotted Horse slowly retraced his steps, trying to think how a criminal's mind might work.

He had dreamed of his wife the long night through.

It had been a distressing, troubling dream, in which he saw her through the falling snow, her arms stretched out for him, beckoning him to come to her.

Then just as he would get to the spot where he had seen her standing, she would dissolve into the falling snow, only an apparition.

Spotted Horse's dreams had also included Sun Bear. Over and over he had seen Sun Bear plummet over a waterfall into the icy depths below. In the dream, Sun Bear's screams were so real that even now the memory of them raised goose bumps along Spotted Horse's flesh beneath the warmth of his fur coat.

Because of this troubling dream, Spotted Horse had forbidden Sun Bear to join him today in his continued search for Marjorie. It was enough to think he might never see his wife again, without worrying about a life without Sun Bear.

Trying to banish his memory of the dream, even though he knew that dreams could mean something substantial to the one who dreamed them, Spotted Horse flicked his reins and sent his team of dogs onward. His warriors followed dutifully behind on their own sleds.

Where would Albert take an abducted woman? Where would he feel safe while hiding her? Where could they have disappeared so soon after her abduction? Where could they stay for so long out of the weather, if not in a cabin?

Spotted Horse and his warriors had questioned all settlers in the area.

None of them had seen Marjorie or Albert.

Spotted Horse slowed his dog team, searching for any signs his wife might have left behind for him to follow, signs that he would not have been able to see yesterday during the storm. She was a clever woman. Had she been given the opportunity, she might have thought to leave a piece of her clothing hanging from a tree limb or bush.

Disappointment swam through him as he saw nothing but snow on the heavy-laden limbs.

Any other time he might have stopped and taken in the beauty of his surroundings, where nothing yet disturbed the snow but for a few deer tracks.

But this was not the time to see beauty in anything! His heart was weary. His very soul ached with loneliness for his woman.

They were still riding across land they had traveled yesterday, though their tracks were hidden beneath a dusting of snow that had fallen earlier in the day before the skies had cleared. Spotted Horse guided his sled out of memory of landmarks they had passed.

When he arrived at the waterfall, he could not help but stop and stare at it. Last night's dream haunted him again, bringing the dreadful sound of Sun Bear's screams as he had fallen.

"Sun Bear is safe at home," he whispered, reassuring himself that it had only been a dream.

Nothing could be as real as knowing that Sun Bear was safe. His son was safely sitting beside the lodge fire.

It ate away at Spotted Horse to know that he could not think the same about his wife!

He lifted his eyes toward the blue heavens. "Where is she?" he cried. "Where?"

His nose suddenly twitched when something wafted through the air, touching his nostrils with its familiar smell.

He looked toward the falls. "Rabbit," he whispered. "Someone is cooking rabbit?"

His insides quivered strangely and he leaned forward and gazed in wonder at a slow spiral of smoke that came from behind the waterfall.

The dream came to him again in vivid flashes. His son. The waterfall.

"It was an omen!" he cried, hope filling him.

Pleasant Moon jumped from his sled and went to Spotted Horse. "Smoke," he said, also watching the slow trail of smoke rising into the heavens. He looked over at Spotted Horse. "Do you think?"

"That my woman is being held hostage behind the falls?" Spotted Horse said, completing his question. A wide smile creased his face. "Yes. I believe we have found White Bird!"

He would not allow himself to feel foolish for not having thought to check the falls earlier. Behind them, in the cave, there would be a perfect hiding place.

And he knew that Albert, a skilled hunter, would surely know of the cave.

His heart pounding, Spotted Horse quickly commanded some of his men to surround the land that looked down on the falls. He sent others down to stand beside the small river below while he and Pleasant Moon made their way slowly down the slippery rocks toward the ledge that would lead them into the cave.

Spotted Horse smiled when he thought again of the dream. He now knew for certain that the dream had not been to warn him of the danger his son might be in, but to guide him to his woman.

He knew for certain that the *Big Holy* had chosen this way to answer both his and Sun Bear's prayers.

He stopped long enough on his descent toward the cave entrance to give a silent thank you to his almighty friend in the heavens.

Then, with a tightened jaw and throbbing heart, his rifle clutched in his left hand, he moved slowly downward. His eyes never left the entrance of the cave that he now could see through the tumbling, half-frozen waters of Minnehaha Falls.

"Soon, *mitawin*," he whispered, "you shall be in my arms safe again."

Chapter Thirty-four

Chuckling, seeing that Marjorie looked dreamy-eyed and tipsy from having drunk so much whiskey, Albert gently took the cup from her and tossed it over his shoulder.

He then took Marjorie by the wrists and with his body shoved her to the blankets spread out beside the fire.

Completely disoriented by the whiskey, since she had never consumed as much as one drop before today, Marjorie was hardly aware of what was happening. Her mind seemed incapable of thinking clearly.

She was just aware of a man's presence, and having missed Spotted Horse so much since her abduction, she somehow confused this man's body with his.

When lips covered hers, she twined an arm

around the man's neck and returned the kiss.

Yet when the kiss deepened, and a hand slowly began sliding up the skirt of her dress, she suddenly realized despite her cloudy thinking that these lips were not familiar to her, nor was the thick, callused hand that was now touching her between the thighs.

This hand . . . *those* fingers . . . were clumsily and hurtfully pinching and probing her secret place.

Enough rational thought returned to Marjorie for her to give a hard shove, which made Albert fall clumsily away from her.

Trembling, she tried to roll away from Albert before he regained his composure. But her strength had been weakened not only by the alcohol, but also by her fear. She was not quick enough. Albert was there again, growling like an animal, his gray eyes cold as his hands gripped her wrists painfully.

"You little wench," he ground out, pinning her down against the floor of the cave, his body like steel as he pressed it against hers. "Do you think you're going to get away that easily?"

He leaned closer to her face and saw that Marjorie's eyes were wide with a mixture of fear and loathing.

"I've wanted you for too long to wait any longer," he said huskily. "I'm warnin' you, Marjorie. If you try to fight me off, I'll not make any of this easy for you. If I have to, I'll place a knife to your throat. Do you want me to do that?"

"Please let me up," Marjorie cried. "What did

I ever do to you to cause you to treat me so unjustly?"

"You made me desire you, that's what," Albert said, his voice thick with lust.

"I didn't do that purposely, and you know it," Marjorie said, a sob lodging in the depths of her throat.

"Just you bein' there, always lookin' so pretty, was all I needed to make my want of you deepen into something that made life almost unbearable at times," Albert said. "Marjorie, please don't fight it. I do love you so. I've never loved a woman like I love you."

"Your sort of love is sick and depraved," Marjorie said in a low hiss. "You should look at me as a daughter, not . . . not . . . like some street whore you can sweet-talk into lifting her skirts for you."

"Just let me show you how much I love you," Albert whined. "I promise not to be rough."

He held his hands away from her. "See? I'm no longer holding your wrists," he said throatily. "If I touch you, it will be with gentleness."

"Your hands aren't holding me down, but your body is," Marjorie said, jerking first one way and then another in an attempt to jar him from atop her.

"I can't let you go," Albert said thickly. One of his hands again slid up inside her skirt. "The first time I'll just get a quick satisfaction and then let you go sit by the fire. Is that all right? Just let me have some satisfaction or I might burst from my need of you."

"Don't you dare unfasten your breeches,"

Marjorie said, her eyes widening as he moved his hand toward the front of his breeches. "Albert, please don't."

"I can't help myself," Albert said, the buttons snapping free and scattering in all directions in his anxiousness to take her.

When she saw him release his thick shaft, she made another desperate effort to dislodge him.

But that only seemed to help him position himself over her. The skirt of her dress was now hiked up past her thighs; his throbbing member was lowering toward her woman's center.

He bent low and kissed her as his hand tried to spread her apart to make his entrance easier. She knew that there was only one thing left to do to save herself.

She sank her teeth into his lower lip.

Blood spilled through her lips from the wound she inflicted before he jumped away from her, yowling.

She quickly lowered her dress and scrambled away from him while he glared at her and shouted.

"You stupid wench!" he cried, blood dripping from his lip.

He yanked his breeches back in place and got a handkerchief from his rear pocket.

"To hell with you! I should kill you just like I killed Snow," he shouted as blood soaked into his handkerchief. "Or maybe I'll tie you back up and leave you to die here where no one will ever find you."

He wiped more blood from his lip and glared down at her as she edged farther and farther away from him. "Maybe the stench of your dead body will attract someone to investigate," he said menacingly. "I just hope it's Spotted Horse. Imagine the look on his face if he finds that all that is left of you is . . . bone."

With Marjorie now on her feet and backing up toward the cave entrance, Albert suddenly realized that while he was so filled with rage, he had not noticed just how far she had gotten from him.

He threw the bloody handkerchief to the rocky floor of the cave and ran to her. He grabbed her wrist just as she was ready to run outside to the ledge.

"You ain't gettin' away that easy," Albert said, half dragging her back to the campfire. He tossed her to the floor. He glared at her. "You do realize that I have no choice but to leave you here to die, don't you?" he said, his hands on his hips. "Why couldn't you give me a chance to show you that lovin' doesn't vary much from one man to another? Each man has the same equipment. There ain't too many varied ways to use it. You might've discovered that my lovin' is as good as the Injun's, perhaps better."

He leaned down into her face. "At least my skin is white," he said, then grabbed her hair, gave a yank, and released it.

He sat down beside the fire. "I'll wait until dark," he said, placing a log on the fire. "I imagine Spotted Horse is out there again today, scouring the land, looking for you. I sure as hell don't want him to find me traipsing in the snow."

Almost every bone in her body ached from his rough treatment, but Marjorie was relieved that Albert had given up on seducing her. She reached for a blanket and placed it around her shoulders.

She knew that he would soon be tying her up again. The thought of dying in the desolate, cold cave made tremors of fear ripple across her flesh. When the fire went out, there wouldn't be much time left before she would freeze to death.

Yet she could not beg this man for mercy. She would not lower herself to asking him for anything. She knew that he would never give her her freedom.

The only way she knew that he would not abandon her was for her to give in to him in every respect. And dying alone was better than being a love slave to this depraved man.

Silence reigned as Marjorie sat on one side of the fire, Albert on the other.

When a sound came to them—the sound of crunching rock beneath someone's feet—Marjorie turned just in time to see Spotted Horse and Pleasant Moon rush into the cave.

Pleasant Moon grabbed Albert and wrestled him to the ground. Spotted Horse reached for Marjorie and lifted her up into his arms and held her close.

"You found me! Oh, Spotted Horse, thank God, you found me," she cried, clinging to his neck. Her eyes searched his, finding it almost unbelievable that he was actually there.

"Has he harmed you?" Spotted Horse asked, his gaze sweeping over her.

"Not so much physically as . . . as . . . he has done me great harm mentally," Marjorie murmured.

She turned to see what was happening to Albert.

She ignored Albert's cold glare and sighed with relief to see Pleasant Moon tying his hands behind his back.

"This white man will never again cause you any harm," Spotted Horse said, gazing down at Marjorie as she turned her eyes back to him.

"My love," she whispered, her lips meeting his.

She was startled when Spotted Horse drew his lips away and gave her a silent, questioning look.

"You smell of white man's fire water," he said thickly.

"He . . . forced . . . me to drink it," Marjorie said, lowering her eyes. "I am so ashamed for you to see me like this . . . and to smell me."

He placed a finger beneath her chin and made her look up at him again. "Feel no shame for what was forced on you," he said, then watched Albert walk past.

"I enjoyed your woman's body," Albert shouted, laughing boisterously. "It's sweet and soft, Spotted Horse. And so young and shapely."

The shock of his words was so intense it stole Marjorie's breath away.

Then rage overtook her.

She jumped from Spotted Horse's arms.

She ran up to Albert and slapped him hard across the face. She grabbed him by an arm and

Cassie Edwards

swung him around to face Spotted Horse.

"Now you tell my husband that nothing sexual happened between us!" she cried. "Show him your lip! Tell him why I bit it!"

"I never got to do nothin' with her," Albert said in a low whimper. "She wouldn't allow it."

"Tell him why I bit your lip!" Marjorie persisted.

"She didn't want me kissin' or touchin' her," Albert said, lowering his eyes.

Marjorie sighed triumphantly.

As Albert was taken away, Marjorie went to Spotted Horse. "Please take me home," she murmured. "I have so missed being there with you and Sun Bear."

Spotted Horse removed his warm fur coat and slid it around Marjorie's shoulders, then grabbed up a blanket and threw it around his own shoulders, tying the ends together beneath his chin.

Then he lifted Marjorie into his arms, and while their eyes held, he carried her outside to the ledge.

"Would it be safer if you placed me on my feet and we went single file across the ledge?" she asked, breaking the spell that had been woven between them . . . woven by the magic of their love for one another.

"I never want to let go of you again," Spotted Horse said, stepping out beneath the soft spray of the falling water.

"Not even while I cook that fish for you that we caught the other day?" Marjorie asked, find-

332

ing it wonderful to be free to tease her husband again.

Her eyes twinkled as she recalled the fun they had had while ice fishing. She had not wanted to clean the fish, but had looked forward to cooking them.

"Your eyes!" Spotted Horse said, stopping to search them for any signs of snow blindness. "You can see now? You can see everything? You have no pain?"

"My eyes are functioning normally again, and, no, there is no pain," she said, smiling.

Then her smile faded, for moments ago, while recollecting their fun day of ice fishing, she had recalled something else.

Snow!

"Spotted Horse, I now know for certain how Snow died," she murmured as he carried her free of the dangerous ledge.

He placed her on her feet so they could climb to the top of the ridge.

"Albert confessed to killing him," Marjorie murmured, clinging to rocks that jutted out from the bank.

"I am not surprised to know that," Spotted Horse said, keeping a protective arm around her waist as they moved slowly up the slippery rocks.

Finally on flat land, Spotted Horse stood with Marjorie as they watched in silence while Albert was tied on a sled.

Then Spotted Horse turned to Marjorie and drew her into his embrace. Gently he held her. Slowly he rocked her within his arms, whispering words of love that made her heart sing.

The ordeal behind her, Marjorie felt as if she were in paradise. But even now, thoughts of Albert troubled her.

Marjorie had to wonder what Spotted Horse's plans were for Albert. Her husband was not likely to forgive him for all of the heartache that had been caused by Marjorie's abduction.

Marjorie would not spoil this special moment with her beloved by asking such a question.

She would know soon enough.

It was enough now just to realize that she had the rest of her life with Spotted Horse, Sun Bear, and. . . .

She slowly slid a hand down to her tummy and smiled. She had just realized that she had missed her very first monthly since she had begun her periods at age twelve. Surely she was with child!

Oh, how wonderfully complete her world would be if she could have a child born of her and Spotted Horse's special love. And this child's life would be nothing at all like Marjorie's.

Their children's lives would be filled with the love of parents who adored them with all of their hearts and souls! Yes, her children would have a mother *and* a father!

Finally Marjorie would know what it was really like to have a father around. She would experience it for the first time through her children!

She smiled.

Chapter Thirty-five

Everyone was quiet in the large council house as they stared at Albert. He stood in the middle of the circle of people, his eyes wide with fear. He had been stripped of his clothes to humiliate him. His hands were tied tightly behind his back. His ankles were tied so that if he tried to move, he would lose his balance and fall.

Freshly bathed, and wearing a warm, long-sleeved buckskin dress, and moccasins that reached up to her knees, Marjorie sat beside Sun Bear as Spotted Horse paced slowly back and forth before Albert, giving him occasional frowning glances.

Four fires burned in the council house, sending their slow spirals of smoke through the smoke holes in the ceiling. Beyond in the heavens, the sky was a delicate shade of blue.

Marjorie reached over and took Sun Bear's hand and squeezed it affectionately. She saw out of the corner of her eye that he kept looking at her, as though he found it hard to believe that she was actually there, safe.

She now knew just how concerned he and everyone else had been about her, and it touched her heart deeply to know that she had been completely accepted by Spotted Horse's people. She could feel their love for her.

"This white man is guilty of many things," Spotted Horse said, finally breaking the silence in the large room. "He is not only guilty of setting traps which gave him easy kills in our forests, always taking more than necessary for his survival, leaving less and less for our own needs."

Spotted Horse turned, stopped, and glared at Albert. "He heartlessly skinned a fox while the animal was alive, not taking into account that it was only following its instincts for survival by killing some of this man's chickens."

He turned and faced his people when he heard their gasps.

He raised a fist into the air, purposely saying things that would enrage them. "A fox!" he shouted. "He skinned a fox alive—the animal of our people!"

He paused, letting his words sink in, then turned and glared at Albert again.

"This man dared to hold a knife to my son's throat!" he shouted, again drawing horrified gasps from his people.

He turned and reached a hand out for Sun

Bear. "Son, come to me," he said softly.

Sun Bear rose and went and stood before Spotted Horse.

"Turn around, Sun Bear, and point out the scar left on your neck from the knife's blade," Spotted Horse said, gently placing his hands on his son's shoulders, turning him slowly around to face the crowd. He knew there wasn't a deep scar, but enough to prove his point.

Sun Bear raised his chin and placed a forefinger just beneath the scar. "This is where the knife threatened my life," he said, glad to be a part of his father's torment of the wicked white man. "He did this to me when I tried to save the fox from being skinned while it still had breath in its lungs!"

The women covered gasps behind their hands as tears came to their eyes.

The warriors' faces twisted with hate, and many put their hands on the knives sheathed at their waists.

Marjorie couldn't take her eyes off Albert. She could tell that he was mortified by what Spotted Horse was doing. Recalling his vile hands and mouth on her, she smiled at his distress.

He deserved even worse!

And perhaps that was where this was all leading, she thought to herself. Spotted Horse had not told Marjorie the sort of punishment that he had chosen for Albert. But she couldn't believe that his choice would be inhumane. Her husband was a man of compassion.

"Go and sit back down with your mother, Sun Bear," Spotted Horse said, nodding at Marjorie.

337

Sun Bear scurried back to Marjorie's side and sat down on the blanket beside her. Again she took his hand. He smiled at her, then they both watched Spotted Horse, and listened.

"This man is guilty of abducting my wife!" Spotted Horse shouted, again raising a fist in the air.

He turned and leaned his face closer to Albert's, their eyes locking. "This man tried to . . . rape . . . my . . . wife," he said, his teeth clenched.

This time the gasps of horror among his people were much more pronounced.

Then Spotted Horse again faced his people. "This man is also guilty of killing the man called Snow and burying his body in a prison of ice," he said somberly.

Then he turned to Marjorie. "My wife, rise and come to me," he said, beckoning toward her.

Stunned that her husband was going to include her in this council, Marjorie hesitated. She just wanted it all behind her so that they could resume their normal lives.

But not wanting to do anything that would delay the council or the decision about Albert's fate, she went and stood before her husband.

"My wife, since you were the one who suffered the most at the hands of this man, it will be your decision how he will die," Spotted Horse said, his eyes searching hers. She paled and took a step away from him.

"Me?" she said in a whisper. "You want me . . . ?"

"It is your decision," Spotted Horse said softly. "Speak it. It shall be done."

Marjorie took a quick step toward Spotted Horse. She leaned close to his face, her eyes softly pleading. "Spotted Horse, please don't put such responsibility on my shoulders," she whispered. "I hate the man, but I . . . but I . . . don't want to be the one to say how he should pay for his sins. God . . . God will be doing that soon enough."

"I have thought much about the choices," Spotted Horse said, gently placing his hands on her shoulders. "As I see it, he must die. But should it be at the hands of our people? Or the white pony soldiers?"

"What do you mean . . . the soldiers?" Marjorie asked, glancing past him at Albert who softly, silently pleaded with her with frightened eyes.

"Before this man's confession about killing Snow, I thought that we, the Dakota, had no choice but to deal with him in our own way," Spotted Horse said. "But now that he has confessed, and we can deliver the casket maker's body to Fort Snelling, so that they can have the responsibility of burying him, why not deliver the man who killed Snow to the white man authorities at the same time and be done with it? Have we not had enough grief caused by this man? Why make it twofold by asking one of our warriors to take his life?"

"Then you think it is best that we hand him over to the authorities?" Marjorie said softly.

"You think the colonel will believe us when we tell him how this all happened?"

"He will have my word, as a powerful Dakota chief, and yours, a woman of much respect in the white community," Spotted Horse said, nodding. "Tell me your thoughts on this. Do we hand down the death sentence ourselves, or give the responsibility to someone else? Either way, he will pay."

"You don't feel a deep need to have the last word about what is to become of him?" Marjorie asked, her eyes searching his. "For you know, Spotted Horse, once we hand him over to the white authorities, it is totally out of your hands."

"My heart is weary," Spotted Horse said, lowering his eyes. Then he slowly looked up at Marjorie again. "My people have had so much to endure these past sunrises. They have seen too many deaths. Why must I force another one on them?"

Hearing his sorrow, and loving him so much her insides ached, Marjorie flung herself into his arms and hugged him. "We will take him and Snow to the fort," she murmured. "Then we will be done with the both of them and can resume our lives without any more interference."

"My wife has spoken," Spotted Horse said, weaving his fingers through her long black hair, then stroking it. "That is how it will be done."

He held her for a moment longer, then eased her out of his arms and held her at his side as he again faced his people. "It is both your chief's and his wife's decision that this man will be taken to the authorities at Fort Snelling," he shouted. "They will be the ones to choose his fate. His ultimate punishment will be decided much later. The crimes a man commits in this world will be punished in the life to come. The crimes a man commits in this world will be carried with him into the next!"

Spotted Horse paused and sighed. "My people, it is time for our lives to be filled with a gentle peace," he then said. "To keep this man one day longer among us, or to have one of you send an arrow or bullet through his heart, would be asking too much of everyone. I have brought Snow's body to our village. Once this man's corpse and this prisoner are taken to the fort, our lives will begin anew. We will smile and laugh again!"

There was a strained silence for a moment as everyone seemed to be weighing Spotted Horse's decision. But soon they all cheered and gave their blessings.

Marjorie turned and slowly gazed at Albert. She could see keen relief in his eyes, and she thought that she might have even seen him whisper a silent thank you to her, which made her grimace.

She had not made this decision for *him*. It had been done only for Spotted Horse's people!

Sighing, she turned quickly away from Albert. She walked outside and stood back with Sun Bear as Snow's body was brought out in one of his pine coffins and placed on a sled.

Scarcely breathing, she watched as Albert was brought out of the council house, clothed, and a warm pelt was thrown around his shoulders as he was taken to the same dog sled on which Snow's casket had been tied.

She gasped and was taken aback when the casket lid was opened and Spotted Horse ordered Albert to climb inside with the dead man.

"You can't do this to me!" Albert cried, his eyes filled with terror as he tried to jerk himself free of Spotted Horse's tight grip. "It's inhumane! Have mercy, Spotted Horse! I don't want to get in that casket! Oh, Lord, have mercy, I don't want to lie down in that thing with a dead man!"

"This man is dead because you killed him," Spotted Horse said, nodding to two of his more hefty warriors to take over the chore of getting Albert in the pine box. "It seems only appropriate that you share his pine box with him, at least until you arrive at the fort. Then who is to say where you will end up? Perhaps the soldiers will decide to place your corpse in the same pine box to save them the cost of burying you."

Goose bumps rose on Marjorie's flesh as Albert screamed while he was shoved into the box atop Snow.

She could even hear him clawing at the top of the box when it was closed and nailed shut.

She was reminded of how Snow's fingers had been bloodied beneath the ice, where he had clawed at it in an attempt to free himself.

She closed her ears to Albert's screams as she climbed onto Spotted Horse's sled beside Sun Bear, for Albert had more of an advantage than

Snow had been given. Air holes had been drilled into the pine box for Albert.

After several other dog teams and sleds were readied for the journey through the snow to the fort, Spotted Horse came and took charge of his team.

Marjorie and Sun Bear huddled closely together beneath a thick layer of furs and blankets as the sled slid smoothly through the snow.

"Will they kill him?" Sun Bear suddenly blurted out. "Will the white pony soldiers truly kill one of their own, or should we have done it to make sure he died?"

Taken aback by the seriousness of Sun Bear's question and sensing that he was not comfortable with the decision today, Marjorie reached beneath the pelts and blankets and took his hand in hers.

"Rest assured that this man will soon be out of our lives, regardless of what the soldiers choose to do with him," she murmured. "He's an evil man. He *will* be punished."

"I have a terrible feeling about this," Sun Bear said somberly. "It is as if something or someone is inside my heart, warning me."

"It's only natural that you would feel uneasy about the man, since you have witnessed so much of his evil firsthand," Marjorie said softly. "But remember, Sun Bear, I have also seen it."

She shivered as she thought back to how horrible it had been to have Albert's hands and lips on her body. "I have experienced the worst side of this man," she said. "And I feel at peace handing him over to those in charge at Fort Snelling.

So, please, Sun Bear, allow yourself to be at peace, also. When we return to our village this evening, we will *all* be finally free of this man."

Tears came to her eyes when she thought of her mother, wishing that she could have lived long enough to see Albert pay for his evil ways.

Chapter Thirty-six

It was a quiet, lovely moonlit night, as though the world itself joined the Dakota in their new-found peace.

Sun Bear was asleep behind his blanket screen.

Spotted Horse and Marjorie were behind their own drawn blanket, their bodies touching and moving against each other's.

"Now that it is all behind us, and Colonel Dalton sympathized with our plight and took Albert off our hands, it doesn't seem as though any of the terrible things that happened these past weeks are real," Marjorie said.

She reached up and framed Spotted Horse's face between her soft hands. Soon he was rocking above her, his strong thighs against her legs, his rhythmic thrusts inside her slow, deep, and wonderful.

"I am so content, Spotted Horse," she purred. "So absolutely content."

"You have brought me much happiness," Spotted Horse said, brushing a soft kiss across her lips. "To have lost you would have been the same as losing my own life."

Then his mouth seared into hers, leaving her breathless and shaking, yet wanting more.

As he slid his lips from hers and moved his hot and hungry mouth over the creamy skin of her breast, she felt a tremor deep within her.

She gasped and tossed her head slowly back and forth when his lips slid gently over her nipple, nibbling.

Again he covered her lips with his mouth. Anchoring her fiercely against him, he coaxed her lips apart.

Their tongues touched and danced. The silvery flames of desire leapt high within Marjorie.

She clung to Spotted Horse and rocked with him. She locked her legs around him and drew him more deeply into her heat.

It was such a splendid joy to be with him again in this way, when only a few hours ago she had wondered if they would ever see one another again! And now she was enfolded within his solid strength.

With each of his thrusts inside her, she knew exquisite pleasure. With each kiss . . . with each caress . . . she experienced a new sweep of desire.

As his hands cupped her breasts and he gently squeezed them, his thumbs circling her nipples, waves of desire flooded Marjorie's senses. She could feel the curl of heat growing to almost the bursting point within her lower body. Her world was melting away into something wild and desperate!

Spotted Horse felt the yielding silk of Marjorie's body as he touched her all over with his hands. He could feel how open she was to him as he drove into her swiftly and surely, her heat matching his.

He could feel her sexual excitement mounting and it pleased him that he could arouse such wildness, such pleasure, in his woman. It made his own pleasure twofold.

As he kissed her, this time with a mindless savagery, he reached beneath her and lifted her soft hips into his hands.

His fingers pressed urgently into her flesh, and he lifted her closer, imprisoning her against him.

Bright threads of excitement began to weave through his heart.

Her mouth was sensuous and demanding.

He felt the urgency building, his passion this time a frantic one!

Only half aware of making whimpering sounds, Marjorie felt the last vestiges of her rational mind floating away. She was aware only of a sweet euphoria welling up inside her, filling her, spreading . . . spreading . . . spreading.

Each of his strokes within her promised fulfillment.

Suddenly her whole universe seemed to start spinning around as she began her journey over the edge into ecstasy. She became engulfed in a rush of pleasure so intense, she felt faint.

She clung to Spotted Horse and cried out as his body began answering hers, quivering and spilling his seed deep within her in an explosion of ecstasy.

Afterward, as they lay together in exquisite tenderness, their fingers intertwined, Marjorie badly wanted to tell him that she was expecting.

But she had thought of a different way to tell him that she might be with child. This evening, when he had been gone for a while after returning from Fort Snelling, she had gone to her paper doll supplies and had made something special for her husband.

Now was the perfect time to give it to him. Her pulse raced to think of the surprise, the joy she would soon see in her husband's eyes.

Gently she slid away from him and placed a blanket around her shoulders.

"Where are you going?" Spotted Horse asked, leaning on an elbow. "The night is yet young. Do you not wish to spend it in my arms?"

"I desire nothing more than that," she said, giggling when he grabbed her hand and wouldn't let go. "Darling, I will be back. I will be gone for only a minute."

"Why must you leave at all?" Spotted Horse said, giving her hand a gentle tug. He nodded toward the pillow at his right side. "Come back to our bed. Perhaps we will make a child tonight. Would that please you?"

It took a lot of willpower not to burst out and tell him. She even had to work hard at not smiling knowingly down at him, for he was so astute about so many things, he might guess her secret.

"A child?" she said, bubbling over inside with the joy of these sweet moments with him. "Yes, I would be so pleased if we made a child tonight."

"Then forget the foolishness that takes you away from our bed," Spotted Horse said, giving her a soft, pleading look. He tugged her hand again. "Time passes quickly. Soon the sun will replace the moon in the sky. Sun Bear will be awake."

"I know," Marjorie said, gently easing her hand from his. "That's why you should just lie there and quit fussing at me and let me go. I'll be back in a jiffy."

"Jiffy?" Spotted Horse said, puzzling over the word.

"That means quickly," Marjorie said, stepping from behind the blanket.

She went to one side of the tepee where she kept her paper doll equipment stored in boxes. Smiling, she picked up one of the boxes. She left the lid closed and took it back to their bed.

Sitting down in the middle of the bed, the blanket sliding from around her shoulders, Marjorie watched as Spotted Horse stared inquisitively at the box.

"Come and sit next to me," Marjorie said, patting the bed beside her.

When he did as she asked, she shoved the box over to him. "Open it, darling," she said, anxiously watching him as he reached for the box and slowly lifted the lid.

"Paper dolls?" he said, staring down at them.

"Take them out of the box, darling," Marjorie murmured, taking the lid from him.

Spotted Horse took out first one paper doll, and then another, until four dolls lay on the bed between them.

"What do you see?" Marjorie asked, her eyes twinkling.

"I see four paper dolls," Spotted Horse said, looking questioningly at her.

"What sort are they?" she asked softly.

"There is what seems to be a mother and father, a young brave perhaps Sun Bear's same age, and then there is a baby," he said softly.

"That family represents ours," Marjorie said, moving to her knees and wrapping her arms around his neck.

"But there is a difference," he said, looking down at the dolls and then into Marjorie's eyes. "The baby is the difference."

"Not for long," Marjorie said, giggling. "Darling, I made these dolls especially to show you that I am with child."

Spotted Horse's eyes widened.

His breath quickened.

Then he reached for Marjorie and drew her onto his lap. He gazed into her eyes, his own dancing. "You are carrying our child within your womb?" he asked, his smile and his voice revealing his intense joy. His hand was gentle as he laid it over her stomach.

She shared his joy. "Yes, and I hope it's a

boy," she murmured. "I want not only to give you another son, but I would like to give Sun Bear a brother. I just know that our son will be as handsome as both you and Sun Bear."

"A daughter in your image would please me," Spotted Horse said, gently tracing her facial features with a forefinger. "Do you know just how beautiful you are? How much you stir me into endlessly desiring you?"

"I believe I know of your desire," Marjorie said, leaning into the palm of his hand as he placed it against her cheek, relishing the very essence of his nearness. "But I have never seen myself as beautiful."

"Never doubt it again," Spotted Horse said, wrapping his arms around her and drawing her closer so that her breasts pressed against his chest. "And you are even more beautiful now with the radiant glow that pregnant women are blessed with. I do not know how I did not notice it sooner, but it is there. I do see it now."

"If I am that beautiful while pregnant, I wish to have many children," Marjorie said, laughing softly.

His hands reached around and cupped her breasts. "Soon these will be filled with our child's milk," he said thickly. "Soon I will be seeing our child suckling from them."

"Not too soon," Marjorie said. "I surely have eight months to go before giving birth to our child."

"Compared to a lifetime, that amount is no more than the blink of an eye," Spotted Horse said, then covered her lips with his mouth.

His tenderness grew slowly into a surge of passion. He stretched Marjorie out beneath him. They celebrated in their own special way the child they would cherish . . . the child they would adore. It would be special, because it would be born of their special, enduring love.

"How I do adore you," Marjorie whispered as his fingers ran down her body, caressing her, making her shiver.

They made love and held each other until the moon's crescent went pale in the sky. Through the smoke hole overhead, as they lay snuggled in their bed, they watched the sky become suffused with the stain of another gentle, rose-tinted morn.

Chapter Thirty-seven

Five years later

Hardly able to believe how quickly the years had passed or with what joy, Marjorie sat beneath a tree with her four-year-old daughter Pretty Star.

Her daughter, whose skin and features revealed her Dakota heritage, was wide-eyed as Marjorie cut out another paper doll from a thin piece of cardboard.

Their attention was drawn away from the task at hand when Yellow Hawk, Marjorie's two-year-old son, who was the exact image of his father, began squealing while he chased several blackbirds from a field of corn not far from where Marjorie and Pretty Star sat.

The birds were a constant nuisance. Some of the Dakota erected scaffolds for watch towers, but in the smaller fields, which sat close together behind the Dakota lodges, the children ran around on foot chasing off the blackbirds.

"Be careful!" Marjorie cried, waving at Yellow Hawk. "Don't trip over the roots that have grown up from the ground!"

Giggling, his hands flailing in the air as the blackbirds swept low, then flew away in a frightened flutter, Yellow Hawk glanced over at Marjorie.

"Mommie, can you see? I'm helping!" he shouted. Yellow Hawk was not truly responsible for guarding the corn today. Several much older braves were there, among them Sun Bear, who kept an eye on his baby brother more than the pesky birds.

"Mother, like my brother Sun Bear, I will be bold and strong!" Yellow Hawk cried.

"Yes, I see how you are helping," Marjorie said, laughing softly as she watched his short little legs flashing. His attire on this warm summer day was only a brief breechclout and moccasins. "And, yes, you will be bold and strong like Sun Bear."

Yellow Hawk's black hair hung long and loose. He wore a colorful headband, and a lone eagle feather, dyed yellow, was thrust in a coil of his hair at the back.

Marjorie could not remember ever having seen a little boy as cute as her son, not only in his appearance, but also his actions. He was quite mischievous, always into one thing or another. Since he had been old enough to walk, life was never boring.

"We are going to have lots of corn this year, aren't we, Mother?" Pretty Star asked in her soft, dainty voice, which matched her tiny form. She wore a soft doeskin dress with pink shells in the designs of flowers on its bodice. She also wore knee-high moccasins. Her hair hung in long braids down her back.

"Yes, and our people will have you, in part, to thank for that," Marjorie said, now slowly, carefully painting a face on her paper doll.

"It was fun planting the corn," Pretty Star said, giggling when her little brother fell clumsily to the ground, rolled over a couple of times, then jumped back to his feet and resumed chasing the blackbirds.

Marjorie nodded, recalling the first time she had stood among the Dakota women helping plant the crops, herself. She had been surprised to know that the women always selected a place for their crops where there was a healthy growth of wild artichokes. She had learned that the reason for this was because they were likely to find the soil in such places richer and more fertile.

Another thing she had learned that year was that the women never planted their corn crops until they had found the first ripe wild strawberries.

It was then that they soaked their seed corn until it sprouted, planting it with their hands quite deep in little conical mounds that they had prepared earlier.

As soon as the corn showed three or four leaves, they loosened the earth around it with their fingers. When the corn was large enough, they hilled it up thoroughly with their hoes.

They planted a small kind of corn that ripened early. "I'm hungry for some corn now, Mother," Pretty Star murmured. "Can we have some for supper tonight? Can we?"

"Yes, I believe that can be arranged," Marjorie said, nodding.

She always preserved some corn by boiling it before it was hard, scraping it from the cob with mussel shells, then drying it.

What was not devoured by the people before it was ripe, they husked, leaving two or three leaves of the husk attached to the ear. They braided the husks together in strings four or five feet long and hung them in the sunshine to dry.

When the corn was thoroughly dry, the women spread cloths on the ground and put the corn on it, then removed the kernels by pounding it with crude wooden clubs.

The corn that was not to be used immediately was put in barrels made of bark, and buried in the ground to be dug up when needed.

The Dakota planted little else besides corn. The vegetables they didn't obtain by trading at the trading post, they found growing wild.

Marjorie enjoyed gathering berries, plums, and nuts.

But she had discovered that the most important plants among the Dakota were the *psincha*, the *psinchincha*, the wild turnip, the water-lily, and wild rice.

Psinchincha was a root in a shape resembling a hen's egg, and about half as large. *Psincha* was another root, about an inch in diameter. They both grew at the bottom of Lake Calhoun, where even today Marjorie planned to wade, to gather these treasures of the deep.

"Mother, so many of my friends have grandmothers and grandfathers," Pretty Star said, breaking through Marjorie's thoughts. "Tell me again why I do not have any."

Marjorie looked quickly over at Pretty Star. Her delicate face was a picture of innocence, even though she had been told time and again why she had no grandparents.

Her constant curiosity about this only proved that it truly bothered her not to have grandparents, especially when her friends' grandparents were an integral part of their lives, living in their lodges, sleeping with them, eating with them.

Marjorie found it hard to understand, though, why Pretty Star found the absence of grandparents so troublesome. Marjorie felt so absolutely blessed to have what she had in life. Throughout her childhood she had never thought she would achieve such peace and have such love as there was in her lodge.

Only occasionally did she allow her thoughts to return to her past, and how lonely she had been while growing up without brothers or sisters.

She had vowed to herself, after finding such a love with Spotted Horse, that their children would never know the meaning of the word "lonely."

But it seemed that no matter how much Marjorie and Spotted Horse filled their children's lives with love, there was, nonetheless, a void left there, without grandparents.

"Why?" Marjorie said, wishing she did not have to go through the explanation all over again.

She hated being reminded of her previous life with Albert.

It was bad enough to know that he had managed to escape from the soldiers only three months after being arrested and jailed. As he had been transported from one fort to another, he had escaped and had never been found or heard from since.

The knowledge that Albert was out there somewhere was the only thing that disturbed Marjorie's serene life with Spotted Horse and their children. She could never be sure that he was out of her life forever. He just didn't seem the sort to give up on things that he wanted . . . namely her.

But it had been five years now. Surely it was foolish to worry about him still.

Her thoughts strayed to Louis Eckert. No man, besides her beloved husband, could be any more kind and generous to her and her children than Louis. He doted on her children as though they were his grandchildren.

He doted on Marjorie as though she were his daughter.

In fact, he had given her a room in his house

where she could make her paper dolls. He had even found ways to sell them. He had hired people to take them on the riverboat to destinations all along the Mississippi and Missouri Rivers.

Marjorie was in heaven, to know that what she did, and enjoyed so much, was so well received. And she had grown to love Louis like a father.

After a life of being cast about as though she were no more than a worm dangling on the end of a fishing line, Marjorie now felt blessed to have so much in her life.

A husband.

Children.

A father figure.

Friends.

And a means to make extra money for her family by her sales of paper dolls.

"Mother, I am going to leave now," Sun Bear said, drawing Marjorie out of her reverie.

"Leaving?" she said, raising an eyebrow as she gazed up at Sun Bear, who was now fifteen. He was lean, tall, and handsome. The young girls in the village hardly left him alone a minute. They were always following him, giggling, watching.

"*Ho*, while horseback riding yesterday I saw a large beehive," he said. "I wish to go there now and steal the honey. It will be good on our breakfast bread, do you not think?"

"Yes, it would be good. But, Sun Bear," Marjorie said warily, "stealing from honeycombs is so dangerous. Don't you remember the last time you tried? You were stung severely by several bees. After the stingers were removed, the welts took days to heal."

"That won't happen this time," Sun Bear said, proudly thrusting out his bare, muscled chest. "I was just a boy then. Now I am a man."

Marjorie laughed softly. "Men can also be stung," she murmured. "But go ahead. I know how overprotective you think I've become of you. I don't want the children to start calling you a mama's boy."

He brought his lips down close to her ear. "Some already do," he whispered. "I have much to prove now to my friends. Thank you for allowing it."

She started to reach up to hug and kiss him, then resisted the temptation. Such kisses and hugs were how he had acquired the reputation of being coddled too much by his white mother.

She watched him walk away, so dignified, so much like his father. He held his shoulders square, his chin high; his eyes were always alert.

"I would like to go with my brother to get honey," Pretty Star said, taking Marjorie's hand to draw her attention back to her. "But I wouldn't want to get stung by mean bees."

Yellow Hawk started running after Sun Bear, crying.

Marjorie smiled as Sun Bear stopped, turned, and whisked his brother up into his arms and brought him back to Marjorie.

Marjorie set her paper doll equipment on the ground beside her. "Come here, sweetie," she said, holding out her arms for Yellow Hawk.

She took him and cuddled him close as he tried to reach out again for Sun Bear. "Your brother is going where little braves should not be," she murmured, holding Yellow Hawk more tightly as he tried to wriggle free. His lungs proved their strength as he screamed and fussed while Sun Bear walked away, then mounted his lovely steed.

After Sun Bear was out of sight, Yellow Hawk's cries softened to sobs.

Then he laid his cheek against Marjorie's breast, and his eyes slowly drifted closed.

"He is tired from chasing birds," Pretty Star said, reaching over to stroke her brother's arm. "Sweet baby brother, go to sleep."

Then Pretty Star gazed up at Marjorie. "You did not answer my question yet," she said softly.

"About grandparents?" Marjorie said, having hoped that through the confusion of these past moments her daughter would have forgotten her question.

"*Ho*, besides Grandfather Louis, who is truly not my blood kin grandfather, I have no other," Pretty Star said. "You have told me often about my grandmother, *your* mother, and how pretty she was. Why did she have to die so young?"

Marjorie's eyes wavered, then she again explained to her daughter about a grandmother whose life had been cut short by a heart that had given out too soon. She explained about how Pretty Star's Dakota grandparents had died.

But she had no way of explaining about a grandfather who had just disappeared those

361

long years ago . . . a father that Marjorie, herself, had never known.

"But, remember, darling, the Dakota people, as a whole, are members of your family," Marjorie murmured. "The grandparents, the aunts, the uncles, the brothers and sisters are also yours. That is the way of the Dakota. We are one large family unit."

"Yes, a *happy* family unit," Spotted Horse said, suddenly kneeling down beside Marjorie. He placed a gentle hand to Marjorie's cheek. "My wife, are we not all one big happy family in our Dakota village?"

"Yes, and I will never forget how I felt when I realized this about your people," Marjorie said, sighing. "There is nothing like it in the white communities. There is much suspicion of neighbors. There is much tension. For certain, everyone locks their doors at night."

"It is good to see how you prefer our way of life over what was once yours," Spotted Horse said softly. He kissed Pretty Star on the brow, then slowly lifted his son from his wife's arms.

As he watched Yellow Hawk in his sound sleep, he slowly rocked him back and forth in his arms. "I shall take Yellow Hawk to his crib and then I am off to the haunts of the muskrat. I have promised a certain number of muskrat pelts to the agent at the trading post. If I fail to make my promise good, the new agent at the post might not trust me again. And now is not the time to jeopardize that relationship. Each muskrat pelt is worth seven to ten cents in white man's coins."

"While you are gone on a muskrat hunt, I plan to gather *psinchincha* in the lake," Marjorie murmured.

She gathered up her paper doll equipment and placed it in a buckskin bag. Carrying the bag in one hand and holding Pretty Star's tiny hand in the other, she walked with Spotted Horse toward their tepee.

"Do not go far in the lake and do not stay long," Spotted Horse said, frowning over at her. "And take someone with you. I always worry about your safety."

She did not tell him that she planned to gather the *psinchincha* at the far end of the lake, where it grew in abundance in the shallowest part of the water. That spot was out of sight of the village. She knew how much he worried about her.

And she was not going to take someone with her. It was not as though she needed an escort. She enjoyed gathering the *psinchincha* alone in the waist-deep water, her bare feet feeling for the plants at the bottom of the lake.

She loved the solace of occasionally doing things alone, especially the serenity she always felt while she was in the lake beneath the shadow of the large trees that hung like umbrellas over the water. There she was at one with the birds, the animals, and the tiny fish that swam curiously around her.

"I shall be just fine," she said, not promising anything.

They went into the lodge and stood over the cradle as Spotted Horse placed Yellow Hawk on the soft mattress made from buckskin stuffed with the fluffy down of cattails.

Out of the corner of her eye Marjorie saw Pretty Star go and stretch out on her side in her own bed.

Marjorie went over and knelt down beside the bed and gently slipped her daughter's moccasins off, then drew a soft blanket over her.

Marjorie watched Pretty Star until she was asleep, then she went and stood in Spotted Horse's embrace.

"I'm going to go and get Blue Flower to sit with our children while you and I are gone," Marjorie murmured.

Her insides melted when Spotted Horse framed her face between his hands and gave her a soft kiss. If the truth be known, she would much rather stay home and slip into bed with her husband.

But she knew that he must hunt, for he did want to keep in good standing with the new agent at the trading post.

"Do be safe while I am gone," Spotted Horse said, his eyes imploring her.

"I will," she said, then placed a hand on his cheek as she brushed a kiss across his lips. "Do you think I would do anything that would keep us from our bed tonight? I so hunger for you, my husband."

"I shall feed those hungers while the stars feed the heavens with their light," he said huskily.

He swept her closer and smothered her gasp of pleasure with another kiss, this one giving her the promise of what he planned for her tonight!

Chapter Thirty-eight

In reckless abandon, Sun Bear had stolen the honey from the bees.

Laughing in the wind, he rode away on his surging horse across an emerald meadowland. With his steed's nostrils flaring, its tail flashing, its long mane flying, Sun Bear rode on through deep, wild dells and past waterfalls and piles of moss-clad rocks. Hanging from the side of his horse was his parfleche bag filled with sweet honey.

Holding the reins with one hand, Sun Bear slid the fingers of his free hand between his lips and sucked honey from them, having dripped much of it on himself while fleeing from the angry bees.

He inhaled the fragrant air of early afternoon and enjoyed the beautiful sights around him as he rode onward toward the lake, which now lay ahead, sparkling like an azure-tinted mirror beneath the sun. Its banks were edged with long grasses, intermingled with wildflowers drooping over and reflecting graceful fringes in the translucent water below.

On his right side, pink clover dotted the land. On his left, a meadow of sunflowers waved in the breeze.

He could hardly wait to get to Lake Calhoun where he would bathe the stickiness of the honey from his flesh on the far side of the lake. He wanted to be fresh and clean when he arrived at his lodge with the gift of honey for his mother. He wanted his horse's mane to shine.

He would even weave a wreath of sweet grass for his horse's neck. He would take the eagle feather from his headband and tie it to his horse's tail, for his horse was a big part of today's success. Had his steed not been quick and loyal to his master, Sun Bear might even now be swollen with bee stings!

Sun Bear sank his heels into the flanks of his horse and sent him plunging into the shimmering, crystal water. The horse's hooves sent up golden fountain sprays into the air.

Surrounded by tall stalks of wild rice that hid his view of his village, Sun Bear leapt from the horse and removed the bag of honey, his rifle, and then his saddle.

Then he swung himself onto his horse bareback and clung to the reins as he urged him further into the water. Grasping his horse's mane, lying low over him, Sun Bear let the water wash them both clean of the honey.

Trout, giant silver fish, gleamed in the clear water of the lake. Tiny minnows darted out of the horse's path.

Feeling as one with his steed, Sun Bear straightened his back, held his head back, and closed his eyes. He envisioned himself in the heavens flying with the mighty eagle.

He felt as free as an eagle. He felt as proud. He felt as happy!

His horse suddenly neighed and jerked its head from side to side, causing Sun Bear to open his eyes with alarm. He knew all of his horse's ways of warning him of danger. This was one of them.

He was now far enough out in the water to see beyond the tall stalks of wild rice plants. And what he saw made him grow cold all over.

White Bird! His mother! She was in danger! A man was approaching her as her back was turned. He was on land, hiding behind one bush and then another, a rifle aimed at White Bird's back!

Panic immobilized Sun Bear for a moment.

Then, knowing that only he could save his mother, for she was quite alone and far from the village, he sank his heels into the flanks of his horse and sent him splashing out of the river.

Still on the horse's back, Sun Bear rode up to where he had left his gunboot and rifle. Without dismounting, he slid over the side of the horse and, clinging to his mane, swept the rifle from the gunboot.

His fingers tight around the rifle, he then rode off toward the man who was stalking Marjorie.

Even as Sun Bear grew closer to the man, the stranger approached Marjorie. It seemed as though the man was purposely delaying killing her, obviously getting some sort of strange, sick pleasure by just watching her.

Then it came to Sun Bear who it might be. His mother's stepfather!

From this distance he couldn't yet see enough of the man's face to know. But Sun Bear knew that Albert had managed to escape the clutches of the white pony soldiers.

And even though that had been several years ago, and everyone thought he was gone from their lives forever, Sun Bear knew that both his father and mother never truly forgot about him and the possibility of his returning to either kill Marjorie, or take her away.

Not wanting to alert Albert that an enemy was bearing down on him, ready to kill him, Sun Bear drew his horse to a quick halt and dismounted.

With his rifle clasped hard in one hand, his heart pounding, he ran stealthily through the thick brush.

When he got close enough to see the face of the man, hate and disgust overtook Sun Bear. Yes, it was White Bird's stepfather.

Sun Bear was now only a few yards away from Albert. He took a steady aim, then started to shout to Albert to drop his firearm.

But Sun Bear paled when he saw that Albert's finger was closing on the trigger of his rifle!

"No!" Sun Bear cried as he pulled the trigger on his own firearm.

He watched the bullet splatter into Albert's back, causing his body to lurch, then crumple to the ground, his rifle flying away from him and landing in the river.

Marjorie heard the gunshot.

Eyes wide, her pulse racing with fear, she turned and stared blankly at Albert stretched out on the ground on his stomach, blood seeping through his shirt.

Then she watched Sun Bear step out into the open, his rifle barrel smoking.

"He was going to shoot you!" Sun Bear cried, his eyes locked with Marjorie's. "I shot him first."

Marjorie was too stunned to move. Her knees were trembling. She felt faint at knowing that she had come so close to dying.

Then thinking about Sun Bear, and how he had saved her life, tears of joy streamed from her eyes as she splashed out of the water.

Sun Bear ran to her. He dropped his rifle and flung himself into her arms.

"Thank you, son," Marjorie murmured, stroking his sleek, copper back. "Had you not been there—"

"But I was," Sun Bear said, easing himself from her arms. He placed a gentle hand on her cheek. "And you are all right."

He took her by the hand as she walked toward the fallen victim.

When she didn't see any firearm, she sent Sun Bear an alarmed, questioning look.

"Are you certain he was ready to shoot me?" she asked.

"His rifle is in the river," Sun Bear said, nodding toward Lake Calhoun. "It fell there when I shot him. I shall retrieve it soon."

"No," Marjorie said, shuddering. "Leave it there. I never want to see it."

She looked up and saw the village people running toward her. The sound of gunfire had drawn them there.

When they came to her and Sun Bear told them what had happened, they took turns hugging her and then Sun Bear.

As a warrior was hugging her, she looked past his shoulder and saw Spotted Horse riding toward her, many muskrat pelts tied to the back of his horse.

She broke free of the warrior and started running toward Spotted Horse, her arms outstretched toward him. They had come so close to losing everything! If not for Sun Bear, their world would have ended!

"Spotted Horse!" she cried, so glad when he came to her and swept her onto his horse with him.

"I saw from a bluff what happened," he said, holding her near to his heart. "I was too far away to stop Albert. You do not know how helpless I felt as I saw him moving toward you. I was even too far away to shout a warning to you."

"Our son saved me," Marjorie said, relishing his closeness.

"I watched him approaching Albert from be-

hind," Spotted Horse said. "I knew then that
you would be all right. That was when I rode
off the bluff and came to you. My woman, you
never should have gone alone into the water so
far from our village. Did I not warn you?"

"Yes, and I shall always heed your warnings
from now on," Marjorie said, smiling down at
Sun Bear as he ran up to the horse, his eyes
beaming.

"My *micinksi*, today you have earned a celebration of courage," Spotted Horse said,
stretching out a hand toward Sun Bear.

Sun Bear took the hand and twined his fingers through his father's.

"You have made your father and mother so
proud today," Spotted Horse said thickly. "And
not only us, but our people as a whole. They will
never forget how you saved your mother. There
will be stories told about your courage for many
moons to come."

"I did nothing that extraordinary," Sun Bear
said, suddenly shy. He slowly slid his hand from
his father's. "I did what any son would do when
his mother was in trouble. I saved her."

"Not all sons would have the courage to do
this," Marjorie said, smiling down at him. "But
you? You are your father's son and would do
anything for your family."

Spotted Horse slid Marjorie from his lap, and
then dismounted.

With Marjorie at his left side and Sun Bear at
his right, his arm around both of them, he went
and stood over Albert.

"He just would not let it rest," he said somberly. He glanced over at Marjorie. "My woman, these past years I am certain your stepfather spent his every waking hour scheming how he would kill you. Revenge was his whole reason for living. And now he is dead, vengeance lost to him forever."

"I truly had thought he had gone somewhere and made a new life for himself, especially after coming so close to being put to death for his crimes," Marjorie said, turning her head away. She did not want to see Albert ever again, dead or alive.

"Never put faith in such beliefs when the man involved has a heart as evil as his," Spotted Horse said.

He turned to Pleasant Moon. "See that his body is taken away," he said somberly. "There is no need to take him to the white authorities. They will only complicate matters. This white man has caused enough pain in our lives. Find a place far from the village. Bury him. His spirit is now dwelling in the land of spirits. There he will be made to pay for his transgressions in life."

He then turned to Marjorie and placed his hands gently on her cheeks. "My hunt was good," he said, in an attempt to draw her thoughts away from what had just happened. "And yours? Did you harvest many water plants?"

"Yes, but . . . but the bag fell from my shoulder as I left the river," Marjorie said. She smiled slowly up at him. "But it is more important that your hunt was successful."

"And *mine*," Sun Bear said, beaming from one to the other. "I brought home much honey for our bread."

He looked over at his horse who stood dutifully waiting for him.

Then he smiled again from his mother to his father. "I shall go and retrieve the bag I left by the river," he said.

An anxious voice shouting Sun Bear's name drew him quickly around. He gave his friend Fire Eyes a questioning stare as he came running toward him.

"A bear!" Fire Eyes cried. "Sun Bear, I was out in the forest playing the hiding game with friends when I saw a bear running through the forest with your parfleche bag. I knew it was yours. It was one I borrowed from you one day when I went berry picking with my mother."

Fire Eyes stopped short and gasped when Albert was carried past him on a horse, blood soaking his shirt.

He then looked questioningly at Sun Bear. "The gunshot I heard killed that man?" he asked softly.

Sun Bear did not even hear him. His thoughts were on the honey that the bear had stolen from him.

And then he found some humor in the situation. The bear had been clever to find honey he did not have to battle bees for, as Sun Bear had been forced to do.

"The man is dead," Fire Eyes said, drawing Sun Bear out of his reverie. "Did your father kill him, Sun Bear?"

"No, it was I who killed him," Sun Bear said, proud to be recognized as a hero by his people.

"You are so brave," Fire Eyes said, smiling broadly. Then his smile faded. "But you lost your bag. What was in it?"

"Honey, but it is all right that the bear has it," Sun Bear said, shrugging as he smiled at his friend. "My mother's bread tastes good without honey."

He placed an arm around Fire Eyes's shoulders and walked away, telling him the whole story.

Marjorie saw the awe in the young brave's eyes as he listened to his friend. She then turned to Spotted Horse. "You mentioned a celebration," she murmured. "When? Perhaps tomorrow? I'm so anxious to help in the celebration. I want everything to be special for Sun Bear."

Chapter Thirty-nine

The celebration of courage was in full swing, the excitement mounting as each moment passed. Because the day was so beautiful, the celebration was not held in the confines of the large council house.

Instead, it was outside where there was more room for a huge central fire, where food could be prepared in abundance, and where people could dance with abandon.

The village herald had stood in the center of the Dakota village just prior to dusk after Sun Bear had rescued Marjorie the day before. The herald had invited each guest by name to to-day's celebration.

After having repeated each name, he had said, "I call you to the celebration of courage for our chief's son Sun Bear!"

Each person had accepted by shouting back to him, saying that he or she would be in attendance.

Early in the morning, several warriors had gone out and shot a fat buck mule deer. A whole forequarter now hung over the outdoor fire, where it had slowly been roasting for hours. It was suspended from a tripod above the blaze, and as it cooked, the women took turns giving it an occasional twirl.

Her back resting against a tripod of wood, Marjorie sat on a buffalo robe beside Spotted Horse close to the fire. Their children scampered around playing with those their same age.

Marjorie searched with her eyes until she found Louis Eckert, who had arrived earlier in the day, but not entirely for the celebration. He was wooing one of the Dakota women, a woman who had been widowed a few years back.

Although nearing her fiftieth birthday, Morning Flame was still beautiful, her eyes the most lovely thing about her. Her mother had married a white man. When her mother's husband had died, her mother had brought her back to live among her true people. The only sign of her white heritage was her violet eyes. They were captivating.

Louis seemed drawn into their violet pools as he listened to her telling him about something interesting in her life as she knelt before him, her delicate hands resting on his knees.

"There will soon be a marriage," Marjorie whispered to herself. "Then I will have not only a man I call my father, but also a woman I can relate to as a mother."

Marjorie felt especially pretty today in her soft deerskin dress and moccasins and leggings, all as white as snow. Her long, black, shiny braids were tied with ornaments made from died porcupine quills strung on dyed deerskin strings. At the ends of the braids were tassels of bright-colored feathers.

She shifted her gaze to Spotted Horse, who would soon be awarding his son a special eagle feather for his deed of courage. Today her husband wore a beautiful headdress of thirty eagle feathers. His buckskin attire was also white. It was decorated with porcupine quills, as were his leggings and moccasins.

She could see the pride in his dark eyes as he watched Sun Bear playing games with his friends. Sun Bear sometimes stopped to grab something to eat, for the boy seemed to have a bottomless pit for a stomach.

Marjorie gazed at the food that had been prepared and for the most part already consumed. She had enjoyed waking at daybreak to join the women in the preparations for this special feast. They had prepared squash soup, cherry wozapi, madbear stew, baked wild rice and carrots, hominy soup, fry bread, dried wild turnips and onions, and a varied assortment of meats.

The venison that was still cooking over the fire was there for the meal that would be eaten in the moonlight later on as the celebration continued. It would not end until tomorrow on the sun's first awakening.

All day the anticipation of Sun Bear's honors had grown throughout the crowd of Dakota, as well as their anxiousness to join in communal dancing.

Up to now there had only been food and games.

But as the young men began gathering around their bass drums, holding their padded drumsticks, Marjorie's heart raced. She knew that the time for the real excitement had finally arrived.

She was aware of the drummers watching Spotted Horse. They were not to play until after he had awarded Sun Bear his special eagle feather.

Spotted Horse had explained to Marjorie about the eagle feather, saying that of all animals, the eagle was most powerful, and that a deed of honor was always rewarded with a sacred feather of Father Eagle.

Her thoughts were interrupted when Spotted Horse rose to his feet.

The villagers grew instantly quiet and sat down on their blankets, their eyes on Spotted Horse, and then on Sun Bear as he walked with much dignity toward his father.

The outdoor fire leapt high in the sky. The clouds overhead swam by in great puffs of white.

Suddenly a large shadow fell upon everyone and the great cry of an eagle filled the air with its shrillness.

Yet no one turned his eyes heavenward. Not even Marjorie.

All attention was now on a young brave whose very soul was bonding with the soaring, mystical bird, as Spotted Horse reached out his hands toward his son, a great feather stretched out between them.

"My son who will soon be a great Dakota warrior, take this feather with great pride and honor," Spotted Horse said, his voice loud enough to reach the eagle overhead. "You have proven to everyone that you are a *wicasa-okinihah*, an honorable and respected individual, a young brave of unbounded generosity and courage. You are a person of undaunted honor. In conduct you never forget your pride and dignity. You accept praise and honor without arrogance. Because of your courage, my wife, your mother, breathes today! She watches today as you are honored. My son, a mark of special bravery is to rescue a friend from danger. Saving a mother is even more commendable!"

His pride and joy spilling over within him, Sun Bear accepted the lovely white eagle feather. Shivers ran up and down his spine when he once again heard the cry of the eagle soaring overhead, as one with him as he accepted the special honor from his father.

"*Ahte*, thank you for this day that you have given me, for this sacred eagle feather which I will keep with me always for guidance, and as a reminder of your love for me, a son who is your son as though I was born of your blood. It honors me so that you are my father."

He glanced over at Marjorie. "It honors me so

that your wife is my mother," he said, swallowing hard as he fought back tears.

Then he again gazed at his father. "*Ahte*, a Dakota boy must choose one of three callings," he said softly. "To be a hunter, or to be a scout, or to be a warrior. To become a great warrior is the highest aspiration, and it is mine. I will continue to make you proud of me!"

Fighting back tears of pride for his son, Spotted Horse placed gentle hands on Sun Bear's shoulders. "My son, my pride could never be greater than today," he said thickly.

Then Spotted Horse dropped his hands away and nodded to the drummers.

He smiled down at Sun Bear. "My son, you might want to take your feather to our lodge for safekeeping, for do you not have many hours of dancing ahead of you?" he said, his eyes twinkling as he caught a beautiful girl closely watching Sun Bear.

Sun Shining.

Yes, Sun Shining had begun to notice Sun Bear more and more. Today her eyes showed just how much she cared for him.

"Yes, thank you, Father, for suggesting it," Sun Bear said, glancing quickly at Sun Shining. He blushed as he caught her steady stare.

He ran off, then returned just as a young man wearing a headdress and bells on his ankles, began dancing around the fire in time with the steady beats of the drums. He was called the starter, the one who initiated the dancing. He went around the circle clockwise two times by himself, the bells on his ankles jangling as he placed his feet on the ground, toe, heel, toe, heel.

Then the old "longhairs," dressed in their full regalia, danced their traditional ceremonial dances. Each one holding some weapon in his hand, they stood with their knees bent and made short, quick jumps, lifting both feet from the ground at the same time.

The motion of the dancers was abrupt and violent. When they stopped to breathe, someone would recount in a loud voice and with appropriate gestures the dancer's past exploits in war.

This dance was a violent exercise and could not be continued long at a time.

The women standing around the edge of the circle rose on their toes and sank down again to the beat of the drum.

And then all but the younger children, who just stood and watched, joined the dancing. The four drummers drummed the rhythm required for each particular song or dance.

Marjorie stood with Spotted Horse, noting, as if it were the first time, the women's dance costumes. The sunflower, which grew in great abundance, was the symbol of the sun to the Dakota. It was used a great deal in their ceremonial decoration. The Dakota adored the flower for its golden beauty, and because its face was at all times of the day turned toward the sun. These women wore sunflowers on their long dresses.

Marjorie loved it when the women really got

into the mood of the music. They danced and pranced to the sound of the drums.

"The name of the dance my people are now dancing is the Rabbit Dance," Spotted Horse said, nodding his head in time with the music.

He turned wide, hopeful eyes down at Marjorie. "Have you watched it long enough to be able to do it, yourself?" he asked softly. "Would you join me and dance? It seems to please my people so much when they see you and me together dancing among them."

"I would not want to do anything to disappoint them, now, would I?" Marjorie said, giggling as she smiled up at him.

She was giddy with excitement, for the first time in years not having to wonder where her stepfather was. Finally, she was rid of him and his threat.

She truly felt as though she had a reason to dance. But she would not dance the night away. She had other things on her mind. She hoped to drag her husband away to the privacy of their lodge where they could have their own private celebration. Sun Shining's mother had already agreed to take Pretty Star and Yellow Hawk home with her.

And she knew that Sun Bear would be occupied the whole night through. If the celebration was to last all night, he was going to be there, for it was being held in his honor.

"Yes, let us dance," Marjorie said, grabbing Spotted Horse's hand and leading him amidst the dancers.

She knew the dance well enough and knew

that most songs sung for it had pretty melodies, which made one want to dance and sing.

Laughing, feeling lighthearted and gay, she and Spotted Horse danced side by side.

During the dance, the young men who did the drumming sang,

"Oh, yes, I love you,
Bunny, I do not care if you are married,
I still love you,
I will get you yet,
Hey-o-la! Hey-o-ha!"

They repeated this song over and over again as they continued their steady rhythm on the drums.

Marjorie joined them in singing what they sang. Then she held her head back and laughed, her braids bouncing on her shoulders.

Finally the songs and drumming ceased. The dancers fell away and sat down, their cheeks rosy.

Mint drinks were passed around, refreshing in their coolness.

Marjorie had been delighted by this unique drink the first time it had been offered to her. Spotted Horse had explained how it was made. A sprig of mint was placed in a cup of water. It lay on the surface, and the water was drawn in the mouth through the leaves.

Before long, another dance was started.

Everyone joined the circle again except for Marjorie and Spotted Horse.

"Darling, I don't think we will be missed if we

return to our lodge for a while, do you?" Marjorie asked as she tugged on his hand to lead him away. "I'm tired. Truly I need to stretch out for a moment of rest. Then I promise I will return and dance the night away, if that is what you wish."

"You know what I truly would rather do," Spotted Horse said, giving her a sly grin.

She laughed softly, their eyes meeting and holding. "Yes, I believe so," she murmured, then broke away from him and ran on to their lodge.

He followed shortly after, panting.

He stood over her inside the tepee, a soft questioning in his eyes. "You say you need rest, yet you run with the energy of a young brave to our lodge?" he said, raising an eyebrow.

"I was only jesting about being tired," Marjorie said, slowly lifting his headdress from his head and gingerly placing it on a tripod beside the door. "I truly had other things in mind which called for privacy."

Her hands slid up beneath his shirt and she ran her fingers across his broad, muscled chest. "Do you think you can guess what I am wishing to do besides dance?" she teased, now lifting his shirt over his head.

When she had tossed it aside, she flicked her tongue over one of his nipples and heard his quick intake of breath.

Then, as he watched, his eyes dark with passion-inflamed emotion, she removed the rest of his clothes.

Her eyes locked with his. She knelt down before him and cupped the heaviness of his manhood within one hand, while with her other she stroked him.

When she flicked her tongue up and down the length of his velvety manhood, and then kissed her way across it, she watched him throw his head back with a guttural sigh of rapture.

Enjoying giving him such pleasure, she used her mouth, tongue, and hands until he placed his hands on her shoulders and gently moved her away from him.

"It is your turn to receive pleasure," he said thickly, taking her hands and drawing her to her feet.

Breathless, her pulse racing, her knees weak from ecstasy, she stood there as he undressed her.

When she was silkenly nude before him, and his eyes raked slowly over her, she reached a hand out and took one of his. She placed it at the juncture of her thighs, where she was already pulsing and wet for him.

"Caress me," she said in a husky voice she only recognized as hers while with him in this special way.

She closed her eyes as his fingers moved over her, slowly yet deliberately, stopping only long enough to occasionally plunge into her moist valley.

When he knelt before her, and his fingers parted the fronds of her hair, which lay like silken flowers over her woman's center, she sucked in a wild breath and closed her eyes, for she knew what to expect next.

The most delirious of sensations rushed

through her as his tongue flicked, licked, and sucked her into mindlessness.

She leaned closer to his mouth and placed her hands at the back of his head to increase the pressure of his mouth where she throbbed unmercifully.

"I am so close . . ." she whispered, her face flushed, her throat dry. "Please—"

She didn't have to say any more to him. He understood her urging.

He placed his hands on her waist and lifted her first, then spread her out beneath him.

Mounting her, her legs wrapped around his waist, he thrust his heaviness into her parted, hot folds.

As he rhythmically stroked within her, he gave her a long, deep kiss, his hands on her breasts, his thumbs circling the nipples.

Lost in the intoxication of the moment, Marjorie absorbed the bold thrusts.

Her fingers ran down his body, touching, probing, caressing.

Their bodies straining together hungrily, he gathered her in his arms.

He kissed the soft hollow of her throat, then the long taper of her neck. He licked his way down to her breasts and covered a nipple with his mouth, his tongue absorbing the heat of the hard, pink tip.

As Marjorie rode the wings of rapture, spasmodic gasps escaped from between her lips. She was in a state of euphoria as his hand squeezed her breast, then rotated the nipple against his palm.

Her hips gyrated as Spotted Horse moved powerfully against her, his lips now stifling her gasps with a hot and frenzied kiss.

He plunged over and over again in a wild, dizzying rhythm into her pulsing cleft, his blood quickening as he felt the moment of completion drawing near.

With a last spurt of energy he thrust himself more deeply into her, his hands cupping the rounded flesh of her bottom, lifting her higher, closer, molding her against him.

Marjorie's spasmodic gasps proved that she was going to reach the ultimate pleasure along with him.

Spotted Horse kissed her long and deep and thrust once more, even more deeply, bringing her to spasms that matched his own.

Afterward, he rolled away from her and collapsed at her side, panting.

Herself exhausted, Marjorie lay beside him on her back, her entire body throbbing from the ecstasy she had shared with him.

"Each time is better than the last," Marjorie murmured. She rolled over to her side and gazed at her husband. "Is it the same for you? Are you forever filled with the spiraling need of me? When we do finally get to be together, is it always better than the time before?"

Spotted Horse turned and faced her.

He moved his body close to hers so that her generous breasts would be touching his chest. He swept a hand down her side, then slowly around to where she was wet from his spilled seed.

"You excite me ever so much," he said huskily. "Each time it is better, for with time comes practice and knowing. Do you not know now what stirs my passion the most?"

She giggled. "Yes, I believe so," she said, sucking in a wild breath of pleasure when he began stroking her fiery flesh.

"As do you know what stirs mine," she said huskily.

She closed her eyes. "Like now," she said, her voice quivering in her mounting sexual excitement. "Your fingers, ah, your fingers. . . ."

She arched toward him. He wrapped his arms around her and drew her closer and moved his body against hers.

She could feel his manhood growing against her. She reached a hand to him and helped him, stroking him until he groaned from the pleasure.

When he gazed down at her, she became transfixed by the smoldering desire in his eyes. She was overwhelmed all over again with sweet longing.

Yes, the savage tears were behind them. Their life together had brought them such peace and joy.

And, ah, they shared such love for their children.

Perhaps tonight, Marjorie thought to herself, they might just be making another child. They both wanted the laughter of many children in their lodge.

Marjorie was almost able to forget the sadness of her own childhood, and her loneliness.

Thanks to Spotted Horse, she now had everything that she had only dared to dream of as a child.

Thanks to her wonderful Dakota husband, she had everything that was good on this earth!

Dear Reader:

I hope you enjoyed reading *Savage Tears*! The next book in my *Savage* Series, which I write exclusively for Leisure Books, is *Savage Heat*. *Savage Heat* will be in the stores six months after the release date of *Savage Tears*.

For those of you who are collecting my Leisure *Savage* Series and want to read about my backlist and future books, please send a legal-size, self-addressed, stamped envelope for my latest newsletter to the following address:

CASSIE EDWARDS
6445 North Country Club Road
Mattoon, IL 61938

I would love to hear from you!

Always,

CASSIE

SAVAGE LONGINGS

CASSIE EDWARDS

"Cassie Edwards is a shining talent!"
—Romantic Times

Having been kidnapped by vicious trappers, Snow Deer despairs of ever seeing her people again. Then, from out of the Kansas wilderness comes Charles Cline to rescue the Indian maiden. Strong yet gentle, brave yet tenderhearted, the virile blacksmith is everything Snow Deer desires in a man. And beneath the fierce sun, she burns to succumb to the sweet temptation of his kiss. But the strong-willed Cheyenne princess is torn between the duty that demands she stay with her tribesmen and the passion that promises her unending happiness among white settlers. Only the love in her heart and the courage in her soul can convince Snow Deer that her destiny lies with Charles—and the blissful fulfillment of their savage longings.

_4176-6 $5.99 US/$6.99 CAN

SAVAGE SPIRIT

CASSIE EDWARDS

**Winner of the *Romantic Times*
Lifetime Achievement Award for Best Indian Series!**

™SAVAGE
SERIES

SAVAGE SECRETS
CASSIE EDWARDS

Winner Of The *Romantic Times* Reviewers' Choice Award For Best Indian Series

Searching the wilds of the Wyoming Territory for her outlaw brother, Rebecca Veach is captured by the one man who fulfills her heart's desire. But can she give herself to the virile warrior without telling him about her shameful quest?

Blazing Eagle is as strong as the winter wind, yet as gentle as a summer day. And although he wants Becky from the moment he takes her captive, hidden memories of a long-ago tragedy tear him away from the golden-haired vixen.

Strong-willed virgin and Cheyenne chieftain, Becky and Blazing Eagle share a passion that burns hotter than the prairie sun—until savage secrets from their past threaten to destroy them and the love they share.

_3823-4 $5.99 US/$7.99 CAN

SAVAGE EDEN
CASSIE EDWARDS

Bestselling Author Of *Savage Passions*

"This is a magnificent, sensitive romance...one of her best!"

—Romantic Times

Alone in the Kentucky wilderness, beautiful Pamela trembles under the gaze of the silent Miami warrior—and hungers for his touch. To Pamela, the virile chief Strong Bear is the ultimate temptation. Melting in his sensual embrace, she dares to surrender her innocence—body and soul.

Pamela and Strong Bear share a forbidden love forged in a breathless rapture of mounting ecstasy. The gleam of her lover's strong, bronzed arms, the touch of his lips, and the heat of his flesh kindle the flames of her deepest desires. And when a murderous tragedy strikes Pamela's family, leaving only Strong Bear to blame, her yearning will not die. For only their passion will conquer all injustice—and free their hostage hearts forever.

_52097-4 $5.50 US/$6.50 CAN